THE TROUBLE MAKERS

Celia Fremlin

DOVER PUBLICATIONS, INC.
Mineola, New York

Bibliographical Note

This Dover edition, first published in 2018, is an unabridged republication of the work originally published by J. B. Lippincott Company, Philadelphia and New York, in 1963.

Library of Congress Cataloging-in-Publication Data

Names: Fremlin, Celia, author.
Title: The trouble makers / Celia Fremlin.
Description: Dover edition. | Mineola, New York : Dover Publications, 2018.
Identifiers: LCCN 2017045403| ISBN 9780486816227 (softcover) |
  ISBN 0486816222 (softcover)
Subjects: LCSH: Suburban life—Fiction. | Housewives—Fiction. | Suspicion—
  Fiction. | BISAC: FICTION / Suspense. | GSAFD: Suspense fiction. | Mystery fiction.
Classification: LCC PR6056.R45 T76 2018 | DDC 823/.914—dc23
LC record available at https://lccn.loc.gov/2017045403

Manufactured in the United States by LSC Communications
81622201   2018
www.doverpublications.com

THE
TROUBLE
MAKERS

CHAPTER I

SOMETIMES KATHARINE felt the evening rush hour to be an almost tranquil thing. These long, devitalised queues provided a massed solitude—a breathing-space; an amorphous, unassailable no-man's-land between work and home, where you had an opportunity, at last, to worry in peace.

Was that what these other dismal, damp, hunched-up people were doing—worrying in peace? Katharine glanced round; and realised at once that the actual queue you were actually standing in was never quite like that. It was the standard, prefabricated image of rush-hour queues that she had had in mind. When you really looked properly at your own special queue, you noticed that a lot of people weren't looking dismal at all, nor hunched up—nor even damp, some of them, in spite of the thin, slowly worsening drizzle. Odd how those bright, smart young girls, with their vulnerable gay clothes and dazzling make-up, and with no umbrellas, never seemed to get wet at all, however hard it rained and however long they stood there. It was as if the gay, inscrutable qualities that had succeeded in getting them up like that in the first place had also provided them with a total shield against the outside world, weather and all; a shield of which the gloomy, defenceless middle-aged knew nothing.

But no; even the middle-aged weren't looking particularly gloomy either. Katharine observed this with a curious, perverse disappointment, as if the ordered course of Nature was somehow being mocked by this discovery. Just listen to those

1

two behind her, for instance, heads together, absorbed, loving every minute of it as they went on, and on, and on, in resigned, kindly, vaguely resentful monotones about somebody called Ede who had done something with some pay slips. And what about that tall, gallantly rigged out woman in front, standing straight and unflinching on both her spike heels at once, instead of surreptitiously resting them in turns, like everyone else. A heroic figure, head up to the rain, and almost spitting her excitement about a lettuce. It had either cost an awful lot or an awful little—Katharine could not quite make out which, and the awed, upturned face of the woman's companion gave no clue.

But what about the silent ones, the ones without companions. Were they, like Katharine, wallowing in a peaceful trough of worry—worry about which, for one blessed half hour, absolutely nothing could be done? Idly, Katharine began trying to apportion appropriate worries to the shadowy faces about her. That defeated-looking blonde, for instance, with too much purple lipstick. Was she wondering desperately if her cooling lover would, in spite of everything, ring her up tonight? Perhaps he hadn't rung last night, or the night before, or the night before that, but all the same, if she sat at home all this evening, by her inadequate gas fire, listening and listening... ? And what about that elderly woman in black, so defensive and suspicious? *She* must be living with a son and daughter-in-law who didn't want her; was going home to them now, defiantly, because, hang it all, it had been *her* house in the first place. And her daughter-in-law would be cooking something that her son always used to loathe, and using the wrong saucepans for it too. . . . Without warning, the woman turned her hostile black eyes straight at Katharine; and Katharine hastily glanced away, guilty and embarrassed. Had she been rudely staring? She could feel the woman's eyes still fastened on her averted profile, and felt herself blushing—though of course it didn't matter now that the sickly sodium lighting had come on. One could blush purple from neck to hairline and still only look ill and greenish, like everyone else.

But she wished the fierce old thing would look away, all the same. Did she know her by any unfortunate chance? That really would have been unforgivably rude—to have stared like that, fixedly, at someone you were supposed to know, and yet to have shown no signs of recognition.

A slow, forward-moving impulse shimmered down the length of the queue, and like a great sleepy beast it stirred, heaved itself a few inches along the wet, shining pavement, and came to rest again, as if in relief. Katharine was glad to find, when her section of the queue had finally shuddered to a halt, that the brief upheaval had been sufficient to put an olive green (or was it scarlet?) umbrella between herself and the old woman. And anyway, she thought, reassuring herself, perhaps the old thing was just whiling away the time by sizing *me* up. Two can play at that game, after all. Wryly, Katharine began to wonder what conclusion the woman would have come to? Did she guess at once that Katharine was a busy, capable mother, working part-time to help with the family finances? Could she tell that Katharine was hurrying back now to her comfortable suburban home, to her husband, and her three little girls? Or—Katharine shivered a little, and clutched her scarf tighter against a draughty sputter of rain—can it be that there is already something in my face to show that Stephen and I are no longer happy together? Is there even now that unmistakable tightening round the mouth, that hooded look about the eyes that mark, like a brand, the discontented woman? Did that nosey old thing even imagine that she saw in Katharine's face the frustrated, hungry look . . . ?

In sudden, idiotic defiance, Katharine wanted to turn round, to crane her head round the umbrella and scream at the old woman: You're all wrong! I'm *not* frustrated! I have children. . . a husband. . . . We aren't getting on too well at the moment, I know, but it's only temporary. What you see in my face is only temporary, you silly old fool; only *temporary*, don't you understand? . . .

A sudden, purposeful surging forward of the queue brought Katharine, like the flotsam of a breaking wave, to the threshold of her bus; and a minute later she was wedged inside it, at the far end, trying with one hand both to steady herself and to extract the fare from her handbag, and with the other to deploy her bulging shopping basket in such a way as neither to annoy her neighbours, ladder her stockings, nor squash her pound and a half of tomatoes. Yet even in the midst of these preoccupations Katharine still found time to glance fearfully at the reflection in the darkened window behind the driver's back. It was all right; with all imperfections dimmed by the dimness of the reflecting surface, she looked pleasant, quite young, even quite happy. Of course she did! That old woman was just a fool—a jealous old sour-puss, thought Katharine, happily savouring the total injustice of her unfounded imputations.

When she got off the bus it was nearly closing time at the local shops, and she still had to buy bread. There had only been the sliced, wrapped bread at the supermarket where she had shopped in her lunch-hour, and Stephen hated wrapped bread. Funny, thought Katharine, as she lumbered with her heavy basket towards the bakers, that the growing coldness between herself and Stephen should have affected her in this way: should have created in her not indifference towards his wishes, but rather a nervous, almost obsessive anxiety to please him in as many trivial ways as possible. Did it mean that she still loved him really? Still cared that he should be happy—or at least that he should enjoy as many small happinesses as she could salvage for him from the wreckage of their relationship?

It didn't feel like love. It didn't feel like caring. It felt more like being frightened, Katharine admitted to herself as she emerged from the warm, lighted shop, clutching the crusty loaf protectively under its paper wrapping lest it grow flabby in the damp autumn air.

As she turned the corner into her own road, Katharine saw ahead of her a slim, neat figure, moving rather slowly under the lamplight, body almost primly erect, but head bent.

4

Mary. Mary Prescott, her next-door neighbour. Katharine hurried to catch her up and fell into step—albeit very slow— beside her.

"Hullo." Mary greeted her in the weary, disillusioned voice which Katharine—with a horrid stab of self-dislike—suddenly realised that she had been hoping for. For it meant that Mary had been quarrelling with her husband again; and what despicable, reprehensible comfort there was in this for Katharine! Why is it that when a woman is getting on badly with her own husband, nothing cheers her so much as the knowledge that another woman is getting on even worse with hers? It ought to make me feel worse, Katharine reflected guiltily, but it just doesn't. It makes me feel much, much better. This is really why I ran after her in the first place, simply in the hope of hearing that she has had a perfectly frightful row with Alan!

"You go on ahead if you're in a hurry, Katharine," Mary was saying tensely. "Don't wait for me. I'm going slowly on purpose."

Katharine *was* in a hurry, of course. But even if she had been less ghoulishly eager to suck comfort for herself from Mary's troubles, it would have been cruel to have ignored so blatant an appeal to her curiosity.

"What is it, Mary?" she asked. "Have you . . . ? I mean, is Alan . . . ?"

"He's going out at six," said Mary, her lips only opening the barest minimum to allow the words to escape. "And I can't—I *won't*—go back to the house while he's still there. If it wasn't for Angela I'd face it—I really would. But it's so bad for her to hear us quarrelling; and she's getting to the age when you can't hide it from her. Alan thinks he can. He thinks that if he talks to me in that quiet, dreadful voice, and doesn't shout, then she won't know anything about it. But of course she knows! She may be doing her homework at the top of the house, but that cold, restrained fury of Alan's—it seeps up, Katharine! It does! Up the stairs. Up through the floorboards. . . ."

5

Something in her friend's intensity disconcerted Katharine for a second. Hastily she tried to bring Mary back on to her usual plane of trivial nattering about Alan and his shortcomings.

And it was not difficult. Soon Mary's light, resentful voice was in full and familiar spate about her grievances: how Alan had been writing letters all yesterday evening, right up till bedtime, and then, if you please, had turned round and complained that she never talked to him in the evenings! *Talked* to him! And he knew as well as she did that if she had dared so much as to open her mouth while he was writing he'd have been furious and told her she was interrupting. If only he wasn't so self-righteous when he was being unreasonable ... so cold ... so impervious to argument. ... By the time their short walk was over, Katharine felt that her troubles with Stephen were the merest trifles in comparison—just superficial bickering, such as you might find in any marriage. And there were lamb chops and mushrooms in her basket, which could be cooked quickly, so that tonight at least there would be none of that sense of rush and strain which so often spoilt their evenings right from the start. Supper would be on time. Stephen would be pleased—and would show it, *he* wasn't cold and undemonstrative, like Alan. Poor Mary!

This invigorating Poor-Mary feeling lasted Katharine for just so long as it took her to find the key in her handbag and to open the front door. For as soon as she came into the hall she knew at once, and with deadly certainty, that Clare was crying over her homework again. Not that she could actually hear the familiar, maddening sniffings and gulpings—Clare's room was upstairs, at the back of the house—but she knew it all simply by the air of modest righteousness, the exaggerated composure, with which her second daughter, Flora, came out into the hall to greet her. Her elder sister's troubles always affected Flora like this. You couldn't call it deliberate unkindness—indeed, Flora had very likely been trying to help Clare to the best of her ability. But all the same, she seemed—there was no other word for it—to *thrive* on Clare's inadequacies. Why, she even looked taller whenever

Clare was crying, Katharine noticed irritably as Flora reached up to kiss her.

"Hullo, Mummy. You're late, aren't you? I've done all my homework except my practising, and I got A for biology. Miss Faith showed it to the whole class. She said my diagram was the only one which . . ."

"Splendid, darling. I'm so glad." Katharine spoke rather perfunctorily. For it seemed to her—Oh, so unfairly!—that Flora wasn't talking about her biology lesson at all. Instead, she was telling her that Clare was, at this very moment, crouched heavily over her books in her chilly, untidy bedroom; the fire not switched on, with no blotting paper or india-rubber to hand; and crying quietly, hopelessly, over her quadratic equations. Or was it Latin again? Those wretched gerunds and gerundives?

"And, Mummy," continued Flora, tossing her shining and unwontedly tidy pony-tail (the little wretch had even brushed her hair in celebration of her sister's trials, thought Katharine ungratefully), "Mummy, I tried to light the sitting-room fire for you. But it's gone out."

Katharine's carefully laid fire. The dry wood—the paper—all would be gone; only the black, hopeless lumps of coal would be left; and the black, dead slivers of burnt paper would float out all over the carpet, gently tinkling, as soon as you disturbed them. More wood—and it would be damp this time—must be fetched from the shed.

"Thank you, darling. Never mind." Katharine hoped that she had kept the irritation out of her voice, for, after all, the child had been trying to help. It was hard on them to have to come back from school to an empty, fireless home. Hard on Stephen, too, to have to come home to a supper always late, a wife always preoccupied—and tonight, on top of everything else, to a daughter crying over her homework.

It was this that was going to cause the row tonight, and for a moment Katharine stood very still in the middle of the hall, paralysed by the total conflict of her situation.

For Stephen always said that she shouldn't help Clare. "Doing her homework for her" was what he called it—deliberately provocative, Katharine felt, for he must surely know that she never actually *did* the homework; just explained it. And explained, and explained, and explained. That, of course, was probably the trouble—not that Stephen really disapproved on principle, as he claimed to do, but simply that he couldn't stand spending his evening listening to his wife explaining about present participles, or square roots, or whatever. And what husband *would* like it, she asked herself, with a deliberate effort to put herself on Stephen's side. Immediately she felt a familiar little stab of pleasure at finding she had managed to see something from Stephen's point of view—followed by an equally familiar little stab of frustration at the fact that there was still nothing she could do about it. For Clare *did* need help—and needed it, as always, just when Stephen was expected home. One should either be a childless wife or else an unmarried mother, thought Katharine rebelliously as she set off up the stairs—and even in the midst of her anxieties, she found herself thinking how well this cynical observation would go down at one of those comforting Aren't-Men-Awful sessions at the launderette or over the garden wall.

CHAPTER II

IT ENDED, of course, in Clare's bringing her books down to the kitchen and spreading them about on the table where Katharine was chopping onions against time.

"It's a kind of verbal adjective, you see," Katharine explained all over again, her eyes smarting with the onion smell. "'To be known'—'Knowable'—something like that. So it has to agree with the noun. It's not a verb in the way 'She knows' is a verb."

"'She *doesn't* know,' I'd say," remarked Flora smugly from where she stood, homework all finished, drawing geometrical patterns in a scattering of spilt salt on the dresser. "Mummy, shall I do my practising before supper?"

Katharine did a swift calculation. If there was to be a quarrel—and what with supper late *and* Clare crying over her gerundives there almost certainly would be—then Flora's practising after supper might well be the last straw ("Why on earth can't that child get her practising done earlier? Can't we have *any* peace in this house, ever?") On the other hand, if Flora was occupied at the piano, then she couldn't also be irritating her father by asking questions, or arguing—unwittingly rubbing salt on the surface of a mind already raw and exposed from quarrelling with Katharine.

Katharine felt real tears for a moment soothing away the stinging pain of the onion-tears. Real tears, and no time to indulge them, what with the chops to get on, and Clare wanting to know how a gerundive was different from a passive infinitive, and the potatoes already melting on the outside, yet hard as rocks in the middle—all this week's batch had been like that—and Flora still leaning on the door waiting for her mother to say Yes or No about the practising, and now—ye Gods, it only wanted that!— now the telephone ringing.

When Katharine put the receiver down and went back to the kitchen, she could only hope that her daughters did not notice the terrible relief that she could not keep from her voice.

"That was Daddy," she told them. "He says he'll be very late, and not to wait supper for him. So leave your practising till afterwards, if you like, Flora—and Clare, you leave your Latin. I'll have plenty of time to help you after supper."

She would, too; because now it didn't matter about lighting the sitting-room fire, or cooking cabbage (no one but Stephen liked it), or making things look tidy and welcoming. It was like a sudden holiday—and all because her husband was being kept late at work. When—where in her marriage had she come to feel like this? When had Stephen's homecoming changed from a pleasant climax to the day, and become an anxious deadline? When had her desire to make things happy and comfortable for him in the evenings changed to a compulsive feeling that she had *got* to make things happy and comfortable for him in the evenings? Was it since she had started working again, and was always rushed? Or had it come gradually over the years? . . .

"Mummy!"

Nine-year-old Jane this time, darting into the kitchen as quick and bright-eyed as a field-mouse, her straight-cut dark hair misted over with raindrops. "Mummy, me and Angela have been having such a *super* time! You know where the lamp shines over the wall at the bottom of their garden? Well, you can *read* by it! Did you know? So we took the little table out of Angela's greenhouse, and—"

"But darling, you're soaking!" Katharine ran her hand over her daughter's jersey. "You'll have to change before supper. I'd forgotten you were at Angela's. You had a nice time, did you? And was Angela's mother there—?"

Katharine cut short the seemingly innocent question. Always, always she must be on guard against pumping Jane for inside information about the Prescotts' domestic troubles, for the temptation to do so was tremendous. This evening, for instance, she was dying to know if Mary Prescott had succeeded in dawdling home slowly enough to avoid seeing her husband; and if not, had there been a quarrel? Had they been shouting at each other, or going about in icy silence? Not being able to ask Jane all was like watching a long-awaited instalment of a serial story disappearing into the dustbin.

But after all Jane very likely knew nothing about the Prescotts' quarrels. Perhaps even Angela didn't, in spite of everything that was said about children's sensitiveness to atmosphere in the home. If children were really so sensitive, mused Katharine ruefully, then how was it that they invariably asked their father for complicated and time-consuming favours at exactly the moment when he had pinched his thumb in the car door, or was frantically searching for an urgently needed book? It often seemed to Katharine that the average child, healthily encased in a carapace of total selfishness, could walk unscathed through a domestic atmosphere that you could cut with a knife.

"No. Yes. I didn't see her." Jane's answer broke in on Katharine's speculations. "A sort of grandmother person gave us tea," she continued conversationally. "A *much* nicer tea than Mrs. Prescott gives us. Toast, and real honey in a honeycomb! I wish *we* had a grandmother."

"I'll put it on the grocery list next week," promised Katharine absently. "The honeycomb, I mean, not the grandmother. That's what you want, isn't it? Now do run upstairs, dear, and take off your wet things. I'm just dishing up."

By nine o'clock the two younger girls were in bed and only Clare was left—no longer crying, but looking pale and inky, and bedraggled, and only just starting on her French. She was still working at the kitchen table, and watching her, Katharine wondered, as she had often done before, whether to curse that triumphant day when Clare had scraped through the eleven-plus and won herself a place at the grammar school. The secondary modern would have presented other problems, of course—but wouldn't they at least have been more cheerful ones? Wouldn't it simply be more *fun* to have a thirteen-year-old that you had to scold for wearing lipsticks and high heels, rather than one like this, inky and sodden with crying, yet still refusing to give up; still bravely, mercilessly, trying to suck encouragement, information and moral support from one's own jaded and depleted store? The pile of ironing to be done on her right—the pile of Clare's difficulties to be solved on her left—and neither seeming to get any less, no matter how Katharine worked on them.

And, of course, into the midst of this depressing scene it *would* be Stella, who must plunge, radiating, as usual, an air of having tramped miles across the moors to get here—actually she came from four doors up. So here she was, bursting uninvited through the back door, surging into the small kitchen, and flinging to Katharine a breezy greeting as from wider, nobler spaces, and leaving the scullery door open into the bargain. Katharine went to shut it, the wind whipping round her feet, and came back to invite her visitor to sit down.

Stella, however, was already seated, her feet stretched out under the ironing board, her eyes greedily fastened on Clare's French grammar. Katharine knew that look. Ever since Stella had sent her own children to a progressive boarding school, snatching them from under the very jaws of the eleven-plus (just in time to save them from failing, said the neighbours, and just in time to save them from the grammar school treadmill, said Stella), she had been bubbling over with self-satisfied condemnation of what she now referred to as the educational rat-race. Since Katharine well knew that this tirade could be triggered off by the mere sight of a tattered geography book on a chair, she waited in trepidation to see what would be the effect of the present scene. The whole thing might have been laid on for Stella's especial delectation—the slouching, heavy-eyed grammar school girl, the inky books, the lateness of the hour. . . . In an attempt to avert the armoury of barbed condolences which were about to descend on the unsuspecting Clare, Katharine resorted to swift diversionary tactics, such as offering her visitor coffee, noisily filling the kettle for same, and then asking loudly and enthusiastically after Jack and Mavis in their co-educational paradise.

Oh, they were fine, Stella assured her. Just fine. Getting on marvellously. Loving every minute.

As to which there seemed no more to be said. That was the trouble with Stella now; by sending her children to a school so remote geographically and so Utopian in operation, she had, as it were, put herself outside the conversational orbit of her former friends. All the dear, familiar topics—the problems about bedtimes, teachers, boy-friends, homework—all these now extracted from Stella only one comment, always the same: "Well, you see, at Wetherby Hall that sort of thing simply doesn't arise". This seemed to apply to absolutely everything, from sexual precocity to not liking custard, and consequently left extraordinarily little to talk about to her fellow mothers. Stella's interest in other mother's problems was still unabated, it is true; but there was a sort of gap where her own should have been.

So Katharine struggled to think of something else to talk about. No inspiration came to her, except to send Clare to bed; and that proved an unfortunate move. As Clare slowly piled one battered book on top of another preparatory to taking them upstairs, Stella's face took on a beaky, excited look, like a terrier, as she scented the educational rat-race:

"Do you always have as much homework as this, Clare?" she asked, with monstrous sympathy. "Don't you get terribly tired?"

Clare thought this over in her slow way.

"Not terribly," she answered at last, as though she had measured the word against some exact scale before rejecting it. "It's just on Thursdays, you see. We have four homeworks on Thursdays, with geometry *and* Latin. Latin always takes me ages."

"Mavis doesn't have any homework at all," responded Stella, as if this fact should somehow lighten Clare's problem. "In fact, she doesn't even have to go to lessons if she doesn't want to. And the funny thing is, she finds she learns *more* that way than when she was being forced into it! Isn't that odd?"

The patronising cat! thought Katharine crossly: she doesn't think it's odd at all; she's just trying to show us how marvellous *her* methods are compared with ours! She was immediately shamed by the look of clear, uncomplicated interest which Clare had turned on their guest. Stella, too, must have been a little taken aback, for she pressed her point home clumsily: "Don't you think *you'd* learn more, Clare, if you were at a school like that, where they didn't *force* you?"

Clare was silent for a moment, her grey eyes thoughtful under the tear-swollen lids.

"No," she said at last. "I don't think I would. I think I'd *mean* to work, but I'd keep not doing it." She smiled a little apologetically: "But I expect that's just me. I expect Mavis is different."

Stella looked almost affronted at Clare's total lack of defensiveness; her complete unawareness that either she or her way of life were under fire. Stella turned towards Katharine almost pleadingly, as to a fellow warrior who, although an enemy, did at least know that there was a war on:

"Don't *you* find it tiring, yourself?" she enquired. "I mean, having them hanging around doing homework all the evening like this?"

"Well, I don't know," said Katharine evasively, picking up the iron again. "It's not much different in the holidays when they're hanging around doing something else. Or doing nothing—that's the worst of all, don't you think? When they have nothing to do."

"Well, of course, with Mavis and Jack that simply doesn't arise," said Stella, stretching out her long legs as smugly and luxuriously as a cat, but with much less dexterity: the ironing board lurched under Katharine's hand and the kitchen table shuddered: "Mavis and Jack come home so full of interests and enthusiasms that they simply don't know what boredom *is*."

"What sort of interests?" asked Katharine, with genuine curiosity, while she readjusted the toppling ironing board; "Things they do indoors, do you mean, like painting and Meccano and things, or do they go out a lot?"

"*Everything*," declared Stella with the emphatic vagueness which characterised most of her assertions about her children. "Every kind of interest you can think of."

Katharine quelled her impulse to meet this challenge by thinking of interests so outrageous as to force Stella to be more specific. Instead, she finished sending Clare to bed—odd how Clare's dreamy obedience took up more time and energy, more nagging and pushing, than all Flora's self-assertiveness or Jane's mischief—and poured out two cups of coffee. Stella stretched again as she took her cup—but Katharine was prepared for it this time, with a firm grip on both iron and board. Soon they were deep in a discussion of the manifold advantages accruing from a coffee-grinder—which Stella had got too—as compared with the superfluousness of a cream-making machine, which only Katharine had got.

Stella was just in the middle of explaining that real cream was quite cheap nowadays, and that anyway the top of the milk was just as good, also that ordinary milk was really nicer than cream anyway, and contained more protein, when Katharine heard a very small knock on the front door. Unfortunately, Stella hadn't heard it, so after one or two vain attempts to interrupt, Katharine simply had to leave the room in the middle of hearing about the vitamin content of skim milk. She hurried across the hall just as the very small knock was being repeated a second—or perhaps even a third—time.

It was Angela Prescott, in bedroom slippers and with a winter coat pulled on over her pyjamas. She looked white and rather wide-eyed against the background of rainy darkness, and at first she seemed to have some difficulty in explaining her errand.

"Please—do you think—? That is, do you know where Mummy is?" she asked. "You see, I don't know what to do. I think something's happened."

CHAPTER III

"COME IN, Angela," said Katharine, reaching out to draw the child towards her. "Come into the warm and tell me what's the matter."

But Angela shook her head. Shivering yet obstinate, she would not even come under the shelter of the doorway.

"No," she said. "No, I must go back. You see, I think something's happened. I—I only wondered if you knew where Mummy was?"

With sudden uneasiness. Katharine remembered her last sight of Mary Prescott that evening—creeping, dawdling, killing time under the street lamp so as not to reach home in time to encounter her husband. She remembered with compunction the gusto with which she had listened to Mary's account of this latest quarrel with Alan—a quarrel which sounded just like all the others that Mary had related over the years. Or did it? Hadn't there been something odd, and strained, in Mary's manner? . . .

Certainly Angela must not be allowed to go back alone to whatever was the mysterious trouble next door. Telling the child to wait for a moment, Katharine hurriedly returned to the kitchen, and explained to Stella briefly what had happened, and that she must go back with Angela at once.

Stella's face lit up. Other people's troubles were like nourishment to her—something concentrated and quick-acting out of a jar. She would listen to no argument but that she must come too—"You might need my help," she explained, with shining eyes.

So it could not have been more than a minute or two before Katharine, Stella and Angela were all filing in through the Prescotts' narrow hall, the facsimile of Katharine's own, and into their living-room, which was cold and untidy, and looked as if no one had been in it all day.

Once under her own roof, and in familiar surroundings, Angela became more communicative. Prompted by a good deal of questioning, she managed to give some sort of account of the situation that was troubling her.

Her mother was out; that was the first thing; had been out all the evening. Not that this was so unusual, but her father was out too, and neither of them had told Angela anything about it, or had left any supper for her, or told her to go to bed at the usual time, or any of the things they usually did. They hadn't even argued with each other about whether they *should* go out and leave her, which was apparently a familiar, and therefore comforting, prelude to their outings. "There's usually such a *fuss,* you see," said Angela nostalgically. "About me, and about Mummy not being ready in time, and about the fires being on, or off, and about locking or not locking the back door. I can't understand how they could have just gone, without any fuss at all."

No, she hadn't seen either of them when she came in from school, though of course her father might have been in his study, she hadn't looked. Auntie Pen had come to give her and Jane their tea, and No, she didn't know if Auntie Pen had been asked to come—she hadn't thought anything about it, and anyway Auntie Pen had seemed in a terrible hurry, she had gone away again while Angela and Jane were still eating. And then they'd been playing in the garden, and then Angela had been doing her homework, and it was only when it was bedtime, and there was no one anywhere, that she'd begun to worry.

"So I packed my satchel and polished my shoes ready for tomorrow," continued Angela. "And then I brushed my teeth and I went to bed. I hung up my dress, too," she concluded, virtuously.

Of course, reflected Katharine. That's what a frightened child would be sure to do—to obey punctiliously, and all by herself, the rules that usually had to be enforced by constant nagging: the rules that hold together the threatened framework.

"But you didn't go to sleep?" prompted Katharine, and Angela agreed that she hadn't. She'd lain in bed for a while, listening, and slowly coming to the conclusion that "something had happened." So she'd got up and come next-door to Katharine. That was all. Angela finished her story and looked expectantly at Katharine, with a child's supreme and arrogant confidence in the adult's power—and duty—to explain, to reassure, to put matters right.

Katharine quailed. Angela's expectant gaze, combined with the total lack of data on which to base any sort of action, intimidated her. But Stella was made of sterner—or more inquisitive—stuff.

"I think we should go all over the house," she announced decisively and with relish. "You never know."

"They might have left a note or something," hastily interpolated Katharine, anticipating that "you never know" might be invested by Angela with all sorts of unnerving implications. She wished she knew the child better, so that she might have some idea of the probable direction and extent of her imagination. She wished, too, that Angela could have been left out of the search; but Stella was already striding up the stairs ("We'll start at the top—do the thing systematically") with Angela close on her heels.

The general aspect of the upstairs rooms was one of untidiness and neglect—bedclothes hastily pulled up, assorted garments draped over the chairs, dust filming all the furniture. Stella was as outspoken in her criticism as she dared to be in Angela's hearing. Too outspoken, it seemed to Katharine; but then Katharine had often reflected that Stella would be a more amiable person if she had either fewer convictions or else less of the courage of them.

"You'd never think, would you," observed Stella "that Mary had *nothing* to do but run the house? No job—nothing! I wonder what she *does* with herself all day?"

"She's pretty busy, you know, really," answered Katharine, rather repressively. It wasn't true, of course, but she felt a good deal of sympathy for Mary's ineffectual housekeeping. For who better than Katharine knew the demoralising effect of a quarrel with one's husband? How it made one no longer care whether the carpets were swept or the furniture shining: whether the cushions looked better this way or that way, and whether books and papers were piled sideways on the shelves. Quarrelling could do more damage to the appearance of a house than a party for fifty people, all drunk. And the *time* it took, too! First the shouting, and the slamming doors: then the angry, secret crying . . . the not speaking to each other. And then the long, long brooding, going over and over what he'd said, and what you'd said, and what you *should* have said if only you'd thought of it in time. Yes, on second thoughts, Mary probably *was* a busy woman.

Downstairs now, with Angela almost falling over their feet with her closeness, they searched first the living-room and then the kitchen, where the remains of the toast and honey tea were still littering the table. Katharine wished that Stella wouldn't keep looking into cupboards and under tables. It was absurd, and surely full of frightening implications for Angela— although the child made no comment, and indeed peered into all these ridiculous corners with an avidity apparently as great as Stella's own.

It was in Alan's study that they came upon the bloodstains: like red ink spilled across his desk, and like brown rust stains on the carpet beneath. For a moment Katharine stared at them quite without surprise, feeling, ridiculously, that this was just what she had expected to find all along. Her total lack of emotion made her glance nervously at Stella, as if seeking some clue as to how she ought to look, to behave, in a situation like this; she felt like an unaccustomed church-goer, surreptitiously watching for clues from his neighbours as to when to kneel, when to stand up, when to join in the singing.

But Stella was staring at the desk just as helplessly as Katharine: her face, too, failed to show any appropriate emotion. If anything, she looked rather disapproving, as if this was just another example of Mary's slatternly housekeeping, like the dust and unmade beds upstairs.

And then, quite quickly, the shock began to lift, and Katharine felt astonishment flowing back into her like blood into a numbed limb. But still she could not feel horror. Once again, and even more strongly, she felt the total lack of data as a constricting force all round her, paralysing action. What *could* you do— what could you feel, if it came to that—when you had no idea what had happened? Ring the doctor? But there was no patient for him to come to. Ring the police? But to tell them what? And anyway, supposing Alan had simply cut himself accidentally? Katharine could imagine his cold fury at finding himself on the front page of the local paper as a result of police intervention. Besides, Mary was Katharine's friend; and *supposing* . . . Katharine would not let herself finish this supposition, even in her own mind, but she knew very well it would all add up to not ringing the police. Not without seeing Mary first, anyway.

But *something* must be done. They couldn't just stand there staring at the bloodstains all night. They must fetch someone— ring someone. Who was this Auntie Pen person that Angela had been talking about? She must surely know something about Mary's and Alan's whereabouts since she had come in to see to Angela's tea—had presumably been asked to do so. Was she on the phone? . . .

It was only now, on turning to ask Angela about Auntie Pen, that Katharine realised that the child hadn't followed them into this room at all. What a terribly lucky thing, considering how she had followed like a shadow in and out of all the other rooms. Motioning Stella to follow her, she walked out into the hall, carefully closing the study door behind her.

"Angela!" she called; and after a moment's pause the child came out of the kitchen, quite slowly, and licking her fingers. She must have been helping herself to the bread and honey still on the kitchen table.

"Angela," said Katharine—a little too brightly, perhaps, a little too reassuringly—and was it obvious that she was standing in such a way as to block the door of the study? "Angela—you know you told us your Auntie Pen was here at teatime. Do you know where she lives? Has she a telephone number?"

Was it only Katharine's anxious imagination, or was Angela looking a little guarded? But she answered quite readily.

"Oh yes. It's in the book. Can she come, do you think? I'd like her to come."

Quite absurdly reassured by this, and feeling that simply by wanting Auntie Pen to come, Angela had lifted an enormous load of responsibility from her, Katharine's shoulders, Katharine went eagerly to the telephone. As she waited, listening to the ringing tone, she remembered that this Auntie Pen must be the "sort of grandmother person" referred to by Jane. Was she an old lady, then? Too old to be expected to help with a problem like this? Katharine's doubt subsided at the warm briskness of the voice that was now saying "Hullo?" Old or not, this would be a person who could cope.

Auntie Pen said she would come at once. That is to say, it would take her three-quarters of an hour, and could Katharine stay with Angela until she arrived? She did not ask what had happened—very luckily, for with Angela hanging around like this Katharine did not see how she could have explained very much. Nor did Auntie Pen seem surprised to be thus summoned: indeed, Katharine could have fancied that she had been waiting for just such a phone call, all ready, and with suitcase packed.

As soon as she heard that Auntie Pen was coming, Angela seemed to relax; to realise suddenly that she was very sleepy. Of her own accord she went back to bed, leaving Katharine and Stella downstairs.

It seemed a very long time that Katharine and Stella were sitting in the Prescotts' sitting-room waiting for the front-door bell to ring. Stella had lit the gas fire, but it was making little headway against the day-long coldness of the room; and, oddly, there seemed to be nothing to talk about. Both women were uneasily aware that the breath of possible tragedy had put Mary temporarily out of range of the light-hearted, catty gossip which usually formed the staple of their conversation—indeed the very cement of their friendship, Katharine sometimes ruefully admitted. It was no longer possible, with those unexplained bloodstains in the adjoining room, to discuss Mary's inadequacies as wife or housekeeper; it was not even possible to remark on Angela's rather odd and secretive demeanour throughout the proceedings. Normally, Stella loved to spot signs of insecurity in other people's children; she brought to it all the enthusiasm and proselyting expertise of a keen gardener spotting greenfly on somebody else's roses. Katharine could already see the beginning of frustration on Stella's face; could hear it in the cracking of her joints as she moved her long limbs restlessly. *Bother* Mary, she was almost visibly thinking: *Why* must she get her wretched husband murdered or driven to suicide or something; now we shan't be able to say anything nasty about either of them for weeks and weeks.

Katharine filled in some of the uneasy minutes of waiting by going back to her own home to make sure that the children were asleep, and to leave a brief and rather confusing note for Stephen explaining where she was in case he came in before her. By the time she came back, Stella had made herself more at ease, sitting on the floor in front of the fire, her legs stretched out before her, and reading a copy of *Health for All*. As soon as she saw Katharine, she embarked on a forceful and argumentative dissertation to the effect that drinking two gallons of yoghourt a day wouldn't necessarily make you live to be a hundred and fifty. Since it had never occurred to Katharine to suppose that it would, the forcefulness of the argument was somewhat wasted on her, but all the same she was pleased to find Stella so much herself again after the shock; and the time passed really quite pleasantly until they were interrupted by a sharp, decisive ring at the front door, and knew that Auntie Pen had arrived.

Katharine could not have said exactly what she had expected Auntie Pen to look like—indeed, she had deliberately not allowed herself to build up too definite a picture on the basis of that reassuring voice on the telephone. But with all her caution, all her refraining from over-optimism, she had never dreamed that Auntie Pen's appearance would give her a shock like this. For there in the doorway, framed unmistakably against the misty rain-drenched light from the street lamp, stood the black-coated woman whose eyes Katharine had so disconcertingly met in the bus queue this very evening.

CHAPTER IV

IN THAT single moment Katharine's sense of recognition was complete and beyond doubt or argument. It was only after they had moved into the brightly lighted sitting-room and the new-comer had removed her coat, that Katharine began to wonder if she had been wrong. For with the black coat gone, with the down-turned corners of the mouth lifted in a smile, with the hostile look in the black eyes replaced by the friendly animation suitable to the first greetings between strangers, the woman did indeed look quite different. Moreover, she showed no signs of recognising Katharine.

Full of uncertainty, Katharine felt some uneasiness about confiding in the newcomer, but Stella naturally had no such inhibitions. Indeed, she seemed by now to have developed a somewhat proprietary attitude towards the whole business, and ushered Auntie Pen into the study and showed her the bloodstains with the air of a house-agent displaying a desirable property.

Mrs. Quentin (for such they had learned was Auntie Pen's name) did not seem shocked, nor even very much surprised; but her face changed in some indefinable way as Stella went on talking, so that Katharine once again felt sure that this was indeed the woman in the bus queue. After staring, thoughtfully rather than with horror, at the desk and at the floor, Mrs. Quentin turned towards Stella, checking her flow of narrative with an impatient half-patronising gesture.

"I see," she said slowly. "I'm beginning to understand." Then, more briskly, and with a hint of apology in her smile: "This has been a dreadful shock for you both, I realise now. I'm sorry. I really am. I should have rung up or something. . . . But do let me assure you that nothing very dreadful has occurred—"

"Then you know—"

"What is it, then—?"

Katharine and Stella both spoke at once, and Mrs. Quentin smiled again, deprecatingly.

"No, no. I don't know *exactly* what has happened, any more than you do. But I do know that no one has been seriously hurt. Mary—Mrs. Prescott—rang up to tell me that Alan—my brother, you know—has had a slight accident with a knife and is in hospital. It's not serious, you understand; he will probably be out again tomorrow. But the wound has to be stitched, you see. Nothing to keep him laid up for long—"

She stopped, and looked her two companions straight in the eyes—almost, Katharine fancied, as if defying them to disbelieve her or to ask any more questions. And Katharine, indeed, could not for the moment think of any more to ask. Her mind was fully if foolishly occupied in calculating how this old—or at least elderly—woman could possibly be Mary's sister-in-law. She could, though. After all, Alan must be at least fifty—it was only because he was Mary's husband, and Mary was so much younger, that they all thought of him as the same sort of age as themselves. He could easily have a sister ten years older than himself, or more. . . .

But while Katharine's mind was tracing out this byway of irrelevant curiosity, Stella's had kept zestfully to the point. She was bombarding Mrs. Quentin with questions of every kind, ranging from the wholly reasonable to the nearly impertinent. When had it all happened? When had Mary rung up? Why had Mrs. Quentin come to give Angela tea in the first place? And then gone away again? *Where* was Alan wounded?

Mrs. Quentin was no longer smiling: she was watching Stella guardedly as the questions rattled forth; and when she replied to this last question she seemed to be choosing her words carefully. Her brother had been wounded in the upper arm, she said, clearly and primly; and it was an accident.

Such finality did she put into the word that even Stella was silenced. For a few seconds no one spoke, though it seemed to Katharine that the whole room was a-whisper with the unspoken question that must be filling the three minds: namely, what sort of task would a man have to be engaged on to wound himself in the upper arm by accident? Pencil-sharpening? Wood-carving? Cutting bread? You'd have to be a contortionist to manage it.

But, anyway, he was all right; no harm had been done. Oddly, all three women broke the silence simultaneously with words to this effect. But the only thing was, where was Mary now? Apparently she had rung up Auntie Pen from the hospital at about nine o'clock, and Auntie Pen had understood from her then that she would be leaving for home almost at once.

"And she still isn't back," commented Katharine, looking at her watch. "It's after eleven. What do you think can have happened? Should we ring the hospital?"

But Mrs. Quentin thought not.

"There's no need to rush her, now I'm here," she said. "I can stay the night if necessary, so Angela will be all right. Mary's probably had to stay to sign forms or something. Or maybe he's been given an anaesthetic, and she wants to see him when he comes out of it. Anyway, there's nothing to worry about."

Nothing to worry about. It was as if Stella had been waiting for these words as for a green light at a crossroads. Now it would be all right to say something a teeny bit nasty about Mary.

"I'm surprised Angela can't come home from school and get her own tea," she commented, cautiously feeling her way out of the unaccustomed charitableness forced on her by the events of the last two or three hours. "I'd have thought a child of ten—a *secure* child—would be able to do that."

Mrs. Quentin looked at her appraisingly.

"Yes—I suppose so," she said non-committally. "But it didn't matter—I was quite pleased to come. I've been out of town a long time, you know, and I was glad of the chance to see Angela again. I've always been fond of the child. Besides," she went on cautiously, "I didn't think it was just a question of Angela's tea. When Mary asked me to come—when she rang me up this afternoon—I got the impression that she was— well—in a bit of a state. You know—well, you must do, being neighbours—you must know that Mary doesn't always get on too well with my brother, so when she rang up sounding so—so upset—I thought perhaps she might have left him again—"

Mrs. Quentin stopped: feeling, perhaps, that she was being indiscreet, carried away by the lateness of the hour and the illusory intimacy of shared anxiety.

"And has she? Left him, I mean?"

Stella's gusto was almost indecent, and Mrs. Quentin stiffened.

"Well—obviously not," she replied dryly. "There she is, in hospital with him, waiting anxiously for him to come round. A devoted wife. She really is, you know, in her own way."

The last sentence was spoken in such a way as to give the lie to any suspicion of sarcasm in the preceding phrase. Stella looked a little downcast. It had been such fun when Mary had left Alan before—she'd cried for nearly a week when she came back, letting the neighbours give her good advice all the time, and telling them about all the awful things Alan did. And now here was Alan's sister who might, handled carefully, be induced to tell them about all the awful things Mary did. Expertly, Stella surveyed the possible openings. Not a blatant question, of course; it would have to be something sympathetic—and it must also suggest that they already knew so much about Mary's affairs that it wouldn't be disloyal of Mary's sister-in-law to discuss her with them.

"Of course, anything like that is so disturbing to children," Stella began. "Particularly to Angela, of course. Being an adopted child, she'd be bound to feel it more."

"Oh—so you knew she was adopted?"

The ruse was working. No, it wasn't. Praise, not criticism was to follow: "I think she's a happy child, all the same. Not an anxious one."

"Not anxious!" Stella was outraged. "Look how nervous she was this evening, just at finding herself alone in the house! Did you notice, Katharine, how she clung to us, following us about every step we took? And so reserved, too, and so repressed. A normal child would have been crying."

"She was shy, naturally," Katharine pointed out. "Any of mine would have been the same if they'd had to go in to Mary in a similar situation."

Stella looked at her pityingly, and Katharine realised that she had merely exposed her own children to similar charges. Shyness was doubtless another of the troubles that simply didn't arise at Wetherby Hall. She shifted her ground. "*Anyone* would have been worried, whatever their age," she argued. "*We* were worried, if it comes to that."

"Yes, of course we were; but then Angela hadn't the same reason. She didn't know about the bloodstains. Didn't you notice that the study was the one room she didn't follow us into?"

Katharine had noticed; and suddenly the oddness of this fact struck her with full force. She had assumed that it was a lucky coincidence that Angela should have tired of the search just then. But was it? Could it not be that Angela was deliberately avoiding that room? Avoiding it because she had been in it already: knew what was to be seen there; and did not want to see it again?

Katharine was just about to suggest this possibility, but something—a sort of weariness—held her back. She would only be told that such behaviour in a ten-year old argued unhealthy secretiveness of a sort characteristic of adopted children who

29

are about to go in for the eleven-plus, and that Jack and Mavis would have behaved quite differently in similar circumstances, and anyway circumstances like these simply didn't arise at Wetherby Hall, as indeed they probably didn't. And in any case, the conversation had now shifted from Angela to the parents.

"Of course, my brother is a very reserved man," Mrs. Quentin was saying. "As well as being so much older than Mary. I don't imagine he is very easy to live with—especially for a girl like Mary, so open and impetuous by nature, though of course marriage has changed her a lot. I always said he should have married a Victorian heroine sort of girl—an ultra-feminine type who would twist him round her little finger. But Mary's the type of girl who never uses her little finger where fists will do: she insists on head-on collisions when she wants her own way. Or did. As I say, she's changed."

"And *I* think she shouldn't *let* herself be changed," burst out Stella. "Head-on collisions are healthy. They're honest. Every marriage should be based on absolute honesty, collisions and all."

Mrs. Quentin looked at her a little pityingly.

"Absolute honesty couldn't fail to wreck even the best of marriages," she observed, with a sort of sad certainty; and then, as Stella stared at her, she elaborated: "Or rather, I should say absolute honesty on the part of *both* partners. It's all right for one of them to be totally honest so long as the other is willing to undertake all the necessary deceptions. By this means one partner is enabled to glory in his egocentric honesty, while the other struggles to keep the marriage going; and for him—or her—there is no glory."

She fell silent, with a look of brooding melancholy which set Katharine speculating about a possibly non-existent Mr. Quentin. Was he—had he been—an inveterate truth-teller? Had Auntie Pen shed him somewhere along the line—divorced or separated? Or was she a widow? Or—possibly—was she just an ordinary married woman, with Mr. Quentin sitting at home right now, with one eye on the clock, waiting to embark on some more than usually forceful truth-telling? Just look at the time—nearly twelve o'clock!

Katharine got up from her chair. There was absolutely no reason for staying any longer, now that Auntie Pen was here. And yet—she hesitated. It was so queer that Mary wasn't back. Her husband's injury was not serious: what could be keeping her so long? Why hadn't she at least rung up—sent some message? As she stood hesitating, Katharine saw Mrs. Quentin's eyes fixed on her just as they had been in the bus queue, with the same thoughtful, faintly hostile intensity. They seemed to be delving deep into her thoughts . . . boring for samples into her very soul.

"Yes—you must be very tired," was all the older woman said at the end of this deep scrutiny. "I'm sure you're both dying to get home and go to bed. Please don't feel you have to stay any longer; everything's under control."

She stood up briskly; and then, as if there had been no interruption of her former train of thought, she added:

"And so, you see, I always feel it is fairer if *both* partners take their share of the necessary deceptions."

Whether this remark was addressed to Stella, or to Katharine, or simply to the world at large, it was impossible to tell. Katharine only knew that it added somehow to the obscure uneasiness she felt about leaving the house with Mary's absence still unexplained. Still, Mrs. Quentin was in charge. She must really be kind and sensible—look how fond Angela was of her; how pleased—how comforted and reassured—she had seemed on hearing that Auntie Pen was coming. Children's instincts could be relied on in these matters—or so everyone said, and who was Katharine to query so universally held an opinion, and at twelve o'clock at night, too.

She ran quietly down the Prescotts' steps in the still, damp air of midnight, and quickly up the adjoining ones to her own front door, closing it softly behind her as she went in.

The light in the hall was still on; her note to Stephen was still lying on the little table where she had left it. Katharine was seized with a sudden anger close to tears. So he hadn't even bothered to read it! He didn't care where she was or what she was doing at this hour of the night. He would be asleep by now, no doubt, and certainly she wasn't going to risk waking him. She did not know whether it was anger at the unread note that brought her to this decision, or fear of starting a quarrel, or even consideration for Stephen's night's rest after his long day at work. What ever it was, she did not go up to bed: instead, she passed a brief, uncomfortable night on the sitting-room couch, waking at half-past six, stiff and dazed, to the unaccustomed sound of someone else doing the washing up.

CHAPTER V

FOR A few minutes Katharine lay still, trying to feel grateful. It was Stephen, of course; Stephen must have noticed that she had gone out last night without washing up the supper things, and had decided to get up early and do them for her. It was terribly nice of him. Any wife would appreciate it.

So Katharine rounded up her thoughts and tried to compel them in the direction they should go. But it was no use. Trying to coerce one's thought was like that frantic stirring of an egg custard after it has already begun to curdle: you know that the change is irrevocable, and that it will never be smooth again, and yet you go on stirring, compulsively.

The trouble was that it always seemed to Katharine that Stephen only washed up when he was annoyed with her. But what could he be annoyed about this time? Something she had said—done? Or something she had not said—not done? Or something about the children? Surely Clare couldn't still have been crying about her Latin when he came in last night? And telling him, with that admirable, catastrophic frankness of hers, exactly how much her mother had helped her with it? Katharine wriggled off her uncomfortable couch, pulled on her dressing-gown, and went out into the hall.

At the kitchen door she stopped, adjusting a grateful smile on her face as she might have adjusted a slipping shoulder strap. For after all, even if Stephen always washed up in anger, it didn't follow that he washed up out of spite. On the contrary, he probably did it rather as she had brought that nice crusty bread last night—a forlorn attempt to make up in trifling material ways for the empty or unkind feelings towards her that were beyond his control. Was he beginning to hate crusty bread, just as she hated being helped with the washing up?

This feeling that they were fellow-sufferers of each other—that they were each painfully evolving the same hopeless techniques for dealing with the same unwelcome emotions—moved Katharine strangely. A stab of rare tenderness towards her husband suddenly changed the carefully adjusted smile on her face into a real smile, bewildered, sad, and loving. If Stephen had turned round at once when she came into the room, he would have seen it. But he didn't; he went on scrubbing fiercely at a saucepan for several seconds. By the time he did turn round, it was too late; everything had already gone wrong.

For Stephen was not looking in the least as Katharine had pictured him during that moment as she stood outside the door. If only he had been padding brusquely and clumsily about in his old brown dressing-gown, his hair still standing sleepily on end! It wouldn't have mattered, then, even if he had looked a bit cross as he turned round. But instead, he was already dressed, neatly and completely, in his dark town suit; his hair was smartly smoothed down, and his face already wore the aloof, preoccupied, business-man look which went with these clothes. Not even the touching absurdity of a frilly apron had been allowed to soften the picture; instead he was protecting his suit with a tea towel tied round so stiff and straight as to seem almost to belong with the rest of the outfit. Briskly and irritably he was pitching knives and forks off the plates into the hot water, and stacking the plates themselves into an angry tower. He hardly glanced at Katharine as she stood in the doorway trying to replace the fading, useless smile in her lips. Perhaps, even now, if she ran across the room to him. . . .

"Why don't we have a washing-up mop, like other people? Just look at this!"

Stephen held up the tattered remnant of old towelling that Katharine had got so used to during its weeks of service that she had not noticed its advancing senility. It did look rather awful; but all the same, Stephen didn't have to hold it out ostentatiously between his finger and thumb like that. He must have been using it without demur all the time until she came into the room; why had it suddenly become so repulsive *now*?

"We *have* got a mop," she countered defensively. "It's——"

But it wasn't, of course. And then Katharine remembered that Jane must have taken it for cleaning her rabbit hutch. It was the only thing that would go right into the corners, Jane said; and though Katharine had told her that No, she mustn't have it, she had known, even at the time, that she wasn't saying it in the tone of voice which would actually prevent Jane taking it; and she knew that Jane knew that she knew that she wasn't; so in a way you couldn't really say that it was disobedience on Jane's part at all.

Though of course Stephen wouldn't see it like that. He would say that it *was* disobedience, and that if there was any more of this sort of thing the rabbit would have to be got rid of; and Jane would cry, and then Clare would butt in with some tactless argument— tactless as only Clare could make it—in Jane's defence; and then there would be a frightful row all through breakfast, and by that time Clare would be crying too, and that would make her forget her hockey boots, and she would miss her train coming back for them, and that would mean she would get into trouble for being late and would come home miserable about it, and then there would be another row about why is Clare always in trouble at school? . . .

This vista of alternate tears and rows, without foreseeable end, seemed to Katharine at that moment to justify any kind of lie, black or white, that she could think of quickly enough.

"I forgot; it was worn out and I meant to get a new one," she improvised hastily, assuring herself by some blurred and devious reasoning that it wasn't really a lie because she really *was* going to stop Jane using the mop for the rabbit hutch in future.

"I can't understand," Stephen was saying, flicking cups upside down on to the draining board with an ostentatious efficiency far greater—it seemed to Katharine—than could possibly be needed for so simple a task; "I can't understand why you don't keep stocks of the things you need, like other women. This mop business is typical. You wait until your old one is worn out and thrown away before you think of buying another. It's the same with everything in this house. There's never any soap in the bathroom. The black shoe polish is—"

"I bought a new tin yesterday," snapped Katharine. "I just haven't put it out on the shelf yet, that's all. And as for the soap, there's been exactly once, in the last six months, when—"

She heard her own voice, rising shrill and shrewish, and stopped in disgust. There was some truth in his complaints, of course. She *was* careless about this sort of thing, and she might have admitted it handsomely if it hadn't been for that infuriating "like other women". *What* other women? On what grounds was he so certain that all other women were such models of house-wifely efficiency? Let him ask some of the other husbands, that's all! What a pity men didn't gossip about their wives the way women did about their husbands, then they would soon learn that their own wife wasn't the only one with shortcomings. . . . What were they really quarrelling about, anyway, she and Stephen? Was it really about soap, and shoe polish, and washing-up mops?

"Didn't you see my note last night?"

She thrust the query without warning into the middle of their bickering, surprising even herself by its irrelevance. It was no wonder that Stephen stared at her stupidly for a moment.

"Your note?" he repeated blankly.

"Yes, I left you a note on the hall table, where I always do. Telling you where I was last night. You didn't notice I wasn't in bed, I suppose?"

She wished she had left out this bitter little tailpiece, but it was too late now. Stephen looked at her wearily, with a quite

36

uncalled-for air (it seemed to Katharine) of being nagged and henpecked.

"Honestly, Katharine, I came in absolutely worn out at God knows what hour, and I staggered up to bed, and when I found you weren't there, I dragged myself back as far as the top of the stairs, and saw that there *was* a note on the table, but I was too tired to bother to go down and read it."

Katharine felt as if she had been slapped. Her spirit tingled like smarting skin.

"You were?" was all she could find to say in her anger and hurt.

"I was. And anyway, I knew what it would say. What your notes always say: 'Gone to Mary Prescott's. Back in half an hour.' Meaning you'll be back in about four hours, as Mary's had another *frrrrightful* row with her *frrrrightful* husband, and wouldn't I like to hear all about it?"

In spite of himself, Stephen's voice was growing amused now, warm. In a moment Katharine too would have been laughing at the absolute rightness of his guess. . . .

"Mummy! Where's my clean blouse?"

But it wasn't Flora's shouting over the bannisters that destroyed the moment: it was Katharine's shouting back. And yet what else could she do, with Flora's breath already indrawn for another, more imperative "Mummy!"?

"Hush, dear, don't shout so! It's in the—"

Oh, bother! She hadn't even ironed it yet; it was still damp and crushed up in the pile left when Angela interrupted her last night.

"Wait a minute, Flora," she yelled—a self-contradictory sort of yell, trying to be loud enough for Flora to hear from the upstairs landing, and yet soft enough for Stephen, right beside her, not to feel that it was interrupting their conversation. "I'll bring it up in a minute," she went on, desperately, and wondered if Flora knew as well as she did that it would be ten minutes at least. And it was already twenty-past seven, and she hadn't woken Clare yet—Clare, who would sleep till lunch time unless roused over and over again.

"Wake Clare for me, will you, Flora," she yelled once more, aware of Stephen's stiffening irritation at the tumult; and switching on the iron, she set to work on the blouse.

And then, like a film unwinding, everything began to happen exactly as Katharine had foretold. First, Clare came down to breakfast very late and very sleepy, carrying a pair of hockey boots so muddy that not even the kitchen floor could reasonably be expected to house them, and Katharine told her to put them outside the back door till after breakfast. In a sleep-walking sort of way, and mercifully without argument, Clare obeyed, and came back looking a little less stupefied.

"Look, Mummy," she announced amiably, "I've found the washing-up mop. It was on top of Curfew's hutch."

She thrust the unwelcome object towards Katharine. Rabbitty sawdust dripped incriminatingly over floor and table, and Stephen looked up sharply.

"I thought you said you'd thrown it away?" he accused; and Katharine clutched the abominable thing almost protectively.

"Yes— I meant— That is—" She stopped; for the mop looked horribly healthy in spite of the damp and the sawdust. New, and plump, and fluffy it was; no one in their senses would have thrown it away. However, Stephen was in the middle of some gloomily absorbing bit of the paper; he might even now have let the whole thing slide if only it hadn't been for the awful lack of any instinct for self-preservation on the part of any of the children.

"Oh, Mummy, I'm sorry!" gasped Jane disastrously. "I *did* mean to bring it back, and I *did* mean to wash it, like anything! I was going to wash it and wash it, so that there *couldn't* be any germs! I'll do it now if you like."

She jumped up, scraping her chair back noisily, snatched up the mop with a fresh shower of sawdust, and tripping over her satchel on the way, she plunged towards the sink. No father on earth, however deeply immersed in however apocalyptic a morning paper, could possibly fail to notice the commotion. Stephen looked up indignantly.

"Have you been using that mop for the rabbit hutch again, Jane?" he asked. "I thought I heard Mummy telling you not to, days ago."

"No, well, you see, Daddy, it was only just for this once," she explained eagerly. "You see, Curfew's sawdust had got awfully wet, and there were all bits of bread in it—I *wish* people wouldn't keep giving him bread, Curfew hates bread—and you see, as it's Curfew's birthday on Saturday—"

If only, thought Katharine, watching helplessly from the wings, if only she wouldn't keep bringing in the creature's name so much. If only she would refer to him as "the rabbit". For among the multifarious aspects of Jane's rabbit that annoyed Stephen, this name "Curfew" was one of the most provocative. Indeed, Katharine herself had been rather taken aback at the time of the christening, and had asked Jane, rather doubtfully, but *why*?

"Oh, *Mummy*," Jane had replied, a little patronisingly. "He's called after the Curfew in the poem, of course. Don't you know it? 'The Curfew tolls the knell of parting day'—?"

She quoted the line solemnly, raptly. It was plain that she found it beautiful. But what on earth did she think it meant? Did she think that a curfew was some sort of small animal? And if so, what did she think "tolls" meant? And "knell"? What, in the name of sense and reason, could be the picture in her mind as she chanted the words in unison with her classmates in 2A? Katharine hadn't quite liked to ask her point blank: it seemed a pity to disillusion her—especially when disillusion would involve a whole new fuss about what the rabbit was to be called, all over again. And anyway, it was all rather sweet, in a way. . . .

But when Katharine told him about it, Stephen hadn't thought it was rather sweet at all. He simply thought that it showed how appallingly Jane was being taught in her primary school, and how appallingly inattentive she must be. He went on and on about it—how heedless and scatter-brained Jane was becoming (which was Katharine's fault); and going on to how crazy the State educational system was (which you'd have thought was Katharine's fault too, the way he glared at her). Luckily, his annoyance wasn't sufficient to make him propose taking Jane away from her school—where, after all, she was very happy, and learned, by fits and starts, a surprising amount of quite complicated arithmetic: but it was sufficient to cause him an extra stab of irritation every time he heard the rabbit referred to by its ridiculous name. The rabbit and Jane's educational deficiencies were now firmly and inextricably intertwined in his mind: and if only Jane could *understand* this—or no—understanding was too much to ask; if only she could have some sort of *instinct* about it, the way children were supposed to have. . . . If only, one way or another, she would stop *saying* it—"Curfew. . . . Curfew. . . . Curfew. . . ." Couldn't she *see* how it was all bound to end? . . .

". . . Any more of this sort of thing, and I'll have the brute got rid of!"

Fatalistically, Katharine waited for the rest of it. Jane in tears. "It's not *fair*. Daddy! Oh, Daddy, you *can't*. . . !" and now here was Clare plunging recklessly, ineptly, to the rescue, like a non-swimmer whose courage in plunging into the stormy sea is only equalled by his nuisance-value in having to be rescued himself.

"Jane doesn't mean it's not fair that she should be punished," explained Clare heavily. "She means it's not fair to *Curfew*. I mean, it's not *his* fault about the mop, is it? It's not even his fault that Jane has him at all."

"Well—for God's sake—! is it *my* fault, then?" exploded Stephen. "Wasn't I against having the beastly creature right from the start? The damned animal has caused nothing but trouble ever since she had it! One fuss after another . . . day after day. . . ."

"He doesn't! It's not!" screamed Jane, beside herself with the injustice. "It's *you* who causes all the fuss, Daddy, not Curfew! There's never any fuss about Curfew when you're not there!"

This was so devastatingly true that for a second everyone was silenced. But of course Jane mustn't be allowed to speak to her father like that.

"Jane! Be quiet!" cried Katharine despairingly. "And you too, Clare," she added, seeing her elder daughter already opening her mouth with her disastrous "But Daddy, Jane only meant . . ." "Be quiet, all of you!" Katharine continued scolding. "And go and get ready for school. Just look at the time!"

And as she began to clear the abandoned breakfast table, Katharine found herself reflecting that not Eve, but Cassandra, should be counted the prototype of womankind. For wasn't this the hardest part of a woman's lot—to know in advance, and in every detail, the exact course of every family row, and yet to be unable to deflect it one millimetre from its preordained course?

CHAPTER VI

KATHARINE DIDN'T have to be at her job till mid-day, and she had long ago worked out a timetable by which all the chores could be finished before she left the house at eleven-thirty. On an ordinary morning, that is to say, when nothing out of the way occurred to interrupt her. But it so happened that during the whole of the twelve months since she had begun working, there had never once been an ordinary morning in this sense. Not once; and Katharine was gradually coming to the conclusion that the sort of morning presupposed by the timetable simply didn't exist in the housewife's world. Take this week, for instance. On Monday the coal-man had rung up to say he was coming, and Katharine had had to clear the seaside spades out of the cellar; and the broken birdcage, and the sodden cardboard boxes, and the wet leaves and bits of paper. And then he hadn't come. He hadn't come on Tuesday either, but on Tuesday she had had to take Jane for her last polio injection, and take her on to school afterwards as she didn't know the way from the clinic by herself. On Wednesday the coal-man *did* come, just after she had washed the kitchen floor, so that on Thursday the kitchen floor had to be washed again, and also the geraniums had to be potted and brought indoors in a hurry because the paper said it was going to be frosty. It hadn't been frosty, in fact it had rained all day and all night, and they could just as well have been left till the week-end, but anyway, here was Friday, and she must—she simply must—pop in next-door and see how Mary was—whether she'd got home all right last night and everything. And hear the end of the story, too, she admitted to herself, as she dried her hands and took off her apron. The kitchen was finished, and she would only stay at Mary's a few minutes, and do the bedrooms when she got back.

There were already three other visitors sitting round Mary's kitchen table when Katharine arrived, and Mary herself, looking a little withdrawn, was standing by the gas cooker refilling a large earthenware teapot. Evidently she accepted unquestioningly the unwritten law of the neighbourhood that the first duty of anyone in trouble or distress is to make endless pots of tea for the people who drop in to hear all about it.

Katharine glanced quickly at her fellow guests. Stella was there of course; she sat leaning her elbows on the table and clasping her teacup in both hands, flamboyantly, somehow managing to give the impression that it was a pint of beer. Beside her, like a bright well-chosen little accessory, sat Esmé, her niece—or was it cousin?—who lived on the top floor of Stella's house. Esmé was small and blonde and recently married, and as she helped herself to three small spoonfuls of sugar she was glancing round a little nervously. As well she may, thought Katharine ruefully, among us skilled and seasoned gossips. And with Mrs. Forsyth here, too, to ensure that the conversation should hinge largely on the shortcomings of the whole male sex, epitomised as they were in the otherwise insignificant person of the absent Mr. Forsyth. Mrs. Forsyth was already wearing that aggrieved yet curiously satisfied look of a woman modestly aware of the prestige conferred by the ownership of a husband with more faults and failings than any other in the whole neighbourhood; and as she stirred her tea with small, jabbing movements she was watching Mary with a sort of eager, prompting look, as if willing her to make some damaging disclosure about Alan which she, Mrs. Forsyth, could then cap with one even more damaging about her Douglas.

But Mary was just now absorbed in pouring Katharine a cup of tea, and in answering once again the questions that she must already have answered three times this morning. Yes, Alan was as well as could be expected. Yes, he was out of hospital already; he was upstairs in bed right now.

"*In bed*?" Mrs. Forsyth had evidently found the required opening. "In *bed*, with just a cut on his arm? You'd think a bandage, or a sling, or something, would be all that was necessary, and he could go about his work as usual. But men are all the same, aren't they. The tiniest thing, and they take to their beds as if they were dying! Goodness, don't I know! Last week-end Douglas had a cold. Just an ordinary cold in the head, like we all get, you know—but he was absolutely convinced that he'd got flu! *Determined* to have it, that's what I say; it nearly drove me potty, having him drooping about trying to get me to make a fuss of him. All Sunday he went about with a thermometer in his mouth, like a baby with a dummy, trying to make it go up to 99. But it never did; I had to laugh, really!"

She laughed again now; and little, fair Esmé laughed, too, nervously. She was too young, too sweet, too newly married for this sort of thing, thought Katharine; the poor child seemed to be trying desperately to find a foothold in this harsh and alien conversation:

"*My* husband was ill too, last week," Esmé ventured bravely; and then, as four pairs of eyes fastened on her with instant greedy expectancy, she sought frantically for a sequel to this rather barren bit of information.

"The doctor thought at first it was laryngitis," she battled on: but still the eight eyes demanded some luscious climax, and at last poor Esmé panicked. "But it wasn't!" she finished helplessly, and hid as much of her confusion as she could behind her cup of tea. Katharine felt terribly sorry for her—and momentarily ashamed for the rest of them—but before she could think of some pleasant, interested remark to make about the girl's abortive anecdote, Mary broke in rather brusquely:

"Alan's not like that at all," she asserted, speaking to Mrs. Forsyth. "In fact, he's rather the opposite, really. He despises any kind of weakness in anybody, including himself. But the doctor insisted that he should stay in bed. There was the shock, you see, as well."

"Of course there was!" agreed Stella enthusiastically. "And of course it's always much worse with that reserved type, who won't let themselves go. If only he'd screamed, or snatched the knife back and stabbed the fellow back—but of course Katharine doesn't know about all this, do you Katharine? Alan was *stabbed* last night. It wasn't an accident at all."

"Then who—? How—?" exclaimed Katharine, and Stella plunged readily into the story on Mary's behalf:

"It was an intruder," she began importantly. "A burglar, presumably, and he walked into the study where Alan was sitting at his desk, and when Alan turned round, the fellow got in a panic, stabbed him, and ran away."

Katharine felt dazed.

"But why on earth should a burglar walk into the study when Alan was there?" she objected. "It sounds quite mad."

"Oh, well, you see," Stella explained—and she seemed as eager to gloss over the discrepancies in the story as if she was herself its author—"you see, Alan always sits there so quietly, I suppose, with that reading lamp with a black shade shining just on to his work. . . . Why, even Angela didn't know he was in that evening, and nor did Auntie What's-her-name. You know, Mrs. Thingummyjig. Anyway, however it was, this man walked in—a dark man, Alan says, doesn't he, Mary? A dark man wearing a raincoat. He walked in, and he stabbed Alan, and then he ran off— What is it, Mary?" For Mary had got hastily to her feet. She was glancing from one to another of her visitors with a curious, trapped look; her hands fumbled nervously with the kettleholder she was clutching as if it was a weapon of defence.

"I—it's all right. Do please stay, all of you—and carry on with the tea. I must go up to Alan for a minute. . . . I think I heard him calling. . . ."

She backed out of the door, facing them all the time, as if they were royalty; and then she either didn't go up to Alan or else she went up very, very quietly; for Katharine, straining her ears, did not hear another sound from outside the room.

But no one else seemed to have noticed anything odd; and Stella was now leaning across the table in an intimate, conspiratorial manner, steering her story into deeper labyrinths than had been possible in Mary's presence:

"When I say it was a 'burglar' I'm only speaking very generally, you understand. There is a burglar in all of us, after all, isn't there, just as there is a sadist and a murderer?"

Sipping their tea, her companions accepted these charges contentedly enough, as people do nowadays. Besides, they guessed that her speech was only a prelude to further exciting revelations, and listened eagerly as she continued:

"It does make you wonder—doesn't it?—whether Alan had any enemies. That reserved, silent type of man—his own repressed hostility tends to become externalised in the form of antagonism among those around him."

"You mean he annoys people by being so disagreeable?" hazarded Mrs. Forsyth, after a few moments' pondering on the translation. "But you wouldn't think, would you," she added, after further thought, "that any friend of Alan's could be so *crude*. I mean actually attacking him *physically*—"

"Stella said 'enemy' actually, not friend," pointed out Katharine mildly; but Stella did not seem at all grateful for the support.

"Friend—enemy—it's all the same," she declared pugnaciously. "Mrs. Forsyth is quite right. A man's enemies *do* have to be in keeping with his character, just as much as his friends have to. After all, love is a form of hate, really, isn't it?"

Stella always made this sort of statement with such a placid, proprietary air as to make contradiction—or even query—impossible. You felt that, to her, an opinion like this was a valuable possession, like a mink coat. If you didn't possess one too, well, it was just too bad, but not a matter for argument.

"And another thing," Mrs. Forsyth broke in, tugging the conversation back within reach as if it was an escaping balloon. "Didn't you notice that Mary seemed—well—a little *odd* just now—when Stella was talking about this man with the raincoat. It occurred to me that perhaps she knew—or guessed—who it might be. Didn't you feel that?"

"Yes, and another thing," responded Stella eagerly. "Doesn't it strike you as queer that she should go off and leave Angela alone in the house like that, knowing that this character with the knife was still around? It only makes sense if—as you say—she *did* know who he was. Knew that although he had stabbed Alan, he still wouldn't harm Angela—"

"Which means she must have known his motive!" squeaked Mrs. Forsyth excitedly. "Yes, it all fits in, doesn't it? For all we know, *she* may have been his motive! I mean, it's not so unlikely, is it? Young—well, fairly young—wife: elderly jealous husband. . . . My goodness! . . ." Mrs. Forsyth began to giggle shrilly as all the interesting implications took hold on her imagination. "My goodness! We're going to see some fun now, aren't we, when all the dark husbands with raincoats who were 'working late' last night are going to have to produce alibis? My! What a joke!"

Her laugh was spiteful rather then amused; but all the same, for poor Esmé's sake, Katharine made an effort to treat the suggestion as really a joke.

"Goodness, yes," she said, smiling. "I hope you had your Douglas tied to the kitchen table all evening, for a start!"

Mrs. Forsyth laughed more spitefully than ever.

"Oh, *him*! The poor fish can't even tell the plumber off for bungling the immersion-heater, let alone stab anybody! He'd expect *me* to do anything like that that needed doing, believe you me! And as to carrying on with Mary—heavens, I'd know soon enough if he was carrying on with another woman; he'd be borrowing the housekeeping money all the time, and getting me to look up the times of week-end trains to Brighton. And she'd always be ringing up asking where he was because of the muddles he'd make about meeting her. I'd have to nurse him through it like an illness, be terribly sympathetic, and at the same time pretend I didn't know anything about it. In any case, he'd be no damn' use to another woman. Why—"

Mr. Forsyth's inadequacies in bed were followed (with equal vehemence) by his inadequacies at finding parking space for the car when he took Mrs. Forsyth shopping on Saturday mornings. And Katharine listened, both enjoying it all and gently priding herself on the fact that *she* wasn't disloyal enough to expose all her husband's weaknesses like this. But paradoxically, as well as priding herself on this loyalty, she also felt guilty about it. If you were prepared to take part in and enjoy these husband-belittling sessions, then you really ought to contribute something—some complaint, some grievance—for the others' delectation. To come merely as a listener like this might be loyal, but it was also mean—like coming empty-handed to a bottle-party.

It was past eleven when Mary reappeared, and by then Katharine was just leaving. Mary said goodbye to her quietly, and with a lack of warmth which yet somehow was not hurtful; on the contrary, it seemed to hold some secret, intimate message which Katharine could not read.

So she was not really surprised when, a few minutes later, as she set off down the road, she heard quick, awkward footsteps behind her; awkward because Mary's supple figure was crippled by a tight skirt and high heels, but quick with a despairing, pattering urgency.

"Wait, Katharine!" panted Mary, like a small child left behind. "Wait! Wait for me!" She drew level; and now Katharine noticed that her face was childishly streaked with tears. "Katharine I must talk to you—*now*! You're the only person who will understand."

Few people can resist the flattery of this sort of appeal; but all the same, Katharine had to catch her bus.

"Mary—of course!" she said warmly. "But I've got to go to work now. Could I come in this evening, on my way home?"

"No, I must tell you—*now!*" insisted Mary with a little gasp. "I'll walk along with you—I'll get on the bus wherever you're going—*anything*. You see, Katharine, I've been telling lies the whole morning. At least—not quite. That is, actually, I haven't been telling lies at all—Alan *did* say it was a dark man in a raincoat who stabbed him. He told the doctors—the police—everybody. But it wasn't, Katharine. It was me."

CHAPTER VII

KATHARINE TOOK her friend's arm, and continued to walk at a steady pace.

"I thought so," she said, quietly, untruthfully, and with absolute certainty that this was the right thing to say. "You mustn't be too upset about it, Mary; after all, anybody can lose their self-control for a moment, and it isn't as if you'd hurt him badly. How did it happen?"

Mary's head was bent, as though she fought her way against a great wind. Her high heels clattered painfully along by Katharine's side; she seemed confused, beaten, unable to find where in her story to begin. Katharine tried to help her.

"You said you'd had a row yesterday," she prompted. "You remember—when I caught you up. You were walking slowly so as not to get home while Alan was still there. *Was* he there after all?"

Mary's head lifted a little, gratefully.

"Yes—yes, he was. That's how it all started. You see, after you'd gone in, I still waited about—walking around, you know—for quite a long time. But at last I *had* to go in. . . ." Her steps dragged slower, as if she was reliving all over again her reluctant entry into her home last night. "And then, the moment I came into the hall I knew—I could feel—that Alan was still there, in his study. As I stood there, wondering whether to slip out again and come back later, the study door opened and he came out and looked at me. Just that. Looked at me. And then he looked at the clock—it was ten-past six by then—and didn't say a word. Oh, Katharine, I know this sounds silly, but you don't know how Alan's eyes are when he just *looks*! Everything he is thinking is right there in them, shining, and I can read it, like some awful language that he has forced me to learn. I was reading it then—how I had been out all day, neglecting the house, neglecting him—how I hadn't lit the sitting-room fire, or got tea ready, or made the beds properly or anything—and I couldn't explain, or argue, or answer back, because he hadn't *said* anything—do you understand, Katharine? You can't contradict someone who hasn't said anything, that's what's so awful about it. So awful. So awful . . . ."

Her voice trailed into a sort of moan, her foot tripped on the kerb as they crossed into the main road, and Katharine steadied her.

"So it was then that . . . that . . . ?" She attempted to prompt Mary again, and Mary raised her drooping head a little and continued:

"No. Oh no. Not then. I didn't do anything. I just—sort of muttered something. Not even an apology, because he still hadn't accused me of anything, had he? It was just a mutter—you know—without any actual consonants or vowels. If you've ever had to mutter like that yourself, you'll know what I mean. And then I slipped off into the kitchen. I thought I'd get dinner ready, and then perhaps it would all blow over, because of course Angela would come down for dinner, and I will say for Alan he's always careful not to be—awful—in front of Angela. But I'd forgotten to do any shopping that morning, and so when I looked in the fridge there was nothing but the cold joint. So I started slicing it up. I don't quite know what I was planning to do with it—I mean, you can't really give your husband just cold meat, can you, even when he's in a good temper, let alone when he's like *that*. But anyway, I thought I'd start by slicing it up, and think afterwards. Don't you think that's quite a good way, Katharine, when you're quite desperate?—*do* something first, and then decide whether to do it afterwards . . . if you see what I mean. . . ." Her voice was growing vague again, wandering

51

evasively down tortuous byways of philosophy as the climax of her story loomed nearer. Katharine forced her to the point again.

"So you sliced up the meat?" she pursued, pulling Mary gently to a halt at the bus stop. "And then?"

"And then I heard the study door open again," said Mary, her voice dropping almost to a whisper, as if even now she had to listen, nerves alert, for Alan's soft movements. "And I heard Alan coming down the hall—very softly, the way he does when he's angry. And then he was standing in the kitchen door, very neat, very calm, and his eyes shining. 'Cold meat!' they were screaming at me. 'Out all day—no fire—no comfort—and now cold meat for dinner!' They *screamed* it at me, Katharine—two or three times! My hand shook so that I cut my finger—my *own* finger, isn't that funny, when you think what happened afterwards? I really did—look!" With a short laugh, she held up a forefinger encircled with sticking plaster for Katharine's inspection, and went on: "And then he spoke to me. Actually spoke, with his mouth, I mean—and you can't think what a relief that was, even though he was still as angry as he could be. 'I see there's going to be nothing for dinner,' he said politely. 'And as I have to go out in a few minutes, perhaps I could trouble you to bring me a sandwich in the study? I'd ask for some coffee too, but of course that would be too much trouble; and no doubt we have run out of coffee.' Absolutely quietly he said it, perfectly civil— and oh, Katharine, I'd give *anything* for a husband who'd stamp, and rage, and throw things at me. . . . Oh! . . ." Tears were swelling her features once more, but with a cruel effort she gulped them back and went on:

"So I began making the sandwiches as quickly as I could—I used the cold lamb for them. Oh, it was such a job, with the bread new, and the butter hard, and my finger bleeding, and trying to make coffee at the same time—and knowing that any minute he'd come back into the kitchen and say in that polite voice: 'I see I'm expecting too much,' or some awful sarcastic thing like that, and go off without anything to eat at all. Anyway,

I did manage to get it ready, and piled it all on to a tray in a great hurry—the carving knife too, just because it happened to be still on the plate with the sandwiches—I didn't mean it to be there, of course—I swear I didn't. And when I put the tray down by Alan as he sat at his desk, the knife was the first thing he saw. He picked it up and handed it to me saying, 'I think this is surplus to my requirements.' And so that's how it happened that I was standing there, with the knife in my hand, when he . . . when I . . ."

"He said something else sarcastic, and it was just the last straw?" suggested Katharine, as Mary's voice ground to a stop once more. Mary nodded forcefully, blinking back a new spate of tears, and tossing her head with an odd, coltish gesture.

"Yes—that's just how it was! Oh, Katharine, I knew you'd understand. You see, as he turned his back to me, and began eating, sitting there at his desk, I felt I ought to say *something*. So I began apologising about not having any dinner ready, and I said that I'd thought he was going to be out for dinner. Well, I *did* think so—he'd said he was going out at six—*you* know that, don't you, Katharine. I told you so at the time. So I said just that: I said, I'm sorry there isn't a proper dinner, but I thought you were going out at six.

"And then, Katharine, he swivelled round in his chair and looked right at me. And his eyes were, blazing, yelling, bellowing, but this time I didn't know what they were saying. And I didn't have to, because again he actually spoke:

"'You thought I was going out, did you, Mary? You actually *thought* about me to that extent? I'm touched beyond words. It's wonderful to have a thoughtful wife, isn't it? And what a sweet, loving thought!. . .' And at that, Katharine—can you believe me?—he stood up and moved as if to kiss me—a sarcastic, poisonous kiss, like a snake.

"And that's when it happened. I simply struck out. I'm not sure I remembered I had the knife in my hand or not, but I struck out. . . . And the next thing I knew, he was slumped in the chair again, staring at me ... and blood was everywhere. And then he didn't cry out, or snatch the knife from me—nothing. He just sat there, looking at me, holding his sleeve, trying to check the bleeding. 'You'd better phone the doctor, Mary,' he said quietly. I was terrified. I rushed to the phone, and when I got back into the study he seemed to have fainted—he was very white, and his eyes shut. And the doctor came at once, he was very kind; he hardly asked me any questions; he said he'd take Alan straight to hospital in his own car. And so we got him into the car, and I went too ... and they stitched him up under an anaesthetic, and when he came to, he told everyone this story that I told you— that a dark man in a raincoat had done it. *Why* does he make up such a story? Oh, Katharine, I'm so frightened!"

Before Katharine could answer, her bus drew up beside them, and she stepped quickly on to it, Mary scrambling up beside her, careless of their destination. By great good luck, the top deck of the bus was empty, and they were able to settle themselves in precarious privacy on the front seat. At last Katharine was free to answer her friend's question—and it seemed to her that the answer was simple and obvious, and that Mary must really know that it was.

"Why did he make up the story? Why, to protect you, of course, Mary. He must have seen that the wound couldn't possibly pass as an accident once a doctor had seen it, and he didn't want you to be blamed. He probably realises, in his heart, that it was at least half his fault—that he provoked you past endurance. He's probably just as sorry about it all as you are. He loves you, Mary—don't you understand? He always has, in spite of the rows, and in spite of his sarcasm, and his reserve, and all the rest of it. He loves you—and this is the proof of it. You should be happy about it—to have him sticking up for you like this."

Mary's answering silence seemed to throb to a rhythm of its own, cutting across the noisy rhythm of the bus, and filling Katharine with new uneasiness. She thought that perhaps Mary was overwhelmed by feelings of guilt at thus escaping scot-free from the consequences of her crime: for crime, of course, it was, no matter how much one might sympathise with her, and understand the provocation.

"Of course," Katharine went on, when Mary still did not speak, "if you're having pangs of conscience about it and are pining to confess, I suppose there's no reason why you shouldn't. I don't imagine anything very dreadful would happen to you in the circumstances, and with Alan himself taking your side and everything. But really, I would have thought you'd do better to leave well alone. Obviously it's what Alan wants—and you have to think of Angela, too. Think how it would upset her to know the truth—and all the gossip she'd have to face at school, too. If it was me, I'd stifle my pangs of conscience and leave it all to blow over. I really would. Unless, of course, some unfortunate dark man with a raincoat really *does* get pulled in—but I'm sure it won't happen. Alan couldn't have hit on a vaguer description—deliberately, of course—and I'm sure he won't encourage the police to investigate too enthusiastically. And there can't *actually* be any clues incriminating a dark man, since there wasn't one. . . ."

But Mary seemed scarcely to be listening at all. Katharine had the feeling that in spite of her damaging and apparently frank confession, Mary was still locked away with some secret fear of which Katharine still knew nothing, and on which all her eloquent reassurance had no bearing. She could do nothing more until Mary herself chose to break the silence.

The bus drew up with a jerk as the lights went red, and Katharine stared out at the hoardings on the wall facing her. Ever afterwards she was to connect the picture of a gigantic, impossibly rosy little boy grinning down at a plate of sausages with the white, agonised face that Mary now turned towards her.

"That would be all very well," Mary almost whispered, low and harsh, "if he just told this story to everyone else. But he tells it to *me* too. It makes me wonder if I'm going mad or if he is. After he came round, you see, they let me go in to him; and when I saw him lying in that stiff, neat bed, looking so white and . . . and sort of *young*,—I suddenly felt terribly, dreadfully sorry. I ran to him crying, and I bent down and began kissing him, and telling him how sorry I was, and that I'd never meant to hurt him . . . . And do you know, Katharine, he just stared at me, sort of incredulously. 'What do you mean?' he said, pushing me away. 'How do you mean, you're sorry? It wasn't *your* fault. *You* didn't let the man in; you didn't even see him. You didn't know anything about it until I called out to you, and you came in and found me with my arm bleeding.' He looked at me then, very straight, right into my eyes. 'How could it *be your* fault?' he said again.

"Katharine, what am I to think? Does he *really* think it happened like that? Did he have some dream under the anaesthetic that has muddled him—made him forget what really happened? Or when he fainted? Can fainting make you forget things, like concussion is supposed to do? And if so, will he go *on* forgetting? Or is it all some awful, complicated, martyred sort of pretence, that he's going to keep up for ever and ever? And what *for*—when he must know that I know?—And know that he knows I must know? Oh, Katharine, what shall I do?"

"Hush," warned Katharine, for Mary's voice was rising, and any moment someone might come up the stairs. "He could have forgotten, I suppose, after a faint—I don't know much about fainting. Or—Mary—are you sure he wasn't saying all that just in case there were some nurses or someone within hearing? Just to stop you betraying yourself then and there? After all, a hospital's not a very private place, is it?"

Mary shook her head decidedly.

"No," she said. "It wasn't that. There weren't any nurses for miles—or any other patients. He was in a sort of little side-room by himself. But anyway, I've talked to him since then—since we've been home, I mean, all alone in the house, and he still says the same—that a dark man in a raincoat attacked him and then ran away. I tried—well, I sort of tried—to tell him what really happened, but he shut me up in a dreadful, icy way, and told me I was being hysterical. Oh, Katharine, it was awful. I just had to give up and accept the raincoat man. He seemed satisfied then. In fact, he really began being very nice to me, in his stiff sort of way. But, Katharine, what does he think? How can I know what he is thinking? Can you imagine what it must be like, to spend the rest of your life with someone who knows that you tried to kill him? Who knows that you know that he knows, and yet neither of you must ever speak of it? To have him watching you—sitting at meals with you—going to bed with you—and to know that all the time he's thinking: 'She tried to kill me once.'"

"But you *didn't* try to kill him!" broke in Katharine vehemently. "You just hit out in anger—and there happened to be a knife in your hand. And even if—in some part of your mind—you knew that you were holding the knife, your subconscious still made very sure that you only hit him in a place where it couldn't possibly kill him. You didn't just miss a vital spot by accident. They say that nothing happens by accident; one's subconscious is in charge all the time."

It might have been Stella speaking. Katharine was aware of an exhilarating sense of power in laying such sentiments, like gifts (and such inexpensive ones), in front of a suffering friend. It must be this feeling, many times repeated, that gave Stella her breezy, muscular look.

Mary looked the gift horse in the mouth, and who could blame her.

"I'm sure my subconscious meant me to stab him right through the heart," she said sharply. "It was *me*, not my subconscious, who—"

But Katharine silenced her with a violent nudge. The young couple trying to settle themselves and their parcels and their Corgi and their two-year-old baby and his iced lolly on the seat just behind probably hadn't heard a word, of course; and anyway, Katharine reflected, snatches of talk heard on buses are always bizarre to the point of making one question one's own sanity. Look at that old woman a couple of days ago, saying as she heaved herself off the bus: "And if it hadn't been for them radiators I'd have had the lot of them landed on me, teeth and all." And the apparently comprehending conductress had laughed amiably, and Katharine had been left to spend the rest of her journey wrestling with unimaginable narratives which could have led up to this sentence as their denouement. Surely nothing she and Mary had said could have sounded, out of context, any more extraordinary than that? Of course it was all right. In brief undertones, she arranged to meet Mary for her short lunch hour at two o'clock; and then it was time to get off the bus. As she stood up, she felt Mary clutch her arm for a second, and something made her glance quickly at the laden couple behind them. She noted with brief, ridiculous shock that the husband was dark, and (in common with nearly every other man in London) he was wearing a raincoat.

Katharine almost laughed aloud. How absurd to let a mere invention of Alan's take a hold on her imagination like this! Followed by Mary, she hurried down the stairs and off the bus; and now she had to rush off to her office, leaving Mary to dawdle through a couple of hours' brooding and shop-gazing before they met again at two o'clock.

CHAPTER VIII

DURING HER twelve months back at work Katharine had discovered, with a sort of uneasy relief, that she could type much better when she was worried, or tired, or preoccupied. It seemed that her fingers, like charwomen, could get on with their work much more efficiently if their mistress did not interfere; and so today she was able to ponder Mary's problem with a clear conscience for a solid hour; and though this hour failed to produce any new or illuminating solution, it did produce three foolscap pages of accurate typing, including several columns of figures whose very existence took Katharine by surprise when she came to check them at the end.

On the whole, it still seemed to her that Mary should leave well alone. In childhood one imagines that an unconfessed crime will weigh upon one's soul for ever; and one of the pleasantest aspects of growing up is the discovery that this is simply not so; that a very few days of not being caught out, of no trouble having ensued, usually suffice to obliterate the whole thing from one's memory.

Surely this would be the best solution for Mary? Alan's reaction, though startling—even bizarre—at first sight, nevertheless might be wise. If he and Mary could, by tacit agreement, talk and behave to each other exactly as if Mary had had nothing to do with his injury, then, within a few weeks, it would really *be* as if nothing had happened, and no scar would be left on their marriage.

Still musing on these lines, Katharine handed over her copy, and took over telephone duties from Mr. Craig's secretary when that young lady sailed in scented splendour out to lunch, radiating from every glint of her nail varnish the superiority of smart young career girls in their twenties over the middle-aged part-timers, with roughened hands, and shopping baskets dumped beside their desks. Katharine's task during the ensuing hour consisted less of answering the telephone than of deciphering the notes on odd scraps of paper by which Mr. Craig intended to convey what he wished said to various possible callers. These notes suggested to Katharine that Mr. Craig communicated with his secretary more by telepathy arbitrarily decorated with red ink than by the actual writing of any known language, so this part of her work demanded a good deal of inventiveness as well as concentration. It took her mind off Mary's problems so completely that by the time they were due to meet, these problems already seemed a little remote—almost trivial, and already solved.

Mary was sitting, hunched and pallid, at a solitary table in the corner of the cafeteria. In front of her was a cup of coffee—no, two cups of coffee—and a plate of cellophane-wrapped sandwiches, still untouched. Skin was forming on both cups of coffee, and it was a little touching, Katharine supposed, that Mary should first have fetched coffee for both of them, and should have then allowed her own cup to get cold in company with Katharine's. After two hours in the bustling office atmosphere, Katharine had to make a conscious effort to recapture the doom-laden mood which was obviously still enveloping Mary.

"How are you?" she said—rather pointlessly—as she settled herself at the table, facing Mary. And then, as a sudden thought struck her, she added: "How's Alan? Is he all right, with you staying out all this time?"

Mary looked a little peevish, as if childishly resenting the deflection on to Alan of any of the concern and attention which had hitherto been focussed on herself.

"Oh, he's all right," she assured Katharine, rather perfunctorily. "Auntie Pen's there. His sister, you know—the one you met last night. She said she'd do his lunch. She wants to talk to him, she said. Do you think—*do* you, Katharine?—that they're talking about *me*?"

Katharine could not help smiling at the naïve egotism of the words—though whether they were prompted by vanity or dread it was hard to tell.

"Why should they be?" she essayed cautiously; and Mary clasped her hands in a schoolgirlish gesture of suspense.

"Oh, I do *hope* they are!" she continued, as if Katharine had not spoken. "If only he's telling her the truth—that it was *me* who stabbed him—than I shan't mind so much if he goes on lying to me about it. So long as *someone* else knows, then it doesn't seem quite so mad. Oh, I *do* hope he's telling her!"

Katharine did not know what to say. She remembered the decisive, challenging way in which Auntie Pen had declared last night that "It was an accident!"—defying anyone to query it. Should she tell Mary that it seemed to her likely that Auntie Pen had guessed the truth right from the start? But of course that wasn't the point. Mary didn't care what Auntie Pen knew—she only cared what Alan told her—what he in fact knew.

"I've been wondering," Mary went on, slightly at a tangent, "whether to tell Auntie Pen myself all about it, and get *her* to persuade Alan to—well—not to be like this about it. Should I, Katharine, do you think? Should I tell her?"

Katharine was silent for a moment, pondering.

"Well—she seems a kind person," she ventured non-committally. "I'm sure she'd want to help you, but . . ."

"But you think she disapproves of me?" flashed Mary; and Katharine was taken aback.

"I don't! I don't think anything of the sort!" she retorted. "As a matter of fact, she was talking about you last night—to me and Stella, you know—and she spoke very kindly of you. I think she's sorry for you—she knows that Alan's difficult—"

"Oh, I *wish* people wouldn't keep telling me that Alan's difficult!" cried Mary—a protest that, in the context of Mary's own ceaseless complaints about her husband, seemed so gratuitously unreasonable that it left Katharine speechless.

"It's not *fair* to say he's difficult!" persisted Mary bewilderingly. "It's not fair! He's strict, that's all. Strict, and rather reserved—like lots of men. *Isn't* he, Katharine?"

Half-dazed by this totally unprovoked attack, Katharine still could not answer; and suddenly Mary's whole face crumpled and dissolved into unrestrained, defenceless weeping.

"I'm sorry, Katharine," she sobbed "But it's so awful when other people say something that suggests he's not—not quite normal. I keep trying to persuade myself, you see, that he's just a bit more pernickety than other men—a bit more reserved. That there's nothing *special* the matter . . . no more than lots of wives have to put up with. . . ."

Her words blurred and mingled with her tears in the depths of a great serviceable handkerchief as Mary tried to hide her tear-stained features. When she looked up, her face was under control again, her voice clear, even argumentative.

"There's one thing Auntie Pen *definitely* disapproves of about me," she declared, as if scoring a point against Katharine, "and that's having adopted Angela. It was my idea, you see. Alan was always rather against it—he said if we couldn't have children then we couldn't, and it was best to leave it at that. He was always very scrupulous about saying 'we', you know—'*we* can't have children'—although we both knew perfectly well that *I* was the one who couldn't. I know it was very considerate of him to put it like that, but somehow it made me feel worse about it, not better. Can you understand that? Anyway, I persuaded him. I thought, you see, that if we had a baby—even an adopted one—it would somehow make things come right. I know they always say in the articles that you shouldn't adopt a baby for that sort of reason, and Auntie Pen said so too, and of course she was quite right—and so were the articles. It seemed so unfair, somehow—so many against one, I mean. Auntie Pen, *and* Alan, *and* the articles all saying the same thing, all lined up against me. And now Angela as well. Did you know that Angela told me the other day that *she* thought we oughtn't to have adopted her?"

"No," said Katharine, smiling. "But honestly, Mary, I wouldn't take it too seriously. Children are always saying things like that. Jane was saying a little while ago that she wished *she* was an adopted child, like Angela, because it would be so lovely if Flora wasn't her real sister. They'd just been quarrelling about something, and Flora had got her own way, as usual. But you don't want to take too much notice when kids talk like that. It doesn't mean anything."

"It means something with Angela," said Mary sombrely. "You see, I can tell for myself that it hasn't really worked out. I'm very fond of Angela, of course, and so is Alan—that is, he's good to her, and treats her well. But it just hasn't—jelled—if you know what I mean. I still feel that she's a sort of visitor in the house. I suppose, really, the trouble was that she was too old. She was past three, you know, when we got her. She can sort of remember the orphanage—though I must say she seems to remember some very queer things about it. As if it was a sort of Paradise, you know, and it just *wasn't*. It was rather a miserable place, actually, and smelt of disinfectant. And when I tell her all the things that you're supposed to tell them—you know, that we actually *chose* her out of all the other babies, instead of just having to take what we got, like other parents—when I tell her that, she just says it's not fair, and that *she* ought to have been allowed to choose *us*. What on earth can I say to that?"

Katharine laughed.

"Offer to play ping-pong with her, I should think," she suggested, "or whatever it is she best likes doing with you at the moment. And don't *worry*. I'm sure it's quite natural that she should make up flamboyant fancies about the orphanage—in fact, I've heard her do it, and it strikes me as perfectly harmless— a sort of game. When she and Jane and Flora were sorting out their fireworks for next week, she was telling them some wonderful story about a Catherine wheel they'd had at the orphanage that was twenty feet across and threw out red and purple sparks as high as a church. And then Flora spoilt it all by telling her that if she was only three she couldn't possibly have known it was twenty feet across, because children of three can't count up to twenty; and they spent the rest of the evening arguing about how far children of three can count. By the way, it *is* your turn to have the bonfire in your garden this year, isn't it?"

Katharine spoke brightly, trying to make it sound like a lovely treat, though she knew as well as Mary that being the one to have the joint bonfire for the two families also meant being the one to have mud all over the carpets, the lawn trampled bare, and hundreds of sodden fireworks cases to clear up the next morning, as well as the wet forbidding remains of the bonfire. It also meant being the one to find stuffing for the guy, to supply paraffin when the bonfire wouldn't light, and to produce endless mugs of cocoa which would get left about, half-drunk, in various obscure corners of the garden. Still, Katharine had done it last year, and fair's fair. Besides, the prospect of all this might take Mary's mind off her present troubles, curtail her profitless brooding over it all.

But it didn't. Mary began to sip grimly at her tepid coffee, as if it was a medicine whose sheer nastiness must somehow cure something.

"I can't think about bonfires with all this hanging over me," she complained. "And I still can't decide whether to tell Auntie Pen about what I did. Shall I? Or not? Would it be better not?"

Katharine suddenly felt curiously strong, curiously certain on her friend's behalf.

"Definitely not," she said firmly. "You see, Mary, it seems to me that you must think first and foremost of Alan, and never mind your conscience. You have to look at it like this: There are two possibilities. One is that Alan has genuinely forgotten how it happened—what with the fainting and the anaesthetic and everything—in which case I can't see any point whatever in upsetting him by telling him the truth. The other possibility is that he *does* know, but wants to put it out of his mind as quickly and completely as possible. And out *of your* mind, too, so that you can both carry on with the marriage as if it hadn't happened. Which seems to me a very sensible way of taking it—"

"But how on earth can he suppose that this extraordinary carry-on *will* put it out of my mind?" protested Mary. "It just makes me worry about it more and more—"

"Only if you let yourself," interrupted Katharine eagerly. "Honestly, Mary, you'll be surprised how quickly you'll forget about the whole thing if you'll only let it all slide, as he obviously wants you to. It's not as if you can do him or anyone else any good by letting yourself be weighed down by guilt for evermore. Why, if you'll only accept his story, back him up in it— even tell it to yourself in your spare time!—why, then, before you know where you are, you'll find yourself actually believing it—and him too! Really you will! And then the whole thing can fade into oblivion for ever—only with both of you that much wiser for the experience. So do stop tormenting yourself, Mary. *Please!*"

There was something dreadful in the way Mary swallowed the cold remnant of coffee skin, as if it was some delicious titbit. Her empty cup clattered down into its saucer, and she stared across at Katharine with large, questioning eyes, seeking, it seemed, to be convinced. For surely Katharine's advice, whatever one might think of its ethics, was offering her far and away the easiest escape from her situation. As she stared, slowly, miraculously, the uncertainty flickered and faded from her eyes, leaving them clear and brilliant, empty of doubt.

"You're quite right, Katharine," she said slowly, almost luxuriously, as if savouring to the last mouthful her victory over her own conscience. "After all, I mustn't be selfish, must I? Alan's own self-respect is at stake as well as mine. I mean, he'd hate it to be known at his job that he had a wife—like that. For a man like Alan—it would hit him very hard. You're right, Katharine; I'll do it! I'll repeat his story to everyone. To him—to myself—"

"Even to me, just for practice!" laughed Katharine; and it was with a feeling of enormous relief—of pride in a job well done, in an important victory gained—that she hurried back to her office that afternoon.

CHAPTER IX

THAT NIGHT Katharine had a curiously vivid dream. Once again she seemed to be in the deserted cafeteria, but this time it was not Mary who was her companion, but a dark man in a raincoat. The raincoat was lightish in colour, shabby, and hung shapelessly from his sloping shoulders; and the man himself was dark, not merely in the sense of having dark hair and complexion, but more as if his whole face was enveloped in darkness; as if a deep shadow was thick upon him, hiding his features. At the beginning of the dream, Katharine was not paying much attention to the man; it seemed natural that he should be there. Her attention was wholly taken up with anxiety about the time. For before she could go back to the office, she must clear these tables; pile on to trays all those dirty cups and plates, and wipe away the crumbs, the flakes of pastry, and the sugary spills of tea. Not just from her own table, but from all the tables—dozens, scores, hundreds of them, scattered in derelict emptiness all over this great, echoing room. And it was then that she noticed that not a single other customer remained—no waitresses—nothing. Just herself and this man. And for some reason, inexplicable to the ordinary waking mind, she knew that she could not start on her task of clearing up while the man was still sitting there. She was impatient for him to go— to leave her—to get out of her dream: for somewhere, already, long before waking, there was growing in her brain a flickering awareness that all this was only a dream.

But the man would not go: and as Katharine turned to look at him more closely, perhaps even to speak to him, the darkness about him grew thicker . . . it was spreading . . . the whole cafeteria was in twilight now, as if night was already falling. And already the man was not quite there any more. . . . Only the raincoat, sitting there, upright and empty, still breathing, and somehow this, too, seemed perfectly natural, and not in the least surprising. What else *would* a raincoat do if its wearer was suddenly no longer there?

"A figment of knives!"

The senseless words leapt into Katharine's brain with that strange, precise clarity, that more-than-natural importance, that meaningless phrases sometimes acquire in dreams. The phrase seemed to explain, to answer everything—the vast room, her own presence there, and even the alert, near-living raincoat . . . which now, after all, lay limp and ordinary over the back of the chair. Only the great, encroaching darkness seemed unexplained . . . the vast, swift twilight swooping . . .

Katharine woke with a feeling of having been roused by a wild storm blowing round the house; a sense of roaring wind, of rattling window frames, of strange, howling hollow sounds in all the boarded-up fireplaces in all the upstairs rooms.

But everything was still, and in darkness. The stillness forced itself upon Katharine's waking mind with strange emphasis; with a shock of sudden stillness like the shock of sudden sound. She lay very still, alert, the dream running out of her, full consciousness swiftly taking over.

And then, clear and unmistakable, there came through the open window the sound of the dustbin lid being replaced on the bin. Quickly, and very quietly, Katharine was out of bed, out on the landing, and peeping, automatically and absurdly, and from an instinct too deep to question, into each of her children's rooms. She knew it was absurd herself; for why in the world should the sound of a dustbin being tampered with outside in the back garden mean that some disaster was being enacted in one of the upstairs bedrooms?

Reassured that all her three children were sleeping peacefully, Katharine set off down the stairs to investigate. Lightly, tensely, she tiptoed down, with feelings more akin to exhilaration than to fear.

The back door was unlocked—was it she or Stephen who had forgotten to lock it?—and in a moment Katharine was standing on the soft, spongy grass of the lawn, the wetness already soaking through her slippers, and the damp, windless air chill and soft about her face. The dustbin stood at the entrance to the side passage; its battered curves shone greyly in the shaft of moonlight that speared through the narrow gap between the houses. Katharine approached it gingerly, wondering what, exactly, she meant to do? What did she hope to discover by lifting the lid and peering into the confusion below?

It was a newspaper parcel, right on top of everything else—but had she put it there herself, last night? There were heaps of things she might have wrapped in newspaper during her hurried evening chores—potato peelings—ashes—the contents of the sink tidy. No—those were still visible just below the newspaper—egg-shells, orange-peel, and a mass of sodden tea-leaves gleaming in the moonlight like seaweed in silvery shallows.

Katharine softly replaced the lid. She would have another look in the morning, when she would be able to see properly. Or—it suddenly occurred to her—had she been mistaken in thinking that the sound came from her own dustbin at all? Didn't the Prescotts keep theirs in almost the same place, just across the dividing wall? It was rather odd of them, of course, to be emptying rubbish at three o'clock in the morning, but it was harmless, and certainly none of her business.

Just to satisfy herself that their dustbin was where she was imagining it, and that the noise might therefore have come from their garden and not from hers, Katharine moved softly across the lawn towards the wall, meaning to look over.

But how was it that these few steps should have set her heart beating in this way? Why should she suddenly feel so weighed down by dread that it was almost impossible to raise herself on tiptoe sufficiently to look over the wall? Was there indeed such a thing as premonition? Or had the misty autumn moon, now shining full across her face, triggered off some ancient fear of leaving cover . . . of showing oneself defenceless in the open . . . a target for watchers in the surrounding darkness?

Slowly, clutching with both hands on the damp, rough surface of the brickwork, Katharine raised herself on tiptoe, and found herself staring into a face so hideous, so motionless, that for a moment her wits completely left her. Just as in her dream, the shabby fawn raincoat drooped from sloping shoulders; but now the wild, mad eyes stared straight into hers with crazed expectancy; the whole figure sagged and drooped against the wall in an attitude of dreadful, senseless leisure. It was a dream again. It could only be a dream because there was Stephen's old frayed yellow scarf knotted round the creature's throat.

It was this final touch of horror that brought Katharine to her senses. It was not madness, after all, which lay behind those expectant cardboard eyes; it was not even sense, nor life of any kind. It was just Jane's and Angela's guy that they'd been making yesterday evening, over in Angela's playroom. They must have brought it outside to work out some way of propping it up on the bonfire, and left it here. It would spoil, left out like this all night. Those painted eyes would run in black and orange streaks; the cardboard cheeks would warp and buckle; it should be brought in at once.

And I wouldn't touch it for a thousand pounds.

Katharine amazed herself with the suddenness and definiteness of this conclusion. After her surge of relief at finding the thing was only a guy, why should she still feel this repugnance—yes, this sickening fear—at the very thought of touching it?

Katharine crept softly back into the house, fastening the back door behind her, bolting it, putting up the chain—locking out the moonlight, and the guy, and her own strangely beating heart as she had stared into its eyes.

But when she crept back to her darkened bedroom, tiptoeing, holding her breath so as not to wake Stephen, she suddenly knew that Stephen wasn't there.

"Stephen!" she cried sharply, and switched on the bedside light. "Stephen—!"

"What is it? Hush Katharine, you'll wake everyone!"

Stephen, blinking in the sudden light, was standing in the doorway behind her.

"Where have you been?" they both asked simultaneously—then both laughed a little, uneasily. And then a sort of paralysis descended on them, which took the form of a halting stilted sort of conversation. Katharine, it seemed, had thought she heard a noise in the garden and had gone to investigate: Stephen, it seemed, had woken and found her gone, and had been looking for her. As simple as that. And with this simplicity they both had to be satisfied, and, much later, in the far, fag-end of the night, to fall asleep.

CHAPTER X

"I THINK you ought to discourage Jane from playing with Angela Prescott," pronounced Stephen; and Katharine felt as if he had pushed her roughly out of the way. For when she had started telling him all this recent gossip about Mary and Alan Prescott, it hadn't been with any intention of asking his advice, or indeed of reaching any practical conclusion of any sort. She had simply been saving it as a possible topic of conversation with which to break the terrible ice of Saturday morning breakfast. This habit of saving up snippets of conversation was one which had been growing on her of late. As her relationship with Stephen deteriorated, she found herself storing up remarks and anecdotes that might form the basis of a conversation with him; hoarding them, like shillings for the gas-meter, furious to see any of them wasted on any other purpose. For one of the most intractable features of a tottering marriage is the swift, relentless narrowing of the range of subjects that can be discussed without causing a row. Months ago it had begun to be impossible to discuss the children in any aspect whatever without starting a row about either Stephen's irritability with them or Katharine's spoiling of them; and not long after, in quick succession, it had become impossible to discuss anything about holidays, or new equipment for the house, or Katharine's job. By now it seemed impossible even to comment on an item in the paper without disaster. Only the other day Katharine had read out a bit about the high rents in the district, and Stephen had commented wearily: "Well, it *is* depressing for a man to feel he's paying out four-fifths of his income to maintain an establishment in which he's never even comfortable, let alone happy." Even the weather was taboo; if Katharine remarked on its being a cold morning, the chances were great that Stephen would start all over again about why couldn't she light the fire *before* she went to work, and leave it banked up. Like *other* women, of course; and that, however hard she tried to prevent it, would bring the resentful look back into Katharine's face. . . .

But amid all these encroaching conversational perils, Katharine had thought that gossip about the neighbours was still safe. Particularly gossip about the Prescotts, since nearly every story about that pair served to underline the pleasing fact that Katharine wasn't nearly such an ineffectual wife as Mary, and that Stephen wasn't nearly as forbidding a husband as Alan. Thus they each tended to emerge from a Prescott anecdote a little mollified; a little better pleased with themselves and with each other. This was precisely why Katharine had saved her story for the difficult Saturday morning breakfast. She was therefore disconcerted in the extreme that Stephen should take her narration not as a pretext for a little much-needed mutual admiration, but as an occasion for positive and disruptive action: action which could only precipitate tears, scenes, recriminations and offence in every direction.

"It sounds to me," pursued Stephen, "as if the atmosphere next door must be very—peculiar. I don't like the sound of it; and I don't want Jane mixed up with it."

Katharine could not allow herself to see that there might be some truth in what Stephen was saying. All she could see was the trouble and upheaval that would be caused in the two families if his suggestion was taken seriously: trouble and upheaval so monstrous, from her point of view, as to swamp all other considerations.

"But Stephen, I *can't*," she protested. "Jane and Angela have played together, in and out of each other's houses, ever since they can remember. I *can't* break it up—make it different—suddenly. And Mary would be so dreadfully hurt. Besides, whatever *for*? After all, anyone can have a burglar breaking in. . . ."

So engrossed was Katharine in making her point, that she almost forgot that there *hadn't* been a burglar. She scarcely remembered even to feel thankful that she hadn't told Stephen the whole truth—and naturally she hadn't. How could she when Mary had made her confession in confidence, to Katharine alone? By the time she had convinced Stephen that nothing had occurred next door that could be classed as "peculiar", she had nearly convinced herself also. Her only anxiety now was that Jane shouldn't parade her friendship with Angela under her father's nose for a while: not until it had all blown over.

It was lucky, from this point of view, that Jane wasn't down to breakfast yet—she'd be sure to have been chattering about the guy at Angela's house last night. But of course you couldn't expect Stephen to see how lucky it was; he was already looking at the clock irritably and asking where were they all? Stephen hated the children's habit of getting up late on Saturdays—or, to put it more fairly, Katharine's habit of letting them. He seemed to set great store by sitting down to breakfast punctually with his family round him, and he apparently didn't notice that this happy family scene nearly always ended in rows, or tears, or both. It must be, thought Katharine, that he had eternally in mind some other, more biddable, family than he actually possessed. He must ever and again be picturing himself sitting down to the breakfast table with three pleasant, well-behaved girls who would ask him (one at a time) intelligent questions that he knew the answer to, like: How high is the Eiffel Tower? Girls who would listen with eager but quiet interest while he explained to them about the inside of a termites' nest.

That this improbable morning vision of his family should still be sustaining her husband after more than a decade of evidence to the contrary, would have seemed unbearably pathetic to Katharine, if only it hadn't been so inconvenient. If only Stephen would accept, once and for all, that breakfast with the children was absolutely frightful, and would avoid it as sedulously as she tried to avoid it for him, life would be much simpler. But no: he was continually urging her to make the girls get up at a proper time at week-ends; and she, not exactly disagreeing with him, was continually compromising by calling them at the proper time and then doing nothing more about it. The net effect of this, of course, was that they didn't get up, and it wasn't exactly her fault, nor yet exactly theirs; and this, she supposed—rather shocked when she actually faced it—was the whole purpose of the manoeuvre.

Oh, well, she reassured herself, most wives probably balance the domestic peace on a series of such evasions and subterfuges, you couldn't always be worrying about these trifles, analysing your motives; and anyway, this Saturday it would have been more awful than usual because of its being Curfew's birthday. She stole a cautious look at her husband. No; he was in no mood to be subjected to Curfew's birthday. Bits of wilting lettuce were probably at this very moment being wrapped messily up in tissue paper on Jane's eiderdown, while Flora lay reading comics in the adjoining bed, and saying "Shut up!" at intervals. And Clare, in the next room, would still be sound asleep. It *was* disgraceful, really, at a quarter-past nine in the morning.

But of course it was worse when they actually came down; arguing, tramping about the kitchen, fishing about in cupboards for packets of cornflakes, warming up rashers of bacon and making toast at the cooker, where Katharine was already trying to put on a stew for lunch. And now Jane was wailing because the grape she'd left wrapped in silver paper ready for Curfew's birthday had disappeared.

Heaven send that Stephen didn't hear her from the sitting-room, where he was now sitting scowling—Katharine could feel it through the solid wall—over the morning paper.

At last even the late breakfast was over to the last scatter of toast crumbs, and what Katharine always thought of as the Saturday Hover began.

"Mummy," began Flora, hovering over her mother's chair and helping herself to a sliver of carrot from the knife, "what are we doing today? Can we go out somewhere?"

"I'm afraid not—at least I can't take you," said Katharine. "I've got to get this stew on, and do the shopping, and I *must* catch up with the ironing today."

"When can we start Curfew's birthday?" demanded Jane, leaning over Katharine on the other side. "He's getting terribly impatient. He—"

"Not till I've got the stew on," repeated Katharine patiently. "Not till this afternoon, really, Jane, because this morning I've got to—"

But of course Jane wasn't listening to what Katharine had to do this morning—nor, indeed, was Katharine herself, for even while she recited her list of tasks, she was simultaneously preparing to parry Clare's request to be shown how to pick up the stitches for the neck of her jumper. It was a shame, really, not to be able to drop everything and help her at once; for Clare had been working for months and months at that piece of knitting: slowly, doggedly, without even any hope, apparently, of ever finishing it, she had been going on, and on, over every obstacle, like a tearful but indefatigable tank. It was a miracle, really, that she should ever have reached the point of needing to pick up the stitches for the neck. But all the same, the stew *must* go on—and any moment now Stephen would be wandering back into the kitchen, folded newspaper in his hand, and saying "Well, what are the plans for today?" All of them, one after another, dumping their week-end leisure in her lap like so many bundles of washing, taking it for granted that it was her job to deal with it.

"Not till after lunch, dear"; "Not till after tea, dear"; "Not till tomorrow, dear"—could she extract from her harassed programme nothing but these negative responses? Katharine took refuge in her usual inadequate solution:

"I'm going shopping in a few minutes," she announced. "Would any of you like to come?"

The response was exactly as she had expected. A long-drawn-out "Uughgh!" from Flora; a blank, slightly disheartened look from Clare as she let her knitting slither into a chair; and a squeal of joy from Jane.

"Oh, yes, Mummy!" she cried, still young enough to see shopping as a magic gateway to unfathomable delights in the way of minor personal possessions; and her delight suddenly lit the morning for Katharine with familiar yet always unexpected radiance. Jane skipped about the house getting ready as if she was preparing for some wonderful holiday; and as the two of them set forth in the golden stillness of the October sunlight, Katharine felt herself sharing Jane's mood. For her, too, Jane's two sixpences shone like newly discovered planets shedding their glory even across the buying of six lamb chops and two and a half pounds of scrag end.

There were four overdue library books to be returned, which together had amassed fines of *2s. 4d.*; and as she fumbled for change, the Librarian gave Katharine that look which always made her feel that they should either raise the fines to a point where they actually enjoyed taking them in, and smiled over it, or else lower them to a point where you felt they were entitled to look as disagreeable as they liked. As things were, you seemed to be getting the worst of both worlds.

Jane loved the library. She always darted instantly and incomprehensibly to the Reference section, dragged out some mighty volume apparently at random, opened it, and pored with catholic enthusiasm over whatever met her eye until Katharine was ready to go.

It was a pity that today Jane should have picked on a particularly gigantic tome, with particularly tiny print, and that she should be positively frowning over it just as Stella came into the library and dumped her pile of books on the counter. None of them had fines, of course—Stella always said that to accumulate fines on library books showed an unconscious resistance to reading them at all; though it always seemed to Katharine that a conscious resistance to making a special trip with them in the rain had exactly the same effect financially.

Stella watched Jane pityingly for a moment, and then hurried over to Katharine.

"It's funny how you can always tell the grammar school children here," she whispered gaily and noisily into Katharine's ear. "Their heads are always bent *downwards,* looking at *books.* It's funny—the children from freer schools always have their heads *up,* looking at *people.*"

It seemed to Katharine that here was a single accusation masquerading as a multiple one. After all, to read a book at all—particularly one of the size Jane had chosen—you would have to bend your head, unless you had quite extraordinarily strong arms for holding it in front of your face; and to look at people you'd have to look straight ahead, unless you were very strangely positioned, somewhere up in the rafters. But it would be difficult to get all this across satisfactorily in a hoarse whisper, so Katharine contented herself with murmuring that Jane wasn't at a grammar school yet, and very likely (would Stella take this as modesty or boasting?) never would be.

"Ah, but she's on the *treadmill* already!" hissed Stella. "You can see it, just from the line of her shoulders! Now, when *Mavis* comes to the library—"

"She chooses books from the two upper shelves, I suppose," murmured Katharine pleasantly—and glanced anxiously across at Jane to see if she *did* look over-studious compared with other children. Was she going to be shortsighted, perhaps, peering and frowning like that, or was it just that the table was rather high and her chair rather low?

"I've just been in to see Mary Prescott," Stella was whispering eagerly. "She seems—don't you think?—in a bit of a state?"

There was an uncharacteristic hesitation in Stella's manner; and it flashed across Katharine's mind that perhaps Stella knew everything that Katharine herself knew—but wasn't sure if Katharine did. Perhaps Mary was one of those maddening people who confide their innermost thought in absolute confidence to absolutely everybody, leaving a trail of gossip-hungry victims who have all promised faithfully not to breathe a word of it to each other, and yet who are all *almost* sure that each other already know.

"Yes—it's all rather a shock for her, of course," replied Katharine, equally cautiously. Unless one of them definitely broke faith with Mary, this could go on for ever. Probably Auntie Pen had been told, thought Katharine crossly, annoyed with herself for having felt flattered at having been specially chosen as confidante from among all Mary's friends. Yes, of course Auntie Pen would have been told: and Mrs. Forsyth as well, very likely; and Mary's daily woman. . . . Oh, well if Mary wanted to *look* for trouble . . .

"The police were there this morning!" Stella was chattering on, in less and less of an undertone as the interest of her revelations mounted. "And it seemed to upset Mary terribly—I can't think why. They'd only come to get a description from Alan of what this burglar person looked like, and Mary was really quite rude to them. Almost as if she didn't *want* them to find out who he was. It does make you think, doesn't it, about what we were saying the other day? I mean this idea that perhaps it was a boyfriend, quarrelling with Alan over Mary. . . ."

So Stella didn't know the truth after all. Katharine felt her vanity restored, and she was also relieved on Mary's account. Better, surely, that Mary should be the victim merely of these idle and quite unfounded speculations than that people should begin to suspect the truth.

For Mary was no actress. Her odd and evasive behaviour over the whole business could not fail to rouse suspicions of one sort or another, and suspicions that are unfounded surely cannot do a fraction of the damage of suspicions based on fact.

"I must go and see her," murmured Katharine, noncommittally. "But I can't quite think when—I'm always terribly busy on Saturdays—"

"Oh, she'll be all right *today*," Stella assured her. "*I* shall be there this afternoon, and I'll stay as long as she likes. I wouldn't let her down at a time like this."

I'm sure you wouldn't, thought Katharine wryly; and nor would any other of Mary's friends. While there was one single crumb of further gossip to be extracted from Mary's cringing and evasive lips, so long would her friends rally round, sympathising, questioning, probing. . . .

Including Katharine herself, of course. Ah, but that was different! *She* was trying to *help* Mary. Perhaps that's what all the others felt they were doing, too? Perhaps, indeed, that was what they *were* doing. For gossip, be it never so unkind, does at least serve to give one's troubles a social framework. It embraces them, takes them to itself, and returns them perhaps a little unrecognisable, but nevertheless cared for, labelled—given some sort of positive status in the drama of the neighbourhood. And might not this be a sustaining sort of thing—a strength and a support whose value is only appreciated if it is at some time withdrawn?

Katharine picked up the two books on which she would be paying 8d. fines around the beginning of December, dragged Jane out of her study of the boyhood of Savonarola—this had followed straight on, without pause or change of expression, from her investigation of the habits of the Australian Brown-footed Rat—and they set off home.

It had been a busy morning, and it was natural enough that among all her other preoccupations Katharine had given little thought to last night's disturbance. Certainly she had done nothing about implementing her midnight intention of examining the dustbin by daylight; and by now, of course, the dustmen had come and gone.

CHAPTER XI

"Happy Birthday to you
Happy Birthday to you
Happy Birthday, dear Curfew
Happy Birthday to you."

JANE CHANTED the words softly as she sat cross-legged on the hearthrug, while Curfew crouched insecurely on her inadequate lap, staring with stupid, lustrous eyes into the flickering firelight. His fast-withering presents, mixed with wet tissue paper, lay neglected on the rug; but Jane didn't seem to mind. He had *had* them—that was the main thing. What "having" them in this context could possibly mean, Katharine herself could not understand, but she knew that to a nine-year-old brain it was plain as plain.

Nearly every member of the family had contributed to the festival; even Flora had condescendingly wrapped a slice of cucumber in a corner of blue laundry paper, and stuck it down with Selotape. And as for Clare, she had gone to a lot of trouble to carve a carrot into the shape of a doll, had wrapped it carefully first in silver paper and then in coloured crepe paper, and had adorned it with a huge postcard-size label saying: "To Dearest Curfew, With Much Love from Clare." in eight different colours. Sometimes Katharine was touched almost to tears by Clare's affection for her youngest sister, her readiness to enter into her childish interests. At others, she wondered if it was perhaps an expression of Clare's longing for her own lost childhood; for the days before gerunds, and stockings, and brassieres, and failing to get into the Middle School hockey team. Was it something to worry about rather than to delight in? No, of course it wasn't ... and now Clare was accompanying Jane's song on the piano, improvising charmingly in the bass: and with sudden, furious longing, Katharine wished that she wished Stephen was there. She didn't wish it, of course; in fact, at this very moment, she was listening nervously for the sound of his key in the lock—but if only she *could* wish it! If only he was the sort of father who would join joyfully in this sort of ridiculous scene—who would sit there with Jane in the firelight, teasing her, talking nonsense to Curfew, examining his presents with laughing admiration. Or—this occurred to Katharine for the very first time—if only she was the sort of wife who could have turned him into a father like that. Could it be *she* who had turned him, instead, into the sort of father who would scowl round the room, maddened by the disorderliness of it all, the idiocy, and the crowning impropriety of bringing a rabbit indoors when it ought to be kept outside in a hutch, if kept it must be?

Heavens! There he was! As Katharine listened to the brisk, firm footsteps coming up to the front door, she was conscious of a physical shrinking behind her ribs. Now this lovely evening would be spoiled, if not by him (for after all he did sometimes restrain his irritation on such occasions), then by her own fear of his irritation—her tenseness—the bright, uneasy way she would speak to him as he came in.

Scrambling over the muddle of greenery in her path, she hurried out into the hall to greet—or did she mean intercept?—her husband. But the footsteps outside were not followed by the expected sound of his key in the lock. Instead, there was a knock, and a ring, and another knock; and who could be thus urgently demanding admittance but Stella?

"Oh—hullo," said Katharine with mixed relief and annoyance; for Stella wasn't an ideal guest at a rabbit's birthday party either. Katharine felt almost sure that Jack and Mavis didn't indulge in anything half so babyish, and it would turn out to be all something to do with going to grammar schools.

So she kept Stella standing, rather inhospitably, in the hall and listened to her message, which came, as Katharine had half expected, from next door.

"Mary says will you go in there for a few minutes, if you possibly can? She seems scared of being alone, poor thing," explained Stella condescendingly. "And the others seem to be out. I've told her I can't stay any longer . . . and actually, I don't understand why she's so frightened, do you? Do you think she can possibly be thinking that—whoever it was—might be coming back? I wonder if she—?"

Stella had lowered her voice a little for the last few sentences, but evidently not enough, for here was Flora, rigid with interest, hovering halfway out of the sitting-room door. If only they'd learn to eavesdrop a little less obviously, reflected Katharine, they'd get away with it a great deal more often, and learn all sorts of exciting things.

"Run away, Flora," she ordered ineffectually. "And shut the door." Flora, of course, did neither. It would have been necessary either to say it much more sharply or else at least twice if it was to have any effect, and Katharine did not want to do either under Stella's assessing gaze. That was the trouble with Stella: whenever she was present, things which had merely been a nuisance before suddenly became a Parent-Child Relationship.

"All right. Tell her I'll come quite soon," she said to Stella, as unilluminatingly as she could for the benefit of the attentive Flora. "Tell her I'll try not to be long. . . ." Hang it all, why should she be apologetic about it! What right had Mary to expect them all to dance attendance on her like this? Anyone would think *she* was the invalid, not Alan. No one seemed to be visiting *him*, or talking about him, or worrying about how he was. Did he mind? Or didn't he notice? Or would he have hated it if people had made a fuss of him? Probably he would; whereas Mary loved it. So it seemed to be all for the best, really, as injustice so often does.

The Prescotts' house was, as usual, bitterly cold. The sitting-room had plainly not been used all day, and Mary lit the gas-fire now for the first time as she brought Katharine in. Katharine sat down in the chair nearest the fire, and leaned towards the chilly blue flame, which as yet made no impact on the big, unwelcoming room. Why had Mary brought her in here, in this formal sort of way, like a visitor, instead of just calling her into the kitchen for the usual gossip over the ironing or the washing-up?

The feeling of constraint increased as Mary seated herself in the chair opposite, with neither knitting nor sewing to soften the growing need for one of them to think of something to say. Desperately, Katharine searched for a subject that would not be so close to Mary's anxieties as to seem inquisitive, and yet not so far away as to make it impossible for Mary to renew her confidences if she wished to.

"So you had Stella for the afternoon?" Katharine took the plunge. "How's she getting along?"

"She seems all right," said Mary unhelpfully: and then, suddenly, she came angrily alive:

"She's been going on and on at me about dark husbands with raincoats! Nobody in the whole neighbourhood seems to have married a fair man, except Stella herself, of course—she *would* be different! She seems to think that I'm playing *Femme Fatale* to the lot of them, and that they've been fighting Alan over me! *Me!*" Mary gave a short, bitter laugh. "A few years ago I dare say I'd have been able to break up one or two happy homes, but not now. Not after ten years married to Alan."

The sheer misery in Mary's voice frightened Katharine. She struggled to keep the conversation on a reassuring, gossipy level.

"Do you mean Stella actually *told* you she thought that?" she asked, ready to be slightly scandalised at such brash tactlessness.

"Oh no. Not point blank," answered Mary quickly. "Haven't you noticed about Stella, that with all her theories about being

84

absolutely frank, and the healthiness of having a good row, and all the rest of it, she's just as cunning as anybody else really. No. She started off by saying had the police got any detailed description out of Alan this morning? And when I told her no, he'd just said it was a dark man in a raincoat, and he hadn't had time to notice anything else, then she began about how impossibly vague a description it was—how it would include practically all the men we know. Fair enough; but then she began *listing* all the men we know—sort of laughing, you know, just to show that she only meant it to illustrate how useless any speculating would be—but actually she was watching me carefully after each name, to see if I blushed. I did too—several times—so I hope she's satisfied! I blush very easily, you know, and I was getting so fed-up with it. So *fed-up!* All these men in raincoats being stood up in front of me like in a police line-up—she made me feel as if they were filing through the room then and there! She made me actually *see* them—she really did, Katharine! I could have screamed! At least, if it was possible to scream in this house. . . . In a house where Alan lives. . . ." Her voice dropped again into the soft bitterness of a few minutes ago. Again Katharine was frightened.

"Scream? Of course you should scream! The very next time Alan annoys you! It would do you both a world of good," she declared bracingly—and cowered before the pitying glance from Mary's unhappy eyes.

"You sound just like Stella," she commented wearily. "Both of you, standing safely outside the lion's cage, and urging the person inside to poke the lion with a stick. That's what half of psychology consists of, it seems to me," she went on accusingly, and a little wildly. "Theories about how other people should poke lions with sticks. . . ." She ran her hand through her untidy hair despairingly; then looked up at Katharine and spoke quite fiercely:

"All right. So the next time Alan says one of those awful quiet, sarcastic things to me, then I scream. Right? So I scream. What happens next?"

She looked at Katharine as if in genuine expectation of an answer; and of course Katharine could not give one. She could not imagine at all what would happen next. One simply could not conceive of someone screaming at Alan. It wasn't in keeping with his character. A man's character, she reflected with surprise, consists a good deal more of the way people feel and behave towards him than of the way he himself feels and behaves.

"I don't know," she said feebly; and a look of unhappy triumph flickered for a moment across Mary's face.

"I want to show you something, Katharine," she said, after a moment's thought. "I've sometimes wondered whether to show it to you before, but—well, I don't know. . . . Wait there. I have to fetch it. . . ."

Awkward, stumbling over the rug as she went, Mary got herself out of the room, and a moment later Katharine heard her moving about in Alan's study.

Left alone, Katharine sat very still, staring into the steady spears of whitish flame that murmured in the bleak grate before her. She felt herself tensed up, expectant—but it was not quite the pleasurable curiosity she would have expected to feel in such a situation. She was aware of a curious sense of misgiving—a growing certainty that whatever it was that Mary was about to show her, she would rather not see it.

It was an envelope that Mary handed to her—a plain white envelope, with nothing written on it but a date—the tenth of August, Katharine, noticed, six years ago. She fingered the envelope rather helplessly, wondering what she was supposed to do. It was a little lumpy—uneven. Something other than a sheet of paper was inside it. Again she felt that inexplicable stirring of repugnance; but it was impossible, of course, at this stage, to withdraw from Mary's confidence.

"Open it," said Mary impatiently. "Open it and look inside. It's not stuck down."

Katharine obeyed, and found herself staring, bewildered, at a tuft of greyish-dark hair, lifeless, and very dry.

She looked up at Mary in bewilderment.

"What . . . ? I mean, where . . . ?" she began confusedly; and Mary gave her a twisted smile.

"It's Alan's of course," she answered, in tones matter-of-fact and yet somehow sounding strained to near breaking-point. "Alan's very own hair. And where did I get it? I pulled it out, with my very own hands. Let me tell you about it, Katharine. Let me tell you about the time when I still dared scream at Alan. . . .

"It must have been six or seven years ago now, I suppose; and Alan and I were having one of our fearful rows—and at the height of it I got so furious that I not only screamed at him, but I grabbed him by the hair and pulled for all I was worth! Quite a handful must have come out, I suppose—I didn't notice, of course, at the time, I was in an absolute rage—and naturally I never thought about it again after the row was over. I mean, I thought about having *hurt* him, of course, and I was very sorry, and I apologised, but I mean I never thought about the actual bit of hair that had come out. I mean, who would? Honestly, Katharine, who *would*?"

"No, naturally not," said Katharine, mystified. "So how . . . ?"

"I'm just telling you. We made it up in the end, as I was saying, and he accepted my apology quite amiably at the time—or seemed to. And really, you know, he wasn't *so* badly hurt—only just for the minute. So of course I never thought about it again. Not for months. For years. Not until last winter, when I was looking through his desk for a bill he said I'd forgotten to give him, and I was sure I hadn't, so I thought I'd have a good look while he wasn't there. Well, so there I was, scrabbling through all the drawers in his desk, and right at the back of one of them I found—*it!*"

She snatched the envelope back from Katharine, and stood staring down at it as if in a trance. Fear, like an infectious illness, seemed to creep from her across the room, towards Katharine.

"You see what it means?" continued Mary. "After the row was all forgiven and done with—or so I thought—he must have gone quietly back to the room where we were ... and collected up the bits of hair ... all by himself ... and put them carefully in an envelope to *keep*! And with the date written on it—the date of the quarrel—written in cold blood, to remind him for ever. ... Do you see, Katharine? Do you *see* ... ?"

Her voice grew shrill as she thrust the envelope once again under Katharine's eyes, stabbing with her forefinger at the brief figures. Before Katharine could think of anything soothing to say, Mary was continuing: "All these years he's kept it—without saying anything—hoarding it up against me. He means to use it somehow—some time. How can I know? It seems nearly mad to me, doesn't it to you, Katharine? Nearly mad. So *now* do you see why I wouldn't scream next time he's angry with me? In ten years time I'd find that scream, in his desk ... bottled somehow ... in pickle. ..."

Mary's wild words dissolved now in floods of uncontrollable crying. Katharine tried to comfort her—to suggest soothing explanations—to assure her that she was making too much of it: but Mary's tears continued for a long, long time. And afterwards, Katharine could scarcely recall whether it was Mary's smothered voice or her own uneasy thoughts which had said to her, at some stage in the evening: And now here is Alan saying nothing about the stabbing ... just as for six long years he has said nothing about the hair. What does it mean? What is he storing it up for? What will he use it for—and when?

CHAPTER XII

FOR THE next few days Katharine did not see much of the Prescotts, and what little she did see was reassuring. She had even seen them, all three together, setting off on Sunday afternoon for some expedition or other, like any other family party. True, Alan's arm was still in a sling, but he did not look ill, or particularly depressed; and Mary's head was bent, looking down at the ground, but then she always walked like that, and with those three-inch heels she probably had to look where she was treading, too. Angela, it must be admitted, looked bored—as if she had been told she would enjoy it when she got there—and who knows, perhaps she would.

Anyway, it seemed as if life next-door was back to normal; and it was not until the following Wednesday—the night of the firework party—that anything occurred to shake Katharine's easy assumption that the whole business had blown over.

Katharine managed to leave work a few minutes early that evening, hoping to avoid the worst of the rush hour; but alas, the queues seemed to be as long as ever. Perhaps everyone was trying to do the same as she was—get home early to scrub potatoes, prick sausages and slit chestnuts ready for cooking on the bonfire. A few for cooking on the bonfire, that is to say; the rest were destined to be actually eaten, and must be properly cooked indoors. As she stood in the familiar queue, Katharine ran over in her mind her share of the preparations. Mary, thank goodness, was doing the hot drinks and the toffee-apples; the children would already be combing the house and garden for burnable rubbish—would Jane, this year, allow the old rocking horse stand to count as burnable rubbish? That was the difficulty about rubbish, that there wasn't really any such thing. That is to say, there was always someone who loved it, someone who thought that it would come in for some thing. . . .

Gradually Katharine became aware of an uneasy, somehow familiar sensation, but so preoccupied was she with her thoughts that it was several seconds before she recognised it for what it was. It was the sensation of being watched. Swiftly she looked up, and met once more a pair of dark, censorious eyes staring straight into hers.

Auntie Pen again. In some confusion, Katharine collected her thoughts, smiled, and dropped back a couple of paces in the queue to join her. Auntie Pen was smiling now, the censoriousness gone, and, half laughing, she called Katharine's attention to a dark, untidy bundle under her arm.

"My old garden coat," she explained ruefully. "Destined for Angela's guy. I don't know why I submit to it, I'm sure. It only leaves me my best one to wear. To tell the truth, I'd really rather have given the guy my best one and kept the other. An old coat is so useful, isn't it, and so irreplaceable? It takes years and years to get another old coat, whereas a new one can be bought in five minutes. Oh, well. I suppose the guy's need is greater than mine," she concluded cheerfully.

"That guy of Angela's must be quite the dandy," laughed Katharine. "He's building up quite a wardrobe. He's already got my husband's old raincoat. Do you think he has to change for dinner, or something?"

Mrs. Quentin turned, and looked at Katharine a little oddly.

"Your husband's old *raincoat*?" she asked, frowning. "Oh. Then that explains—that is—I wonder—?"

Katharine glanced at her companion enquiringly. The lined, strong face was no longer humorous. It looked calculating, almost defensive, in the sick light. Then Mrs. Quentin laughed, not quite convincingly.

"Poor Mary! She's such a child, isn't she? And of course, I let myself in for it, really—simply stuck my neck out. I rang up yesterday, you see, to ask them if they wanted me to bring anything. I have a lot of old hats, you know, and of course you can't give that sort of thing to your charwoman any more—even the rag-man won't take them. There aren't the poor any more, you see. That's the trouble with progress—it has abolished the poor without providing any substitute. Substitutes for coal, yes: and for tablecloths, and for soap, and for real pork sausages: but no substitute for the poor. Well, anyway, I thought it might amuse Angela to choose one of these hats for the guy, but she said no: the guy was already finished, and had all the clothes he needed. And just then there was a sort of clamour down the phone—a crashing and a clattering, though I expect it was just the receiver getting a little knock—you know how these sounds get magnified—and then there was Mary's voice, asking me to bring an old coat for the guy, the one he had wasn't suitable. *Suitable!*—I ask you—for a guy! I must say I was puzzled at the time. I'm afraid it made me laugh."

"I'm still puzzled now," put in Katharine. "I wonder what was wrong with the coat I gave her? It—"

"Oh, my dear, don't you see? Or perhaps you don't know Mary as well as I do. She can be very childish in her outlook sometimes, and it's my belief that she feels superstitious—sort of scared—about burning a figure in a raincoat after—what happened last week. Don't you understand?"

In a way, Katharine understood. But it seemed a bit silly. After all, it wasn't even as if there *had* been a man with a raincoat. Still, Mrs. Quentin wasn't to know that. Naturally, she had been told, and had believed, the same story as everyone else.

Or had she believed it? The older woman was looking at Katharine rather strangely now. . . . Not quite suspiciously, but—carefully . . . as if studying her reactions to this slightly far-fetched interpretation of Mary's behaviour. Katharine thought quickly, and decided to brandish unshakeable belief in the Man with the Raincoat.

"Yes, of course. It must have been such a shock for her," she lied placatingly. "I mean, to feel that a stranger can come into the house and attack someone like that . . ."

Had she sounded convincing? And convinced? Or had all this headlong guilelessness been a bit overdone? For Mrs. Quentin was still looking at her in that speculative way.

"*You* didn't see anything of this man, did you?" she asked suddenly. "I mean, living next door, you might have noticed someone going in . . . or coming out . . . or hanging about in some way?"

Was it Katharine's fancy that the question was less a question than a veiled piece of prompting? Was Mrs. Quentin hinting that it would have been a most convenient, a most neighbourly piece of observation on Katharine's part to have seen a suspicious figure, and thus have backed up the Prescotts' story? And were her next words the truth, or were they merely intended to make up for Katharine's unneighbourly omission?

"Well, *I* saw him," she declared, almost condescendingly, as one who knows the right thing to do even if the younger generation doesn't. "As I came out of the house, after doing Angela's tea, I saw a man of middle size, with the collar of his raincoat pulled up, hanging about under the lamp-post. Of course, I didn't think anything about it at the time, but, looking back, I feel sure it must have been the same man."

"But surely that would have been much earlier?" began Katharine—and stopped. Why should she call the old woman's well-meant bluff? It must be that Auntie Pen knew—or guessed—what had really happened, and for the sake of her young sister-in-law was trying to bolster up the official story with this clumsy but well-intentioned fabrication. It would be cruel to point out inconsistencies—and pointless, too, for Katharine was quite as determined as Auntie Pen could be to protect Mary's secret. And anyway, here was the bus, goading the flaccid queue into frenzied life; pushing, struggling, crushing out all possibility of further communication.

The fireworks party had gone well, without a single disaster of any kind. No one had burnt their fingers, or got anything in their eye, or had been grossly unfairly treated in the matter of being allowed to light things. None of the food had got burnt—except the things cooked on the bonfire, of course, but that was different. Even the customary floods of tears at the poor guy being burnt passed off quite lightly, because this year, with Jack and Mavis away at boarding school, Stella wasn't there to say that all this tender-hearted crying about the guy was really a sign of repressed sadism.

And above all, the fathers had been wonderful. Watching Alan, competent and almost gay as he set up rockets with his one good arm, Katharine caught herself wondering whether Mary didn't, after all, invent or imagine half her troubles. But then, anyone watching Stephen would have thought the same of Katharine. How bronzed and handsome he had looked in the bonfire light. He seemed to have forgotten all about his strictures about Jane's friendship with the Prescotts. Absorbed, happy, and efficient, he had explained to his daughters exactly how they should light this or that firework—how they should hold it— where they should stand. And the children, in their hearts a little frightened of the fireworks, had done exactly what he said: had treated his superior skill with the admiring deference for which in ordinary life he longed in vain. This was the sort of setting in which fathers could thrive, Katharine suddenly realised; a setting which really *is* a little dangerous, a little beyond the skill of the women-folk. Once upon a time nature provided just such a setting for every father everywhere, but this is something that civilisation has systematically destroyed, reducing every daily activity to something well within the powers of a woman, or even of a child.

And now the fireworks were over, and everyone had gone surging indoors into the Prescotts' kitchen, to drink cocoa and hot punch. Only Katharine lingered for a few moments outside, to savour the quietness of the November night. Well, partly to savour the quietness, and partly to avoid the argument about how much, if any, of the punch Flora should be allowed to drink. If she simply wasn't there, then Stephen couldn't complain afterwards that she'd said Yes when she ought to have said No, could he?

But all the same, the darkness and the quiet out here in the narrow suburban garden were bewilderingly beautiful. Odd that one should feel that it was quiet, when voices and laughter were coming from the lighted house; when cars were still passing outside, and occasional rockets from other people's gardens were still swooping up here and there into the empty sky. But the night has a quietness of its own that seems to have nothing to do with the presence or absence of sounds, as if the darkness pressed upon the ears as well as the eyes, shutting one off from the small, lighted world, and bringing one close to the surrounding emptiness.

It was a fine night; and yet the wetness of November was everywhere; squelching up from the ground, hanging still and heavy from every twig, not dripping in the windless air but sodden, all-pervading. Even the ashes of the dying bonfire were growing damp already; Katharine could hear them stirring and shuffling unhappily in the encroaching wet. From below, from above, from every side, the wetness was winning, coming back into its own.

A sound of heavy movement nearby made Katharine start; and there, pushing down the dripping, overhung path beside the lawn came Mrs. Quentin. Had she just come from the lighted house, or had she, too, been hanging about in the peaceful darkness? Katharine hadn't heard the side door open, but then she hadn't been listening for it. Mrs. Quentin came close, breathing heavily.

"Come over to the wall, could you please, for a moment?" she asked, in an undertone: an unnecessary precaution, surely, except as a mark of deference to the huge autumnal night. "That wall down at the end where the lamp shines over."

The Prescotts' house stood on the corner, a wide residential road running past their wall on the side away from Katharine's house. That must be the corner in which Jane and Angela had so joyfully discovered that they could read by the light of the street lamp, mused Katharine; and—yes—here was the little table from the greenhouse still standing where they had dragged it, and two rickety chairs as well. Heavily, but with surprising sureness, Mrs. Quentin climbed on to one of them, and peered over the wall into the street.

"There!" she whispered triumphantly over her shoulder. "*That's* where I saw him—under that lamp there." She spoke aggressively, as though clinching a long-standing argument between herself and Katharine. Just as if Katharine had been going on and on for days trying to prove that there *hadn't* been a man there.

Katharine was annoyed. She hadn't questioned Mrs. Quentin's story and anyway what was it to her whether it was true or not? Why make such an issue of it, when the whole thing was over and done with? Nevertheless, she climbed up on to the other chair and leaned precariously over, staring obediently down at the undistinguished blur of wet pavement indicated by her companion.

"*That's* where he was standing," Mrs. Quentin insisted, as if Katharine was even now denying it. "Just there by the lamp-post—standing as if he was waiting for a bus, only of course there aren't any buses down this road, are there? I've been telling Mary about it, and she says—"

A slight sound behind them made both women jerk round, clutching the wall for balance as the chairs lurched in sympathetic shock. Angela, pale and shiny-eyed, in a dark jersey and jeans, stood dimly silhouetted behind them on the wet path.

"*I* saw him too," she announced—had she heard the whole conversation, then?—"Standing under the light just like you said, Auntie Pen. Wearing a raincoat. And he kept looking at his watch—I suppose to see if it was *time!*" Her eyes grew rounder, more brilliant; her stance more self-important as she went on: "And then he began to walk away—slowly. I'll show you *exactly* where he was, if you like—"

Effortlessly, Angela skidded up the six-foot wall and seated herself astride it, apparently all in one movement, with that total communion between a child and its own home wall that goes beyond mere gymnastic skill, and seems more like a sort of symbiosis between the two.

Now Angela, from her point of vantage, stared gleefully down at the pavement.

"He was carrying a small dark bag," she continued "Well—fairly small, sort *of narrow,* you know; and every now and then he *looked* in it—to make sure he hadn't forgotten anything. I saw something shiny there, and of course it must have been the knife. He put his hand in and ran his fingers along the edge once or twice, seeing if it was sharp enough, I suppose. . . ."

Was Angela making all this up as she went along, or had she got it out of a comic? Or was she, perhaps, even believing it? . . .

"He was muttering to himself," proceeded Angela fluently. "Queer words that I couldn't understand. Not French, or German, or Italian, or any *proper* language, but something very, very queer. And he kept making faces to himself, showing his teeth in a dreadful grin. They were long yellow teeth, like fangs. . . ."

Katharine began to feel that this had gone quite far enough, especially as Jane would certainly be regaled with the same story, even further embellished, within the next twenty-four hours.

"Don't be silly, Angela," she said briskly. "You're making it all up. If you'd seen anyone half as queer as that you'd have been terrified. You'd have rushed in and told somebody."

"I didn't want to frighten Jane," explained Angela virtuously. "She was here that evening, you know, and she's younger than

I am. She gets frightened very easily, you know," she went on, patronisingly. "*I'm* not frightened of *anything*!"

Having flung this fearful challenge into the vastness of the autumn night, Angela slid swiftly off the wall again and darted back into the lighted house. Katharine gazed after her.

"We shouldn't have talked so loud," she said reproachfully. "Now she's got all sorts of nonsensical ideas into her head."

"Children *should* have nonsensical ideas in their heads," retorted Mrs. Quentin, clambering down from her perch and feeling with her solid, lace-up shoe for a safe footing in the treacherous dark flower bed. "Man can't live by truth alone, you know, and children even less so. *You* should know this—a mother of three!"

"Yes—I know what you mean," laughed Katharine. "And I wasn't thinking of Angela coming to any harm. I think this business of keeping unsuitable topics from children is more a matter of expediency than for *their* sake. I mean, take this business tonight, for instance. Angela will go straight off and tell Jane all this rigmarole, and then they'll both tell all their friends at school, piling up the horror as they go; and then the friends will tell their mothers—"

"And why not?" demanded Mrs. Quentin, picking her way along the muddy path in front of Katharine. "Why not? All those people passing on to each other more and more colourful lies, brighter and brighter, in the ever-widening, brightening spiral. Can't you see it as an enrichment of life—of all their lives? Isn't that how you *do* see it?" She threw the last words over her shoulder like missiles, carelessly aimed in the darkness, and Katharine was silenced. Was Mrs. Quentin being sarcastic? Or perhaps—it occurred to her—Mrs. Quentin actually *wanted* this rumour to be spread as widely as possible, simply to distract people from guessing the truth. Probably she had started the rumour herself, on purpose. Yes: studying the sturdy figure in front of her, picking its way heavily and skilfully through the overgrown garden in the darkness, Katharine realised that Mrs. Quentin would certainly be capable of it. For a cause she felt to be worth while, this woman would certainly be prepared to start rumours, tell lies, back up false witnesses, without the faintest qualm of conscience. For that very reason, she probably told lies very well.

Though, come to think of it, she hadn't told this evening's lies very well. In fact, they had been rather unconvincing. So perhaps they were just simply true. Perhaps, by coincidence, there really *had* been a man loitering under the lamp on the night when Mary stabbed her husband?

Well, and what of it? Either the tale was true, and a mere coincidence, or else it was false, and a tribute to Auntie Pen's loyalty to her brother's family. Either way there was no harm done. The whole thing was trivial, and a bit silly.

Why, then, should Katharine feel that some irrevocable decision had been reached that night. That under a quiet November darkness, lit here and there by a flashing, fading firework, something had been set in motion which none of them now could reverse, no matter which of them might wish to do so, nor how soon.

CHAPTER XIII

KATHARINE STUFFED the shirts and the towels and the pillow-cases into the great gaping mouth of the washing machine, slammed the door, and sat back on the nearest of the row of chairs to watch the revolving garments in stupefied fascination.

The launderette was fairly empty at this time in the morning, and where she sat Katharine had no immediate neighbours, but all the same she did not dare take her eyes off her machine until the red light had gone on. It was not that the red light was such a *very* peremptory signal; after all, it stayed on for two or three minutes, during any of which time you could quite well put in the greyish crystals labelled "First Wash". But Katharine knew by experience that if you didn't leap to it the very moment the light flicked on, then some public-spirited benefactor (or some self-righteous busy-body, according to how you felt) would lean towards you and hiss urgently, smugly, and absolutely incontro-vertibly: "Your light's on, dear."

Funny, really, that it was so annoying, because it was very harmless, and very well-meant; and after all, you really might not have noticed the light in time. But it was like having a door held open for you by your predecessor in a corridor when you are still a good many yards away. Having put you to the trouble of hurrying so as not to keep her waiting, your benefactor is now entitled to your gratitude.

It was mean to feel like that, thought Katharine, as she sat there feeling like it, and watching nervously for her light. She fancied that the Light Brigade (as she called them in her imagination) were already on the watch—sharp-eyed, alert, every muscle at the ready, determined to say, "Your light's on, dear," quicker than she could leap to her feet; like some awful game of Snap. Once that was over, the red light safely on and off again, then Katharine could settle down to the real happiness of these weekly visits to the launderette: namely, reading a book, solidly, for twenty minutes, without feeling that she ought to be doing something else.

"Hullo, my dear! Fancy you being here so early."

Mrs. Forsyth's voice came from behind a mound of coloured blankets which she clutched precariously against her. Katharine had to lean over sideways to get a glimpse of a face to which to address her reply.

"I always come early," she answered, from this awkward angle. "I have to be at work by midday, and anyway, it's always much less crowded at this time, don't you find?"

Mrs. Forsyth dumped her load on a chair—or rather on three chairs—with an ostentatious sigh of exhaustion.

"I left His Lordship still in bed," she commented, in oblique reference to the aforesaid sigh. "Reading the papers and drinking his fourth cup of tea! 'Goodbye, breadwinner!' I said to him. '*I've* got to go and do some work!' Do you know, he doesn't leave the house till nearly ten these days—and quite often he's back by teatime! It makes me laugh, when he flops into an armchair as if he'd been heaving coal all day and was enjoying a well-earned rest. Well-earned rest, my foot!—he's been resting all day; I know that for a fact. He spends all his time at the office gossiping and drinking tea—I know one of the girls there, and she tells me. And then he expects *me* to wait on *him*!"

"And do you?" Katharine was aware of the familiar feeling of comfort, of self-satisfaction, even a sort of low-grade self-respect, which she always felt on hearing another wife complaining of another husband. She, Katharine, would of course never stoop to such treacherous revelations about Stephen—fancy gossiping about his shortcomings with a girl from his office, as Mrs. Forsyth must have done. Katharine herself would never be so disloyal, but all the same it was tremendously satisfying to encourage Mrs. Forsyth's disloyalty.

"And *do* you wait on him?" she prompted eagerly; and Mrs. Forsyth's self-pity boiled up like a pan of milk.

"*Wait* on him! It's not the word for it! Who brought him four cups of tea in bed this morning, as well as cleaning out the grate and washing the breakfast things? It gets me down sometimes, it really does. Do you know, he was home by ten minutes past four yesterday; and so when he did his tired breadwinner act, flopping into the armchair and gasping for a cup of tea, I simply glanced at the clock and said: 'What a shame, they *have* kept you late, you must be worn out!' I meant to be sarcastic, of course, but believe it or not, he took it seriously—he absolutely lapped it up! You should have seen how he smirked as he said yes, well, I *am* a bit exhausted, and blah blah blah about some chap called Cooters or some thing. All Douglas's clients seem to have the most ridiculous names, like something out of comic opera. The last one—"

"Your light's on, dear."

"Oh, Thank you. Thank you so much."

Katharine got the words out somehow, hoping that they conveyed appropriate and insincere gratitude rather than inappropriate and sincere hatred, and jumped to her feet. By the time she had scooped the crystals into their steaming destination and come back to her place, Mrs. Forsyth had gathered up her blankets and gone to weigh them. She came back with a look of such truculent malice on her face as seemed to Katharine disproportionate to anything that could possibly have happened in this humdrum setting.

"How much would you think these weigh?"

The truculent look was straining itself round the pile of blankets to get a good view of Katharine's response; and Katharine imagined that the blankets must weigh either very much more or very much less than one would suppose. But since she didn't know which it was, Katharine was at a loss as to how to guess so as to give her companion maximum satisfaction. Safest, really, to say exactly what she *did* think.

"Just about the nine pounds, I should say," she hazarded. "I should think you'll just get them into one machine."

Mrs. Forsyth was enchanted.

"That's right! Exactly nine pounds! Nine pounds to the ounce! Do you know, Douglas was saying it would be more than that! He said it would be at least twelve pounds, and I'd need a second machine. I *told* him I wouldn't, and I was right! Exactly nine pounds!"

The jubilation in her face would have suggested to a stranger that Mrs. Forsyth had just won a football pool rather than merely the prospect of telling her husband at ten-past four that afternoon that he had been wrong about something. Katharine watched her pushing her blankets—her faithful vindicators—lovingly into their single machine, and slamming the door with joyous finality. They began slowly to revolve, gathering speed until they became a gorgeous whirl of rainbow colour, quite inappropriate, Katharine reflected vaguely, to Mrs. Forsyth's spiteful and ungenerous nature. You'd be reading articles about it soon—how you could tell people's character just by looking at the contents of their washing machines. It used to be just by looking at their shoes, or their window curtains. And people's characters stayed just as complicated as ever—just look at Katharine's own wheeling medley of off-whites, right next to all this peacock glory.

Katharine picked up the local paper, which had been left on a chair nearby. She would much rather have read her book, but Mrs. Forsyth was going to come back and sit beside her at any moment, and for some reason it always seems much ruder to read a book in company than to read a paper. The paper was folded back to the advertisement page, and

Katharine, not being in need of a studio flat, or a second-hand grand piano, or an expert landscape gardener, readjusted it to begin at the beginning. As the front page came unwillingly into view under her flailing arms, she experienced a sudden shock.

"MAN STABBED IN CAFÉ," read the headline—and really, it was absurd to have been shocked, because of course Alan hadn't been stabbed in a café. All the same, reading of stabbing at all was oddly unnerving. . . . Police seeking information . . . description of assailant . . . all the rest of it. Katharine became aware that a stout, middle-aged woman on the seat behind her was breathing interestedly over her shoulder.

"Awful, innit?" commented the owner of breath cheerfully. "Just round the corner from us, it was. Not five minutes away. Awful, innit?"

Katharine agreed noncommittally; and her companion went on: "Not safe, are you, not anywhere, these days, not after dark. I'm always telling my daughter, I tell her——"

But what the good woman always told her daughter, and with what (if any) effect on the young lady's leisure activities, would never be known, for just then Mrs. Forsyth came back and settled herself once more next to Katharine, craning over at the paper, and beginning to talk immediately.

"Funny, isn't it, two stabbings in one week. Though of course the Prescott one isn't in the paper . . . is it? *Is* it? . . ."

She moved as if to take the paper right away from Katharine but Katharine hung on to it—why, she was not quite sure.

"No, of course it isn't," she said decisively, and without looking. She tried to turn the page, but Mrs. Forsyth put out her hand and arrested the movement. Evidently she wanted this page left uppermost—not to read, as it transpired, but as a sort of introduction to the subject uppermost in her mind.

"I suppose you've heard?" she murmured to Katharine, very softly. "You've heard that they think they know who it was?"

"Who what was?" Katharine was startled. "Do you mean. . . ?"

"Who stabbed Alan Prescott, of course." Mrs. Forsyth continued, rather less cautiously. "The man who broke in and stabbed him. They've an idea who it was."

Katharine was dazed, and somehow frightened. She felt, quite illogically, that Mary's secret was somehow being attacked, though in fact, of course, the exact opposite was happening.

"They haven't actually mentioned any names yet," Mrs. Forsyth was saying happily. "But they have reason to believe that it was a local man—someone who knew Alan well. It's just what I was saying, isn't it? Do you remember my saying that? . . ."

Yes, of course Katharine remembered; but she also knew that hypothesis was totally untrue.

"It's all nonsense," she asserted loudly. "I *know* it is. They can't have found it was a local man, because—"

She stopped in time. Surprising how difficult it was—and how annoying, too—to keep a secret in the face of this sort of provocation: when you knew that with a single forbidden sentence you could wipe the whole of that smug, patronising smile off Mrs. Forsyth's face.

"Well, I hope you're right, I'm sure," lied Mrs. Forsyth tolerantly. "I'd hate to think it really was—well—any of the men we know. But I heard it from a very old friend of mine whose child goes to Angela's school. Apparently Angela actually *saw* this man actually entering the house—"

Katharine burst out laughing.

"Oh, you mean *Angela* is at the bottom of all this? My dear soul, you mustn't take the slightest notice of anything she says. She's a nice child, but very imaginative, and she can't resist a good story—like a lot of us. Why, I was there myself when she was making it all up. Simply making it up, as she went along, the way kids do. And by the time a couple of other children have improved on it, and passed it on . . ."

Mrs. Forsyth was looking at her, scornful and patronising.

"Oh, my dear, I *do* understand how you feel," she allowed, with ghoulish sympathy. "After all, living right next door . . . I do understand how unpleasant it is for you . . . any sort of enquiries, I mean . . . just routine enquiries, of course, but I'm sure you won't have any trouble—after all, your husband was at home all the evening, wasn't he, when it happened?"

Did Mrs. Forsyth *know* that Stephen hadn't come home that evening, or was it a shot in the dark?

"No, he wasn't," snapped Katharine. "He was out with a gun the whole evening, shooting up the neighbours. Didn't Angela tell your sister-in-law's charwoman? Surely she did?"

Mrs. Forsyth looked annoyed; and really one could not blame her.

"All right," she said huffily. "I only thought you'd be interested. After all, you're a friend of the Prescotts'—supposed to be. . . ."

"I *am* interested—I'm sorry," Katharine apologised. "I was only joking. . . ."

This, the commonest and feeblest of all excuses in this sort of situation, was accepted by Mrs. Forsyth with almost ludicrous alacrity: and for a moment the two women stared at each other, each nonplussed by her own forbearance and readiness to make amends. It's because we can't *afford* to quarrel, suddenly thought Katharine. It's not a real friendship between us; we don't even like each other. The tie between us isn't friendship at all; it's a sort of trade agreement, and that's why we can't afford to break it. *She* needs to get her grievances about her marriage off her chest, and *I* need to listen to them to make my own marriage seem good by comparison. I'm a parasite, really, on other people's troubles . . . and yet, if it helps them as well . . . ?

In sudden compunction, Katharine changed the subject. As if she was restoring a confiscated toy to a child, she brought the conversation back to Mrs. Forsyth's favourite theme, and soon she was listening to bitter little anecdotes about Douglas's uncooperativeness over Christmas, already looming now that bonfire night was over. How he wouldn't help with the shopping, wouldn't put up decorations, couldn't even be trusted to put the right cards into the right envelopes. In her eagerness to re-establish their former profitable relationship, Katharine now caught herself chiming in with *her* husband's annoying ways relative to the festive season: how he refused to do anything whatever about presents for the children, saying that they already had far too much; and then, suddenly, after she had already bought and wrapped presents on behalf of both of them—then he would dash out just before closing time on Christmas Eve and buy a whole lot of large, expensive presents, so that the children ended up by getting even more too much than that he had at first complained of. And no, he couldn't be *counted* on to do this, she always had to have something else ready in case. And then, again, there was the way he hated having the family to Christmas dinner, saying that the only guests he disliked more than her relations were his own; and when, on the strength of this, she didn't invite anyone, then he complained that Christmas wasn't nearly as festive now as it used to be when he was a boy.

Was she being disloyal? Or was it just casual, half-humorous nattering? Hastily Katharine put a humorous note into her voice, and kept it there, conscientiously, until the end of the recital. But still she felt unhappy, almost degraded. Oh, Stephen, why have I done this to you? Why have you made me do it to you? And with Mrs. Forsyth looking on, too, with her mean, exultant eyes?

Her washing slumped to a stop in the machine, and Katharine hastily extracted it and trundled it across to the spin-drier. It was all right; of course it was. All wives talked about their husbands like this sometimes; it was just a safety-valve, a necessary letting off of steam. Healthy, that's what Stella would call it, and why shouldn't Stella be right sometimes, like anybody else? Just because her children were so annoyingly perfect, it didn't mean that she was wrong about everything. The spin-drier began to throb reassuringly under Katharine's hands, like a great cold kitten, and Katharine leaned on it, comforted, relishing its effortless energy as she herself enjoyed her last minutes of idleness.

CHAPTER XIV

As Katharine came up the steps after work that evening, she became aware of voices on the threshold of the house next door. Mrs. Forsyth's voice mainly, comforting some unseen sufferer in a voice shrill and purposeful as some predatory night bird.

"My dear, I *do* know how you feel," she was saying—and now Katharine could see the thin, neat figure poised dimly in the Prescotts' doorway. "Douglas is exactly the same. If *he* feels like going out in the evening, why, then out we have to go. It doesn't occur to him to think that *I* might be tired, or busy, or not in the mood. The trouble with men is, they have so little to do that they're really killing time for more than half their waking hours. Yes, it really *is* more than half. I've worked it out. A man in an ordinary, average job has seventy hours' leisure a week, apart from sleeping! Seventy hours! Imagine it! I'd think the world was coming to an end if I had as much as seven!"

Katharine could not hear Mary's softer response from indoors, but it went on for quite a long time, and it was tantalisingly just possible to hear the unmistakable cadences of self-pity at the end of every few sentences. A lovely, anti-husband natter was in progress, and Katharine felt herself drawn by the sound like an alcoholic by the clink of glasses.

The aggrieved pair did not seem to feel that Katharine was intruding. Indeed, from the moment when she settled herself leaning against the other damp pillar at the entrance of the Prescott home, she seemed to fit into the pattern of the conversation like a stopper into a bottle. It was a little disconcerting in a way: as if she had recently passed some test for total membership of an exclusive club: the club of the Unhappy Wives. For a long time she had been as it were an associate member—her temporary differences with Stephen had been just sufficient qualification. Was she to be considered a life member now? Was that how they now regarded her?

". . . so when he rang up and said he'd got tickets for the theatre tonight, and wanted me to meet him in town, I didn't see how I could refuse. How *could* I?"

Mary's wide, beautiful eyes stared out bewildered into the damp night. But Mrs. Forsyth was once again ready with reassurance of her own inimitable brand.

"Of course you couldn't! I know just how you felt. They know they've got you—like *that*—(she jabbed her thumb downwards, as if nailing the idea to its appropriate place) when they do something like that to settle an argument. They know there's no answer to it."

Mary looked uncertain.

"But he must be doing it to please me, after all, mustn't he? That's the awful part. I *ought* to be pleased. And of course I would be if only I didn't know—I mean, if I didn't feel—I mean perhaps all the time he's thinking—"

She stopped. Only Katharine could appreciate the cause of her confusion. However, Mrs. Forsyth *thought* she could, and that was quite sufficient to enable her to answer in accordance with the principles (few and simple) of the Unhappy Wives:

"Oh, that's how they always try to work it," she assured the wavering Mary. "When they know they're in the wrong. If there's one thing I can't stand, it's when Douglas uses a bunch of flowers or a trip to the theatre as a last word in an argument. It *infuriates* me! If he knows he's in the wrong I want him to admit it, not to silence me with sentimental gestures!"

Katharine was in the middle of wondering what kind of sentimental gesture would in fact succeed in silencing Mrs. Forsyth, when Mary turned to her:

"Oh, Katharine, perhaps *you* can help me? I didn't ask you before, because I seem to be *always* dumping Angela on you; but if you could possibly have her for this evening, then I wouldn't so much mind going out. That's half what I'm worrying about, I think—leaving her alone."

"Of course," said Katharine warmly. "Tell her to come over as soon as she likes. We could put up the camp-bed in Jane's room, and—"

She stopped. Only a few days ago Stephen had been urging her to discourage the friendship between Jane and Angela. True, he hadn't said anything since, and Katharine was beginning to hope that he had forgotten all about it; but surely this would be the height of tactlessness—gratuitously to remind him of it by inviting Angela to stay the night with them? With prac-tised skill, she proceeded to get herself out of it by sheer reckless improvisation. She was terribly sorry, but she had spoken with-out thinking; just tonight of all nights it would be impossible to have Angela, because Stephen might be bringing two old college friends back with him for the evening, and he might want to ask them to stay the night, which would mean using the sofa *and* the camp-bed.

The main thing about this sort of story was not so much that it should be credible as that it should be impervious to evidence of any kind, for or against. She had carefully only said that the friends *might* be coming, that they *might* be staying the night. By the time they hadn't done either, the whole thing would be over and done with.

But all the same, Mary was looking so disappointed that Katharine impulsively added: "But if you like, I'll keep an eye on Angela for you. I'll pop in at intervals and see that she's all right. Will that do? Stephen and his friends won't mind my not being there all the time," she added, rather perfunctorily. She realised, with a mixture of relief and chagrin, that no one but herself cared a hang whether her story held water or not. Consistency in lying is an essentially solitary craft, usually quite wasted on its audience.

Mary seemed to be weighing up Katharine's offer.

"Ye-es," she said, rather doubtfully—indeed grudgingly, Katharine felt. "Yes—I suppose that would do. I mean, thank you very much, that would be marvellous," she amended, with unconvincing enthusiasm. "The only thing is," she continued, with renewed hesitancy, "that—that Angela really seems nervous tonight. Nervous of being left alone, I mean. You see, she thinks . . ."

Her voice grew vague, lost in hesitations, and Mrs. Forsyth eagerly broke in:

"Yes, did you know, Katharine, Mary's just been telling me: Angela thinks she saw the dark man in the raincoat *again*. This evening! Hanging about outside the house, just like last time. Of course, as I tell Mary, it must be all her imagination mustn't it? You were saying, weren't you, that she's very imaginative. . . ." Her eyes held Katharine's in a meaning glance which Mary was somehow supposed not to notice, though how she could fail to do so it was hard to see, since they were both standing right in front of her.

Katharine ignored the look, and spoke directly to Mary:

"Of course the child's nervous, all alone," she agreed briskly. "And I expect you'll be out pretty late. I'll tell you what I'll do. I'll collect up all my mending and bring it in, then I could stay the whole time." She was about to invent hastily some further reason why Stephen's friends could totally dispense with their hostess, but thought better of it; everyone but herself had forgotten about them so completely. Instead, she went on: "I certainly think you ought to take this chance, Mary, and go out and have some fun. It will do you a world of good—both of you."

This time the meaning glance excluded Mrs. Forsyth, and serve her right, thought Katharine cheerfully, as she hurried back to her own house and set about preparing supper.

This must be done even more hastily than usual if she was to be free in time to fulfil her promise to Mary: so she found it hard not to show her impatience when she turned round from tipping the potatoes into boiling water and found herself confronted by Clare's face, at its very gloomiest, peering with maddening hesitancy round the kitchen door.

Gerunds? Compound Interest? The Anglicans and the Rump Parliament? How could *anyone* be expected to cope with it while mincing Sunday's joint with enough onions and breadcrumbs to make it stretch for five? But the poor child looked so woebegone, so sure that she was going to be snubbed.

"What is it, Clare? Do come right in, and don't hang about in the door like that. The draught'll put the oven out."

Like a general deploying his troops to face a new threat, Katharine consciously rearranged her faculties so as to release a proportion of them from attention to the mince and the onions and the chopping of cabbage, and laid them at Clare's disposal.

But it wasn't homework, apparently. It was something much, much worse, to judge by the slow widening of Clare's already horror-stricken eyes, and by the increasing confusion of her speech as she came, via innumerable detours and irrelevancies, to the crux of the disaster.

She had been invited to a party. It was out at last; and Clare gazed at her mother with despairing expectancy, as if awaiting a flood of commiseration.

"But that's nice, darling," said Katharine obtusely. "Your red dress will be back from the cleaners by then, and we'll get you some new shoes, something pretty—"

"But, Mummy, I haven't got to *go*, have I?" interrupted Clare, incredulously, as if she had not known before that such ruthlessness existed in the world. "You don't mean that, do you? I've got to *go*?"

"But why not, darling?" asked Katharine helplessly, flinging into the pan an assortment of vegetables further to eke out the mince. "Why don't you want to?"

"But it's *Sandra's* party!" explained Clare, with such an air of having clarified the whole problem that Katharine began to feel that she must be being unforgivably stupid. Fancy not understanding why it is utterly impossible to go to the party of someone called Sandra.

"You see, Mummy..."

The explanation that followed, comprising a minute-by-minute account of the complex and fluctuating exchanges of best friends that had been taking place since the beginning of term, left her little the wiser. She could only take Clare's word for it that going to the party would be "*Awful. Mummy. I couldn't!*"

Clare paused, twirling the handle of the mincer. "And anyway, Sandra doesn't want me."[5]

"Then why has she asked you?" asked Katharine reasonably—or so she naïvely supposed.

"Oh, *Mummy!*" Clare stared at her parent forlornly. Language contained no words in which to explain anything so obvious as why someone called Sandra should invite you to a party when she didn't want you and you didn't want to go.

"Well, tell her you can't go," suggested Katharine, abandoning the impenetrable maze into which the contemplation of acceptance was leading them. "Tell Sandra—nicely, of course—that you have a previous engagement."

"But, *Mummy*, I've already *accepted!*" wailed Clare; and then, in touching, total surrender, she flung the whole matter into Katharine's lap. "Mummy, will you ring up Sandra's mother and say I can't go? *Please!*"

"But what shall I say? *Why* shall I say you can't? I mean, if you've already told Sandra that you can?"

"Oh, *anything*." The situation was plainly desperate. "Say you don't let me go out so late. Say you're ill and I've got to stay at home to look after you. Say *anything*, except don't say I'm going out somewhere else, because they know I'm not. Oh, *please*, Mummy! You must! Oh, it'll be so *awful!*"

Wondering how many other mothers gain their reputation for possessiveness and over-protectiveness in this sort of way, Katharine gave a half-hearted promise to ring up the unknown Mrs. Sandra and say something appropriate. And by now it was time to put the meal on the table; to summon the rest of the family; to serve out helpings which unobtrusively avoided giving onions to Jane, cabbage to Flora, or anything at all to Clare, who was still brooding over her only partially averted doom. The conversation also had to be steered away from channels which could lead to such subjects as Curfew, or parties, or homework, or why Clare wasn't eating anything, or to anything at all which Flora would be likely to contradict in that know-all manner which always infuriated Stephen. And on top of all this, Katharine had to tell Stephen that she would be spending the evening next-door looking after Angela; tell him, too, in such a way that he didn't really quite take it in—not enough to protest then and there, anyway.

And so, what with one thing and another, by the time Katharine was staggering down the front steps with her gigantic pile of mending, she felt exactly as if she was setting off on holiday.

CHAPTER XV

MARY'S WHITE, anxious face broke into an astonished laugh as she opened the door to Katharine.

"My goodness, you look like a refugee!" she exclaimed. "As if you were escaping with all your bedding, or something."

"I *am* escaping," replied Katharine, laughing, as she staggered after Mary into the sitting-room. "It's always an escape, don't you think, to get away from your family for a bit?"

But of course Mary was the wrong person for a joke like this just now; the laughter had already left her face. How careful you had to be when someone was in real trouble. Trying to mend matters, Katharine hastened on: "But don't be frightened. I'm not moving in. This really *is* my mending." She dumped her load on to the floor beside the sofa, and stared at it a little unbelievingly herself as it swelled and spread in the manner of miscellaneous objects once they find themselves on a floor. "You'd think it was enough to last me a year, wouldn't you?" she admitted. "But actually I shall be able to finish it all this evening. My mending is always like this. Isn't yours? You know, mountains of gigantic garments each needing one tiny thing done to them."

Katharine bent over her pile, and began fingering it through distastefully, like a reluctant buyer at a jumble sale.

"Just look—this is the sort of thing, I mean. A winter coat with the sleeve lining torn. Another with the tab off. Jane's satchel with the strap broken. Flora's jeans wanting a new zip. The loose cover of the armchair with half its tapes off. I do envy those women in books whose mending always seems to consist just of darning socks, don't you? Why, they can keep it in a mending basket! I'd need a van to keep mine in. Of course, our whole house is a sort of glorified mending-basket-cum-washing-box when you come to think of it. . . ."

Katharine had been chattering on, hoping to bring the smile back to her friend's face. But Mary seemed not even to be listening. She was fidgeting about the room, restlessly, in a semblance of tidying, and now she had moved over to the window, latching it, testing the firmness of the latch, and then just standing there, staring out into the darkness. The long, heavy curtain had fallen back over her slight figure, and all Katharine could see of her was a beautifully shod foot, tapping uneasily. The curtain twitched a little as Mary's shoulders moved behind it—perhaps in a shrug, perhaps in some less definable restlessness.

Mary remained behind the curtain so long that Katharine grew puzzled. She went over to join her.

"What are you looking at?" she asked casually, pulling the curtain a little to one side. She was quite unprepared for the startled terror with which Mary whirled round to face her.

"*Oh!* How you startled me!" cried Mary—unreasonably, it seemed to Katharine, for surely she must have remembered that Katharine was in the room? "Oh—you gave me such a fright!"

"Who on earth did you think I was?" laughed Katharine. "And what *are* you looking at, anyway? Are the neighbours dancing naked in the garden, or something?"

Standing beside Mary, cut off by the curtains from the lighted room behind them, she, too, stared out at the dark gardens—Mary's, her own, and then the Pococks', with its eternal line of washing, forever renewed and yet for ever the same, like the tissues of the body. A little while back someone had tried to get Katharine to sign a petition about getting the Pococks to take their washing in on Sundays, but Katharine had refused. She felt that by now it would be like asking them to take in their lawn, or their toolshed, or any other permanent feature of their garden.

Anyway, once neighbours got into the habit of signing petitions there was no knowing where it would stop. Before you knew where you were there would be petitions about people keeping rabbits in ramshackle hutches in the back garden, or letting their children practise the piano at all hours of the week-end.

Anyway, the Pococks' washing looked very nearly beautiful just now as it billowed white and ghostlike in the gusty November darkness; and beyond it the houses and the small bare trees faded into a medley of dark and darker angles and smudges.

She could see nothing that could have riveted Mary's attention for all this time; and indeed Mary herself confirmed this.

"I'm not looking at anything," she declared, a little sulkily, and swished back through the curtains into the lighted room. "I've got to go now," she went on, suddenly quite bright and practical. "Will you be all right, Katharine? Angela's upstairs, finishing her homework, and then she'll go straight to bed. You needn't bother about her at all, so long as you'll just *be* here. And help yourself to anything you like to eat or drink, of course, won't you? There isn't anything much, actually, I somehow couldn't get around to doing any shopping today. . . ." She moved hesitantly towards the door, and stopped again.

"I *must* go," she repeated, as if somehow Katharine was detaining her; and then: "I must just go and make sure I've bolted the back door."

Katharine followed her through the kitchen and into the scullery, and it turned out that she *had* bolted the back door. And locked it, too, and put up the chain. But Mary examined her handiwork a little sceptically, pressed the bolt home more securely, and then latched the tiny window that looked out on to the dustbins. Then she stood staring at the refrigerator as if she wanted to lock that too; as if she suspected that it concealed a trap-door to a secret passage under the road.

"I think there are some cold sausages left," was the conclusion of her anxious scrutiny; and Katharine laughed, and hastened to assure her that she had already had a meal.

But Mary still hung about in the scullery, intent and very still, as if waiting for something. Under the glare of the white, unshaded bulb she looked strained and almost ill, despite her sparkling eardrops and the sequin-spangled black jersey she was wearing.

The refrigerator jerked into its periodic bout of humming, and this seemed to rouse Mary. She moved back into the hall.

"Well, goodbye, Katharine," she said, in her normal voice. "And thank you most awfully. We'll try not to be late." And then, silencing Katharine's assurances that she didn't mind how late they were, she added: "Bolt the front door after I'm outside, won't you, Katharine? And don't let anyone in. Just take no notice if anyone knocks."

Katharine was startled.

"Why ever not?" she asked. "I'm not Angela, you know—I'm not a child!"

"No. But you're alone in the house *with* a child," said Mary. "And you heard—didn't you?—that Angela saw a man with a raincoat hanging around the house this evening?"

"Yes—but for Heaven's sake—After all, *we* both know—"

"Hush!"

Mary's voice was not merely peremptory; it had a wild despairing quality, as if it had been forced out from some baffling depth of agony. "Hush, Katharine, *please!*"

Katharine realised, with some confusion, that she must have been talking rather loud, and she glanced up the stairs, expecting to see Angela leaning zestfully over the bannisters, as Flora would undoubtedly have been doing in a similar situation. But there was no sign of her; and anyway, Katharine hadn't said anything incriminating, had she? She hadn't even been going to finish the sentence which Mary had interrupted with such unnecessary urgency.

And now Mary had gone, tap-tapping off into the darkness to meet the husband she was afraid of. Or hated? Or was trying to get on better with? Katharine shrugged off the problem, closed the door and bolted it, according to her instructions, and went back to the living-room.

For a few minutes she sat idly on the sofa, looking through a magazine. There was more than enough time for the mending in the four hours or so before the Prescotts could be back, and it was so restful to sit in someone else's house doing absolutely nothing. You could never do this at home; there was always something, somewhere, nagging at your conscience—usually in full view, too, no matter where you sat. Curtains that needed washing if you faced the window; a grate that needed black-leading if you faced the fire: books that needed sorting and dusting if you faced the wall: the threadbare piece of carpet that needed patching if you faced the door. But here nothing mattered at all. Indeed, the blemishes in someone else's home can be a positive delight to a jaded housewife's eye. The black smudge on the wallpaper that *you* don't have to rub at with breadcrumbs; the vase of wilting flowers that *you* don't have to give fresh water to; the dust in the carved table legs that *you* don't have to poke at with a duster wrapped round a stick. Bliss! thought Katharine, looking ecstatically round at each of these flaws in turn: such peace and quiet as she had not experienced for months! And it was only after several minutes of revelling in it that Katharine began to feel that the quietness was too complete.

What was Angela doing? Homework, Mary had said; but surely homework wasn't done in such total silence as this? Most certainly it wasn't in Katharine's own home. True, with an only child one wouldn't expect arguments about ink, and taking too much room at the table, and who had borrowed whose protractor; but all the same, there should be *some* sound from upstairs, surely? The shutting of a book—the dropping of a pencil. Or had Angela already gone to bed?

Reclining at ease on the sofa, Katharine worried about it a little, but not enough to make her shatter this enchanted idleness by actually getting off the sofa and going to look. Give it another ten minutes, she thought drowsily. If by then there had been absolutely no sound. . . .

Katharine woke with a start, and with the feeling that she had been asleep for a very long time. She started up, and looked at the clock on the mantelpiece.

A quarter past three! Had she been drugged, or something? And why weren't Mary and Alan home long ago? But almost coincidently with the dismay of this discovery, Katharine recovered full consciousness and remembered about the clock—Mary's idiotic clock which always said a quarter past three. They couldn't get a new one, Mary had once explained, because she particularly wanted a chiming clock that would ring out delightfully every quarter of an hour, and Alan particularly wanted an electric clock that wouldn't. So they had compromised by not having a clock at all. Sad, Katharine remembered reflecting at the time, that so many compromises in marriage are of this empty and destructive kind.

So whatever the time was, it wasn't a quarter past three. It must be late, all the same; it *felt* late, somehow. Half-past eleven, perhaps? Even twelve? Mary and Alan would be back any moment now, and Katharine was guiltily aware that she hadn't looked after Angela in the least. She hadn't even *seen* the child. And what about that strange silence at the beginning of the evening—almost as if Angela hadn't been in the house at all?

In sudden panic, Katharine scrambled off the sofa and hurried out of the room. Of course, when she got upstairs she would find Angela in bed and asleep; but all the same she must reassure herself about it. How absurd to have let her half-waking imagination run riot about a dark man in a raincoat kidnapping the child, when the dark man in the raincoat didn't even exist! How suggestible could one get?

Angela's bed was empty. But somehow the shock of this discovery was less than the shock of finding, a fraction of a second later, that the reason for its emptiness was simply that Angela was still up. Up and dressed—or partially dressed—in a shapely bathing suit of Mary's surmounted by a glamorous gold lamé stole. Thus accoutred, she was posing on tiptoe in front of the long mirror in her mother's bedroom, her white, bony little legs mottled with cold, and her arms outstretched, the wide, glittering stole draped insecurely over them so that they looked like great floppy, pleading wings.

Her back was to the door, so Katharine was able to watch her for a moment unnoticed, amusement swiftly obliterating her terror. But all the same, it was much too late for playing about like this.

"Angela," she called, and the little girl whirled round, her draperies whirling with her. Whether all that graceful amazement was real or feigned it was impossible to say. "Angela, it's much too late for all this. Why aren't you in bed?"

The outspread gold wings buckled and drooped. Angela's whole body abandoned its pose of floating grandeur, and took on a posture appropriate for dealing with something that simply wasn't *fair*.

"But it's not my bedtime yet," she protested, aggrieved. "It's only twenty-past eight."

At first Katharine did not believe her, so strong was her sensation of having slept for a long, long time; and even when a glance at the little bedside clock had confirmed Angela's statement, she still felt somehow dismayed—at a loss, uprooted. To find that her long, deep sleep had lasted less than a quarter of an hour, and that the whole evening was, after all, still in front of her, was an extraordinary sensation—as if she had actually travelled in time, forward to midnight and then back again.

"Look how well I can do a Soutenu Turn," Angela was saying, twirling with lightness, precision, and very nearly grace in front of the mirror. "Auntie Pen says I'm good. She says that if I was *her* child she'd let me have ballet lessons."

"And won't your parents let you?" asked Katharine, surprised: for whatever Mary and Alan might be failing to give their adopted daughter, they had never seemed to grudge her any material advantages.

"Oh, they don't not *let* me," explained Angela. "It's just that they don't . . . they aren't . . ." Vocabulary failed her when it came to trying to express in words the narrowing whirlpool of self-absorption into which she sensed that her parents were being sucked, leaving them with no energy to spare for her and her needs.

"It's not that they *won't* do it," was the nearest she could get. "It's just that they won't *do* it." And then, reverting to the other theme: "I wish I *was* Auntie Pen's child."

She said it simply, as another child might say, "I wish I lived in the country." Katharine supposed that Angela's background had led her to feel that a change of parents was roughly equivalent to moving house—something not very likely, but perfectly possible, and rather exciting.

"Well, anyway"—Katharine evaded the issue—"hadn't you better take those things off now, and begin getting ready for bed? Does your mother let you borrow her clothes like this?"

"She doesn't stop me," Angela responded cautiously, and slowly removed the stole from her shoulders. "All right. I don't mind going to bed *now*. Now it *is* half-past eight."

Honour thus being satisfied, Katharine went downstairs and resumed her place on the sofa, this time with Flora's jeans on her lap. Also needle, black cotton, and the new zip.

But no scissors. Fancy having forgotten to bring something as indispensable as scissors, thought Katharine crossly, getting off the sofa once more. If she went home to fetch them, she would only get entangled in some wearisome problem or other of her family's: some argument to settle; some question to answer; some object to find—something they could perfectly well cope with for themselves so long as she simply wasn't there.

Mary must have some scissors somewhere, surely? Katharine began vaguely looking around the room, but after a minute's fruitless search she gave it up and called up the stairs to Angela.

Yes. Mummy kept her scissors in the table drawer, Angela informed her, pattering swift and light down the stairs in pyjamas. In the corner of the drawer . . . just *here*. . . .

But they weren't. Angela rummaged deeper and deeper, shuffling paper, string, and many varied objects to the front of the drawer as she did so. Among the flotsam Katharine recognised with surprise a photograph of Stephen. It was one he had had to have taken some time ago, for a centenary publication at his firm, and he seemed to have worn for the occasion an expression of unrelieved gloom and misery.

"How did it get here?" she asked, picking it up, and Angela glanced back casually.

"Oh, I expect it's the one Jane brought to school," she surmised vaguely. "We were all bringing all the photographs we could find of dark, criminal-looking men, you see, so as to have an Identity Parade in Dinner Play. *He* wasn't chosen as the criminal, though," she added, with a patronising jerk of her head towards the photograph in Katharine's hand. "Mandy Callaghan's brother got the most votes. He has a most dreadful, grinning face as well as two teeth missing where he fell off his bike. He looked ever so criminal; and so Mandy won. It wasn't fair, though, really, because . . ."

"Jane shouldn't have taken it without asking," protested Katharine absently, her attention returning to the question of the scissors. "Isn't there anywhere else where your mother keeps scissors?" she asked. "They don't seem to be in here, and I'm sure she won't like us muddling up the whole drawer like this. Aren't there any others?"

"There's a pair in the kitchen that don't cut," volunteered Angela, after a moment's thought. "And *I've* got a pair that don't cut, too," she added generously, and waited expectantly for Katharine to make her choice.

"Well—can I borrow both of them, do you think?" said Katharine, smiling. "I'll see which works best."

Angela ran off; and in a few minutes Katharine was once again settled on the sofa with the jeans and the two blunt pairs of scissors, one of which worked quite well if you pulled on the upper blade with your forefinger, inserted the cotton exactly one and a half inches up, and held it taut with your other hand.

For the next couple of hours she worked steadily, without interruption. After the jeans the chair-cover. After that the winter coats. Apart from the rustling and heaving of the great garments as she shifted them about on her lap, the house was quite silent; and after a while Katharine began to be aware again of that odd sense of having lived through the whole evening once before. For a second time, surely, she was mending this lining . . . that sandal strap . . . soon, for a second time, it would be half-past eleven, and she would be wondering why the Prescotts were not back yet.

And if now, in the midst of this quietness, she were suddenly to hear a knock on the front door, would that be for the second time? And would she—for a second time—sit here not answering it? Just listening, tense, terrified, knowing that the knock would come again?

No, of course not. None of this had happened, or was going to happen. This queer sense of familiarity was neither memory not foreknowledge, but simply imagination—imagination triggered off partly by that useless clock and partly by Mary's ridiculous instructions about not answering the door, for all the world as if she was Snow White in the fairy story. As if there might really be a witch out there in the damp suburban night, who would try to sell her a rosy apple to choke her, or a pair of stays to squeeze the breath out of her—or what was that third thing? . . .

Drowsily Katharine chopped at her last fastening with the annoying scissors, dropped the last garment on the pile at her side, and leaned back against the cushions. And it was then that a wild, desperate knocking at the front door thundered and rattled through the house.

CHAPTER XVI

KATHARINE SAT quite still for a moment, trying to control the ridiculous beating of her heart. Her brain told her, clearly and positively, that she should simply go and answer the door in the ordinary way; that Mary's warning had been so much hysterical nonsense, to be totally ignored. But not one single organ in her body seemed to be paying any attention to this sensible message from the brain. Her limbs trembled, her stomach clutched and stiffened, even her head, the container of that clear sensible brain, throbbed and thundered its own independent warning.

The knocking came again, wilder and more imperious, and suddenly Katharine remembered that it might be one of her own family come to fetch her. . . . Something frightful must have happened at home. . . .

She darted across the room, across the icy, darkened hall, wrestled frantically with the unfamiliar bolts and latches . . . and a moment later Mary herself was stumbling, half falling, into the hall. Her breath was coming in quick gasps, as if she had been running for miles, and she seemed unable to speak as Katharine helped her across the hall and into the lighted sitting-room.

Limp and unresisting, Mary flopped into the armchair towards which Katharine urged her, and now, between her gasps, she managed to say: "Bolt the door, Katharine. Bolt the front door again—*quickly!*"—and, without pausing to think or argue, Katharine ran to do so.

When she returned, Mary was already sitting up straight, her composure returning as she recovered her breath. Under Katharine's gentle questioning, she even began to smile at herself a little, and to admit that the cause of her panic had really been nothing more than her own silliness.

"It was when we got off the Tube," she explained, a little shamefacedly. "Everything had gone quite well, really, until then. I mean, Alan wasn't being exactly festive, but—you know—we weren't having any awful row or anything. In a way we'd had a very nice time, and so as we came home on the Tube I was feeling really rather pleased about it all. Until we got to the ticket barrier coming out. I'd got the tickets in my bag—he hadn't had any change left, you see, and so I'd bought them—and as I handed them over I suddenly got the most awful feeling. Oh, Katharine, I just can't describe it. A feeling of most dreadful imminent danger, and I suddenly knew that I couldn't—I just *couldn't*—walk all alone, just me and Alan, along that little, dark, fenced-in footpath—you know, the short-cut past the bridge into Archdale Road. I just couldn't—and yet I couldn't possibly explain to him how I felt. So I tried to think of some excuse for going round the long way by the shops, but it would have been just silly—I couldn't think of *any* sensible reason. And all the time I could feel the danger growing . . . growing . . . coming nearer, like some great dark thing with footsteps striding towards me across the houses . . . across the railway lines. . . . It was coming, and I was the only one that knew it was coming, and so I knew I must do something. . . . And so, just on the spur of the moment, I told him that I'd forgotten to tell him that Auntie Pen wanted him to ring her up just exactly then—eleven o'clock it was—and that it would be too late if he waited till we got home. He was dreadfully cross and puzzled, and kept asking questions, but I practically pushed him into the telephone box, and the moment he had his back to me I turned round and ran out of the station. I ran and ran all the way home. I don't know *what* he'll say. Oh, Katharine, aren't I a fool?"

Katharine could not deny it; but she consoled Mary as best she could, pointing out that everyone behaves foolishly sometimes, that Alan would surely realise that Mary had been through great strain lately, and that anyway no particular harm could come of it; at worst, Auntie Pen would be annoyed for a moment at being disturbed for nothing. And all the time she spoke, Katharine was listening, and knew that Mary was listening, for Alan's angry footsteps on the pavement outside.

But they did not come; and gradually Mary grew calmer, even ready to laugh a little at her escapade; soon she was asking, a little tremulously, about Katharine's own evening, congratulating her on the amount of mending she had done.

"Though I nearly didn't do any," commented Katharine. "First I went to sleep, and then I found I'd forgotten to bring any scissors. I tried to pinch yours for the evening, but Angela could only find these two poor old pensioners. Where *do* you keep your proper scissors, by the way?"

Mary leaned towards the drawer in which Angela had searched unsuccessfully; and then stopped, with an apologetic laugh.

"Oh—how silly of me! I've got them here in my handbag. I noticed them when we got to the theatre, and wondered why on earth I'd put them there. I suppose I must have slipped them in absent-mindedly after fixing the hem of my dress, but I don't remember it. Funny how you do these things."

She extracted from her bag a long, efficient pair of dressmaking scissors—exactly what Katharine had needed. She handed them belatedly to Katharine—and as she did so an uneasiness, a flicker of returning fear came into her eyes. She repeated, a little more forcefully:

"I *must* have put them there myself, mustn't I, Katharine? Why on earth should anyone else put a pair of scissors in my bag? Why *should* they? . . ." Her voice held a sort of suppressed shrillness now, and the fear darted sharp and unmistakable across her features. Katharine hastened to reassure her.

126

"Of course! Of course you did it youself! It's the easiest thing in the world to do something absent-minded like that when you're in a hurry. Why, only last Monday I—"

But at this moment the phone rang, and Mary darted out into the hall to answer it. She came back looking relieved but perplexed.

"It was Alan," she said wonderingly. "And he's not cross after all. Would you believe it, Auntie Pen *did* want him to ring. Wasn't it an extraordinary coincidence, when I'd simply made it up on the spur of the moment? But she did, and he's gone round to her place, and he'll be very late back—he may even stay there for the night. Can you imagine it? Such an amazing coincidence! There must be a Providence that looks after liars, is that it?"

"Speaking as a hardened liar myself, I'd say, No," pronounced Katharine judicially. "On the contrary, I'd say Providence rather has it in for us—the most unexpected things usually crop up to catch you out. However, I'm glad luck was on your side this time!"

They both laughed; and feeling quite easy in her mind about Mary once more, Katharine gathered up her unwieldy belongings and went back to her own home, Mary waving to her almost cheerfully from the adjoining doorway.

CHAPTER XVII

"BUT, KATHARINE, you can't mean we actually have to *go*? *This evening*?"

For a moment Stephen looked so much like his eldest daughter that Katharine could have burst out laughing. She could also have quoted in advance his next words, his last, hopeless protest: "But you never told me! This is the first I've heard of it."

It wasn't, of course. This was in fact about the sixth time that Katharine had warned him that on Thursday—tonight, in fact—they were engaged to have dinner with Stella and her husband. But so reluctant had he been to take it in on the over five occasions, and so reluctant, for that matter, had Katharine been to make him give his full attention to the unwelcome news—surely *telling* him was bad enough, without forcing him to *listen*?—that, in a sense, his protest was justified.

"I *did* tell you," insisted Katharine. "Heaps of times. Anyway, we can't get out of it now. We have to start in about ten minutes. It'll give you just time to get ready while I see to the girls' supper."

She tried to escape further argument by darting into the kitchen and starting a daunting clatter of crockery; but Stephen followed her, still complaining.

"I suppose that what's-his-name fellow will be there," he complained—a trifle unreasonably, it seemed to Katharine, since the what's-his-name fellow was Stella's husband and lived there. "And I'll have to listen to him calling her—what is it? What's that ridiculous name he calls her?"

"'Jag,'" said Katharine apologetically. "And she calls him 'Bloke'. But it's only their way of—"

"'Jag,'" repeated Stephen savagely. "'Jag' and 'Bloke'. My God, and it suits them, too! *Why* does he call her 'Jag'?"

"Well—short for Stella, I suppose," said Katharine inanely. "I mean—I suppose it's a pet name, or something. How should I know?" she concluded with more spirit, suddenly remembering that after all it wasn't *her* fault. "Do get ready, Stephen. If we get there late we can't possibly come away early as well. And whatever the dinner's like, it'll be worse if it's spoilt."

With these and similar blandishments, Katharine succeeded in getting her husband out of the house and down the road; and the moment they got inside Stella's front door, she knew that her troubles were over: it was obvious at once that Stella was in one of her cooking moods. An exotic and promising smell of garlic, bay leaves, tomatoes, and many strange spices filled the air, and Stephen's expression changed dramatically.

"I say! Isn't it all tidy!" he exclaimed wonderingly as they entered Stella's sitting-room. "Just look at it, Katharine! Why doesn't our sitting-room look like this?"

Because our children aren't at boarding school; that was the answer, of course, though it was hardly for Katharine to give it. But she did think Stella might have done so; instead, Stella just looked inordinately pleased with herself, gave Stephen the most comfortable chair by the fire, and remarked smugly: "Oh, there's nothing to it, really, you know. I always think that tidiness is just a state of mind. If your mind is uncluttered and at peace with itself, then your home will be uncluttered and peaceful too."

What a lie, thought Katharine crossly. What sort of a fool was going to believe that it was an uncluttered mind that had black-leaded the grate, polished the tiles, and cleaned all the paint-work. It didn't need an uncluttered mind at all; it needed several absorbent rags and about two hours of leisure, and Stella must know this as well as anybody. And what made it more annoying still was that it seemed out of character for Stella to be a good housewife. With her breezy, aggressive opinions, her unorthodox manners, she should have been living in Bohemian squalor, not in this pretty, polished room with its chintz curtains and chair-covers. And Stella didn't have any domestic help, either. Or said she didn't; but of course you couldn't be sure nowadays, when not having a domestic help or a car is becoming almost as potent a status symbol as not having a television.

But it didn't do to think such catty thoughts about one's hostess, however brightly one kept a smile on one's face. "Catty thoughts *show*"—that should be the motto engraved above all our mirrors, reflected Katharine ruefully. She turned her attention dutifully to the immediate task of getting acquainted with the fellow-guests that had been wished on them, a silent, wary pair called Plumber.

Stella had already charged off to the kitchen, abandoning them to each other's company with no more of an introduction than "These are the Plumbers". Not for her the more subtle reaches of hostess-craft, which might have added something helpful like "Mr. Plumber is just back from a trip to Iceland" or "Mrs. Plumber is very keen on tight-rope walking". Or even the information that one or other of them taught in a secondary modern school in Ruislip. Or didn't. Anything to provide a starting-point.

As it was, the whole universe was open to them in which to find a common interest, and patiently Katharine set to work to find out. But it was uphill work, for Mrs. Plumber's powers of conversation seemed to be limited to "No, I didn't see that," and "No, I haven't been there," and "No, I don't read that sort of book," and Mr. Plumber just kept humming to show how much at ease he was. Katharine wished that the host or hostess would return, but the sounds from the kitchen did not suggest an early rescue: "Pass that damned jug, Bloke. Where the hell do you think I'm going to put this juice?" and "For God's sake, Jag, can't you clear those blasted onion skins out of the way?" . . . None of this suggested that preparations were very near completion.

Nor, on the other hand, did it mean that Stella and her husband were panicking and getting on each other's nerves. Katharine knew that they habitually swore at each other on principle, in the interests of a frank and honest relationship. They sprinkled their remarks to each other with insults dutifully, as other people sprinkle theirs with "Please" and "Thank you" and "Do you mind?" The basic intention—that of improving relations—was the same in both cases.

Katharine plunged once again into conversation—if such it could be called—with the Plumbers. As one subject after another dropped limply into oblivion, she found herself wondering uneasily why she and Stephen should have been singled out to meet this deadly couple? Was it because Stella thought that they were equally boring, and wanted to get them both over together? Or did she—happy thought!—feel that Stephen and Katharine were such scintillating conversationalists that they would be able to draw out even the Plumbers?

Stimulated by this improbable hypothesis, Katharine redoubled her efforts: and by the time Stella finally summoned them to dinner, Katharine and Stephen had between them managed to discover that Mrs. Plumber didn't keep a cat, couldn't drive a car, didn't prefer coal fires to central heating, had never used emulsion paint, and didn't think the weather was specially cold for the time of year.

Armed with all this data, Katharine felt that they should soon be making real headway with their companion, but happily it was no longer necessary, for as soon as they sat down to dinner an animated conversation sprang up about the rare and interesting dish that Stella set before them—Italian, or Greek, or something, Katharine surmised—and accompanied by a mighty pile of beautifully cooked rice, fluffy and steaming.

"Oh, well, it hasn't a recipe really," explained Stella deprecatingly, as the compliments showered round her. "Actually, I never plan meals at all. I just look round the larder and see what I've got, and then I just throw things in as the inspiration moves me.

It's funny, but I often think food turns out better that way, if you just don't bother."

Stephen and Mr. Plumber both nodded in admiring agreement, and Katharine succeeded in hiding her total disbelief. Fresh prawns—button mushrooms—thin strips of veal wrapped round black olives—these are not the sort of items a housewife's eye lights on when she looks round her larder to see what she's got. It would take a lunatic to believe it—or someone else's husband.

". . . And of course the tomatoes are out of our own garden," Stella was saying. "We always get the most marvellous tomatoes from our plants; they last us right through the autumn. Don't they, Bloke? We never look after them at all, don't ever water them, and yet we get this marvellous crop. And the funny thing is, our next-door neighbour is always fussing over his, giving them fertiliser and potash and God knows what, and watering them every single evening, and he never gets a crop at all! Isn't if funny how things work out like that?"

They didn't work out like that for Katharine, of course. She also didn't water or look after their tomato plants, and the result for her was that she didn't get any tomatoes off them. But you could hardly say something like that when everyone was nodding awed agreement with Stella's proposition. And Stella's tomatoes *were* delicious—indeed, the whole meal was delicious, and Katharine decided to stop being annoyed and enjoy it. The conversation, too, was enjoyable; it soon became so engrossing that even the Plumbers allowed themselves to be drawn into it at various unperilous points. Mrs. Plumber informed them, of her own accord, that she'd never been to Spain, and that she didn't think her greengrocer sold garlic: and Mr. Plumber, even more ambitious, told them quite spontaneously how best to get from Holland Park to Mornington Crescent on a Sunday morning.

After dinner, they sat round the fire drinking sweet black coffee into which Stella claimed to have put crushed egg-shells to enhance the flavour. She probably hadn't, thought Katharine grudgingly, but no one could possibly tell one way or the other when they didn't know what the coffee tasted like before it was enhanced. However, the remark had the desired effect of rousing the wondering admiration of both the male guests, and it extracted from them the ultimate compliment, treasured by all hostesses everywhere. "Why don't *you* do that?" they said in unison, turning to their wives.

Shortly afterwards the party was joined by Esmé from the flat upstairs. She entered timidly, clutching a yellow satin workbox, and explaining to Stella that Harry was on duty tonight, and so would Stella mind if—?

"Oh, cut it out!" said Stella cordially. "Just barge in, like everyone else." Not that anyone else *had* barged in, or anything like it, but Stella always liked to feel that she ran her home like that. "Come on. Squat." She kicked a low cane stool invitingly, but rather hard, and Esmé timidly set it upright again, settled herself thereon and accepted a cup of coffee.

"Do you taste anything special about it?" prompted Stella hopefully; and on Esmé's replying that it was very nice, she started all over again about the crushed egg-shells. Esmé looked a little frightened, in an undefined sort of way, but told Stella that yes, it was an awfully good idea, and drank the liquid thoughtfully, while Stella called gaily across the room to Bloke to hurry up for Christ's sake into the kitchen and stop the damn kettle boiling over.

"Why the blazes couldn't you have turned it off when you brought the coffee in?" asked Bloke amiably, heaving himself out of his chair: but before Stella could explain exactly why the hell she couldn't have, a small voice piped up to ask if it could borrow some scissors.

Esmé had her workbox open now, and a piece of embroidery canvas spilling out of it. She paused nervously before the word "scissors", as if wondering whether she should have said "damn scissors" out of deference to her host and hostess.

"Of course, kid. Don't bother to ask. Just grab 'em," replied Stella, tossing a pair across with a generous disregard for aim that made Esmé start like a frightened bird, and actually roused the adjacent Mrs. Plumber to a spontaneous expression of opinion. "Ooo!" she said; and then looked round anxiously, as if afraid someone might disagree.

Stella laughed reassuringly. "Rotten shot, aren't I?" she apologised cheerfully. "Might have killed someone. By the way, that reminds me—"

She was turning towards Katharine as she spoke, but stopped, very suddenly, in mid-sentence. "I'll tell you later," she murmured hastily, and changed the subject by dropping on her knees by Esmé's stool.

"What is it? What are you making?" she asked the girl; and Esmé, proudly and a little shyly, spread out her canvas, displaying a half-worked clump of pansies, a glorious medley of blues and purples seeming to melt into each other, so cunning was the lie of the stitches.

"Isn't it lovely!" exclaimed Katharine sincerely; and "But what *is* it?" persisted Stella; and Esmé's eager face, which had grown rosy and shining under Katharine's praise, now looked a little deflated.

"It's a—well—it's just a picture, actually," she said. "A needlework picture."

Stella stared. "Do you mean to say it isn't *for* anything?" she asked accusingly, and Esmé nodded guiltily, like a schoolgirl caught out at last in some habitual breach of rules.

"It's just to *look* at," she confessed. "We thought it would be nice in our bedroom."

"Fancy! All that work—and it's not even Art, either, is it?" declared Stella judicially. She stared at the gay scrap of cloth as if it was quite painful to her—the waste of so much precious time. It was painful to Katharine, too, but not because of the waste of time. How happily married you must have to be, she was thinking, to spend all those hours embroidering something just to hang in your bedroom to look at. Suddenly her eyes were stinging with tears, the pansies blurred and dazzled into an amorphous purple glory, and she was thankful that Stella chose that very moment to beg her to come into the kitchen and see how well the washing-up stacked into the new washing-up machine.

Stella was a great one for machines. That is, she was a great believer in the time-saving properties of the ones she had got, and in the nuisance value of the ones she hadn't. She could prove conclusively that a washing-up machine saved hours of work and never broke anything, whereas a clothes-washing machine demanded endless attention and all the clothes came out grey. Up to a year ago she had been able to prove that you could get to absolutely anywhere more easily by public transport than by car; but that argument was over now, silenced for ever by the Ford Popular now standing in the road outside.

Katharine watched with interest as Stella groomed her crockery for its venture, scraping, emptying, arranging it this way and that in what looked to Katharine like her own private idea of a space-ship. Indeed, Stella's portentous manner, her air of pride and excitement as she made her preparations, so added to the illusion that when the machine was finally switched on, Katharine found herself quite surprised that the whole thing didn't thereupon rise off the kitchen floor, plough its way through the upstairs rooms, and disappear into the rainy November sky.

"What was it you were going to tell me just now?" asked Katharine suddenly, through the murmur of the machine. "You know—when you threw the scissors across to Esmé."

"Oh yes. Yes." Stella leaned her full weight against the throbbing monster, crossing one foot over the other as she stood, and staring at Katharine appraisingly. "I didn't want to talk about it in front of the others, because it's about Mary," she explained virtuously. "Something that she told me in absolute confidence."

Some women, reflected Katharine guiltily, would have stoically answered: "Well, don't tell *me*, then, either," and would have meant it. And they would have been right, these excellent women. That would have been the right, the honourable thing to have done. But surely there must be millions of others, just like Katharine, who would have stood there expectant, unprotesting, waiting for the intriguing revelations! You didn't need to be *very* wicked, did you, just to refrain from self-righteous protest? So Katharine salved her conscience and also heard the story, which Stella was only too willing to divulge.

"You know Alan and Mary went to the theatre together last night?" she began. "Well, of course you do, because you were looking after Angela, weren't you? Well, just about half-past twelve, just when I was thinking about going to bed, there was a knock on the front door, and there was Mary, all pale and shaken, and carrying a suitcase, and asking if she could spend the night here, with us. Well, of course, I asked her why on earth, and what was the matter, and so forth, and at last I got it out of her that she was absolutely terrified of staying at home alone. I suppose Alan hadn't come back with her, or something—I couldn't make head or tail of that part of it. Anyway, I kept asking her what she was afraid of—though of course I knew really, I just wanted to make her put it into words because I thought it would be best if she made herself face it. That's what she needs, you know, really; to face up to her own fears and aggressions. So in the end I got it out of her—she's absolutely terrified of this dark man with the raincoat. She hates to admit it, because of course in a sense it's an irrational fear—unless, of course, she really *does* know who it is. . . . But I couldn't get her to admit that, though I did try. . . . Still it did her good even to talk about it as much as she did. She represses too much, you know, Katharine. She frightens herself. Did you guess why it was that she wouldn't use that raincoat you gave her for the guy? It was because, to her, the burning of an effigy in a raincoat would have symbolised the burning of this man she is so afraid of! And of course the thought of such an act of aggression towards him made her feel even more afraid. Naturally. This sort of thing is well known. But she *should* have burnt it. I told her so, and I think in the end she saw my point. She saw that such a release of aggression would have enabled her to face her fears squarely. Do you understand?"

"Yes," said Katharine blankly: and Stella seemed satisfied with this senseless tribute to her psychological acumen. Senseless, because what Katharine was understanding was something quite different from what Stella had been telling her. Katharine was understanding—or trying to understand—how Mary must have felt about this onslaught of amateur psychology on a situation which didn't exist at all: when all the time she was faced by another situation, much more frightening, much more intractable, and which actually did exist.

And here another point struck Katharine—struck her with a sudden strange chill:

"Did you say all this was *last night*?" she asked—stupidly, because she knew quite well that Stella had said so.

"Yes. Last night. After they'd been to the theatre," recapitulated Stella. "Why?"

But Katharine did not answer. She remembered how she had left Mary at nearly midnight last night, apparently quite comfortable, reassured by Alan's telephone call, and ready to go to bed. Within less than half an hour from then, Mary must have gone upstairs, packed her suitcase, and rushed in terror round to Stella's house for protection—from what? What could possibly have happened in that brief time? And besides—

"But what about Angela?" The words burst from Katharine in her bewilderment. "How could Mary run away and leave her alone all night if there was something frightening going on?"

Stella's blank, astonished stare interrupted her.

"But Angela was staying *with you* last night," she protested. "That's what Mary told me . . . . "

"Oh yes. Of course. How silly of me." What else could Katharine do on the spur of the moment but back up this bewildering lie of Mary's? Baffled, uncomprehending, she followed Stella back to the sitting-room; and it was not till she was settled there, surrounded by the others, and with all possibility of further confidences at an end, that another curious point struck her. Throughout her narrative, Stella had nowhere explained how it was that the throwing of a pair of scissors across the room should have reminded her of it all.

CHAPTER XVIII

IT WAS the week-end again, and Katharine surveyed the chaos in Jane's and Flora's room with that satisfaction so familiar to mothers and yet so bewildering to outside observers. For, to the mother, most kinds of mess and pandemonium simply mean that her children are happily occupied and aren't going to be trailing about after her saying, "What shall I do?" The gulf between this point of view and that of the neighbours—or even the husband—is so unbridgeable that few women ever attempt it—certainly not Katharine, and certainly not on a Saturday evening, when Stephen was likely to be at his most edgy, and most likely to start a great thing about why don't the girls help more in the house instead of causing all this work? Which would simply end in Clare's breaking the best teapot while she sobbed into the washing-up, with Flora's arguing her father into a fury, and probably with Katharine and Stephen not speaking to each other for the rest of the week-end. Much simpler just to clear up the mess straight away now, while Jane and Flora were still out at their party, and before Stephen came back from his after-noon conference. A little extra tidying was a small price to pay for such a joyful, fully-occupied Saturday as the children had just spent, not bothering Katharine at all.

This, mused Katharine, as she began stuffing the ragged witch's cloak back into the dressing-up box, this was her main preoccupation at week-ends—keeping everyone, including Stephen, happily occupied at something which wouldn't encroach too much on her own precious, carefully budgeted time. This problem of leisure that they talked about nowadays: it was other people's leisure that was the problem, not one's own. Did everyone find this, she wondered: that most of their own leisure was used up in defending themselves against other people's, against the demands that other people's leisure made on one's attention, inventiveness, and conversational powers? Because if so, then the more leisure you give to one person, the more you are automatically taking away from someone else; it all cancels out somewhere, and that's why life never gets any easier, no matter what is invented. This, mused Katharine, is a problem that the politicians never got around to—just as they had never had to decide what should be done with eight battered picture hats bought for a halfpenny each at the Guide jumble sale. You couldn't possibly stuff *them* in the dressing-up box, and there was no room in the wardrobe. . . . Really, you'd think a reputable organisation like the Girl Guides would have more *sense*. Oh, well, they'd just have to go on lying about on the chest of drawers, just as they had done ever since Flora brought them so gleefully home that broiling August afternoon ("Just *look* what I got for only 4d., Mummy!").

Undeterred by these accustomed obstacles, Katharine proceeded systematically with her task, and soon tracts of bare floor began to appear. Seats of chairs were reclaimed, and even a sizeable stretch of table. Books went back into the shelves; hundreds of coloured pencils without points went back into their dozens of boxes without lids, and old Teddy went back on to Jane's pillow, where he lay staring rather sadly up at the pink-shaded electric bulb. Jane still liked to find Teddy on her bed at night, but the days of his glory were over, and he knew it; and Katharine knew it; and probably even Jane knew it. He no longer toured the house under her arm, up and down and up and down, as he had once done. He no longer got left under the kitchen table, or gave tea parties, or had chicken-pox. Was it two years ago—or more like three?—when he had had chicken-pox so badly, and Jane had made Katharine promise not to wake him when she tidied the room. "You must *tiptoe*, Mummy, and be ever so quiet!" had been Jane's parting instructions as she went off to school; and Katharine, all alone in the empty house, had, ridiculously, obeyed. Like a lunatic she had crept softly about the curtained room as she made the beds, had closed the door softly as she went out. . . . Gently, Katharine arranged Teddy's balding, upstretched arms more comfortably, and for a moment she felt that he and she were the sole survivors from a Golden Age. *Had* it been golden, though? And anyway, wasn't it still going on, for all practical purposes? The same sort of muddle of cut-out paper, paint, and dressing-up clothes; the same squashed tubes of glue, half-used notebooks, and tangles of coloured wool; the same plastic things out of past crackers, which no one wanted either to keep or to throw away. Even the same need to watch the time for going to fetch them from a party. The only definite difference here was that nowadays no one would be found crying about her balloon having burst; but it seemed perverse to count crying over balloons as the defining property of a Golden Age.

Katharine looked at her watch. It *was* time to go for them, of course, but if she hung on a bit longer perhaps Mary would come and offer to do it instead. Angela was at the same party, and there was no point in both mothers going. On the other hand, perhaps Mary was cherishing the same hope about Katharine, and if it was to be a question of whose nerve broke first as it got later and later, Katharine felt pretty sure it would be her own. She might just as well go straight away, and get it over.

Besides, it wasn't really fair to expect much of Mary these days, when she was so distraught and unhappy. Katharine told herself this, and tried to feel only sympathy, but she could not help being aware of a stab of annoyance. Unhappy and distraught was all very well, but was Mary proposing to carry on like this for ever? Admittedly her experience had been distressing, but it was days ago now. Surely the time had come to forget the whole episode, and return to normal existence? What good could Mary think she was doing by allowing her feelings of guilt to cloud her whole life like this? A tender conscience was all very well, but when it came to a conscience so tender as to ensure that its owner should never again have to take her turn at fetching the children from parties. . . .

Katharine checked herself, shoved the last partnerless glove into Flora's top drawer, and went downstairs to put on her coat. Fair or not, the children must be fetched. She would just call in next-door and tell them that she was going and that they needn't bother—just in case they *were* bothering, and not absorbed in quarrelling, or not speaking to each other, or some similarly time-consuming occupation.

But there was no answer to Katharine's knock, nor to her two sharp rings; and looking up at the windows, she saw that the whole house was in darkness.

Bother! One or both of them were probably on the way to the party right now. Really, they might have told her, and saved her the journey! As things were, she must still go, just in case they hadn't. How *selfish* unhappiness makes people, thought Katharine crossly, and was instantly ashamed of the thought, yet could not quite withdraw it.

It was a dull, drizzling night, clammy and windless. The low sky hung black and heavy above the houses, dimly reddening towards the horizon, where it dully, grudgingly reflected the vast lighted sprawl of the city. Katharine shivered, wondered whether to go back indoors for an umbrella, but decided against it. The wetness of such a night as this was too vague, too directionless, to be warded off by so naïve a device as an umbrella, which assumes that water, being heavier than air, will fall. Not in November it doesn't, thought Katharine, as she set off down the street, huddled into her coat. In November the water creeps, and drifts, and glides, from here, from there, as unpredictable as thought. The only thing to do was to walk as quickly as possible by the shortest route she could take. Yes, she would take the short-cut across the Building Site.

Nobody knew what Building it had been the Site for during all these years. It simply *was* the Building Site, and always had been—a desert stretch of elder bushes, old bedsteads, tin cans, and tufts of dry, battered grass—dry and battered even in springtime. Legends had grown up about the Building Site as the years went by; about the dreadful things that happened to little girls who played there on their way back from school; about the damage done by teenage boys (though one never actually saw any teenage boys there; most of them, understandably, seemed to prefer the bright streets and the coffee-bars). And, above all, legends had grown up about Allbright and Frost, the cryptic and evocative names that could still be deciphered on a decaying board. Some people fancied that the owners of these names really existed; that the pair of them were actually sitting, alive and well, in some dark office somewhere, working through their Pending trays as the decades passed till they should reach the documents relative to the Building Site. Others thought that they were long dead, and that the ownership of the Building Site was therefore in dispute. Others again thought it was all something to do with the Council.

Be that as it may, the Building Site afforded a convenient short-cut between the High Street and Chatsworth Avenue; and as Katharine set foot on the muddy, officially forbidden path that had been worn into reluctant legality by countless unprosecuted trespassers over the years, she felt that the worst of the expedition was over. Why, there might be someone with a car who would give them all a lift back, she reflected cheerfully as the sparse, shadowy bushes of the Building Site engulfed her.

It was dark in here, and growing darker. Every step was taking her further away from the busy, lighted street, deeper and deeper into the waste land. For the first time, Katharine began to feel a little frightened.

But it was silly. Naturally, one wouldn't let the children come through here after dark, but it was all right for a grown woman. The whole area couldn't be much more than a couple of hundred yards across—as soon as you were out of shouting distance of one road, you were within shouting distance of the other.

But it was queer how lonely a place could be, so near to busy roads: lonely, and deeply, mysteriously alive in its own right. Even though there was no wind, the bare twigs of the elder bushes were for ever moving; twitching, stirring, shuddering against the heavy reddish clouds. Even the ground itself was not quite still. All round her, far into the darkness on every side, there was a something less than rustling, less than pattering or dripping—the vast, indefinable stir of autumn wetness soaking its way into the earth: rotting its way through old newspaper; rusting its way through old cans; somehow, by some route, reaching its victorious end in the deep ground.

Katharine stood still and listened to the huge, faint tumult of the dying season. It was a mistake, of course; for as soon as she stood still and listened she began to fancy she heard other sounds, too—definite, yet inexplicable. Was that a drop of water falling, sharp and hollow, on some tinkling metal surface? Could it really be the damp, windless air that set yonder bush stirring—and what was that sharp crack, as of a snapping twig? Of course, dead twigs *do* fall off old trees and bushes—otherwise how would you find them littering the ground?—but somehow you don't expect to be there when they are doing it. And now Katharine's eyes, too, were accustoming themselves to the darkness, peering deep into dim shapes and dripping hollows. It was with a real effort of will that she made herself realise that the strange dark blob on the path in front was only an old boot; that the queer, crouching shape among the bushes ahead of her could only be another discarded mattress, thrown in some awkward way so that in the darkness it seemed to have shoulders, and a drooping, listening head.

As she stood, Katharine felt her fear growing. If only she had kept walking briskly on she would have been in Chatsworth Avenue by now, under the bright lights and with the long shining cars whizzing by. How could she have been so foolish as to stand like this, letting her fear catch up with her—for all the world as if Fear had been following a few yards behind ever since she had left her home. And yet how difficult it was, having once stood still, to dare to move again. And to move, too, in the direction of that dim, crouching figure, mattress though it must be. Katharine forced herself to take a step . . . and then another . . . firmly, confidently, nearer and nearer to that lumpish shadow. Alongside it . . . and now, thank God, past it. . . . And now simply to walk and walk, and not look back, no, not look back even though a new, a different rustling sound seemed to come from the bushes . . . a scrambling sound . . . and now, Oh God, a thudding. . . .

Katharine felt her coat grabbed from behind, a hand clutched her shoulder, and before she could cry out a hand came over her mouth.

"Hush, Katharine!" came Mary's voice, hissing into her ear in the darkness. "Don't speak! He'll hear us!"

Katharine felt quite giddy with the fear and tension somersaulting out of her body, and bewilderment replacing them.

"What on earth, Mary?" she whispered, pushing Mary's restraining hand away from her mouth. "What do you mean? What are you doing here? *Who* will hear us?"

"Hush!" repeated Mary once more, as Katharine turned to face her. "He *will* hear you! He was hanging about under the lamp, just as Angela said. And Auntie Pen said. Oh, Katharine, I didn't believe it, but they were right. He *was* there!"

"*Who* was?" repeated Katharine stupidly. "What are you talking about—"

But Mary interrupted, in a fierce whisper.

"*You* know who I mean, Katharine," she declared hoarsely. "I'm telling you. He was under the lamp-post by our house, just as Angela and Auntie Pen described. I saw him myself, just as I was starting out to fetch Angela from this party. A dark man wearing a raincoat, Katharine! Oh, I was so frightened!"

"But what *of*?" persisted Katharine, in deepening bewilderment. "Surely you, of all people—And anyway, why should he be here, in the Building Site, if you saw him at home? Do you mean he's been following you? If so, let's for goodness' sake get out of here." She took Mary's arm and almost dragged her towards the lights of Chatsworth Avenue, scolding her roundly—and no longer in a whisper—as they went.

"Honestly, Mary, I do think you're silly. I don't for a minute suppose that this man of yours is after any harm, but if you were feeling frightened of him, then what on earth possessed you to come across the Building Site? Why didn't you go round by the road—or by bus, if it comes to that? Honestly—of all the crazy things to do if you're afraid that a man's following you!"

Katharine almost laughed, so safe did she feel now, and so near to Chatsworth Avenue. She turned, smiling, to look at her companion; and was met not, as she had expected, by a look of rueful apology, nor even by one of continuing fear—but by one of total puzzlement.

"But, Katharine," Mary protested, stumbling up the tufty bank towards the road, "But Katharine, he wasn't following me. Don't you understand? *I* was following *him*!"

CHAPTER XIX

"MARY! WHAT do you mean?"

Katharine stared at her companion in total bewilderment. Under the dazzle of unaccustomed light, she fancied for a second that Mary's face looked strangely smooth—almost tranquil. But no; the familiar troubled look was back again, sharper than ever, as she began to speak.

"But Katharine, of *course* I had to follow him," she protested. "I wanted to know who he was—why he was hanging about there. I mean, he's been seen three times now, by one person or another, as well as the night that Alan was stabbed."

"But—" Katharine stopped, her mind spinning. Surely Mary must realise that all these dark men in raincoats who had been seen were simply the outcome of people's imaginations, stimulated by Alan's faked story? The world was absolutely full of dark men in raincoats, and at any given moment some more or less calculable number of them would undoubtedly be found standing under lamp-posts, just as a calculable number of them would at that same moment be found eating pork chops, buying ties, or winding up clocks. But none of this was sinister coincidence, it was merely sociology, or statistics, or something: the sort of thing you read about when you had finished everything else in the paper. Katharine opened her mouth to explain (as well as she could) this reassuring aspect of the situation, but Mary interrupted.

"I know what you're going to say, Katharine," she complained. (Did she know? Ever afterwards, Katharine was to wonder whether, if she had forced Mary to listen to her, it would have made any difference to the events that were to follow.) "I know what you're going to say, but truly, Katharine, you don't understand. Such queer things have been happening to me lately . . . and now this man under the lamp . . . he was the last straw. Can't you understand that?"

"Yes, of course I can," lied Katharine, without stopping to consider whether she understood it or not, so convenient a foothold did it offer for bringing in what she wanted to say. "But you see, Mary, what you must realise is that in a case like this people are bound to chatter—to spread rumours—exaggerate everything. You see, *they* can't know that—"

"Oh, *people!*" interrupted Mary scornfully. "It's not *people* that are worrying me any longer, Katharine; it's *things*. The queer things that have been happening. . . ."

"What sort of queer things?" Katharine took her friend's arm and urged her gently along the pavement, for after all they *did* have to get to the party. "What kind of things do you mean?"

"There's a strange raincoat in our house," blurted out Mary abruptly. "Hanging on the pegs in the hall. It's not Alan's, and we haven't had a visitor lately. What's it doing, hanging in our hall? Eh?"

Katharine decided to ignore the uncalled-for aggressiveness of Mary's tone. She laughed, lightly.

"There's about a dozen strange coats in our hall, I should think," she declared cheerfully. "And Wellington boots, too, and odd gloves. You must be a terribly good housewife, Mary, if you're surprised to find just *one* old coat that you can't account for. I thought everyone had them, by the dozen."

"You can joke about it," responded Mary sourly, "but it's not happening in *your* house. I tell you, I *don't know* where this raincoat came from. It suddenly appeared, a day or two ago. From nowhere. Whose is it? Why?"

"Could it be the one we gave Angela for the guy?" Katharine asked suddenly. "She didn't use it, you know, in the end, so I suppose it must be somewhere in your house. Couldn't Alan or someone have found it and hung it up just for tidiness?"

"You mean it's *Stephen's* coat?" asked Mary sharply. "But that makes it queerer still. Because, do you know, I found a photograph of Stephen in my little drawer this afternoon. As if it had been planted there. Because *I've* never possessed a photograph of your husband. Why should I? Why on earth *should* I? It seems so queer. . . . And now you following me tonight. . . ."

"Well, *honestly*, Mary, this is too much!" exploded Katharine. "I might as well accuse you of following me! I'm going to fetch the girls from the party, of course. You're just working yourself up deliberately—distorting things and talking nonsense—just for the sake of causing a scene. I'm not surprised Alan gets furious with you. . . ."

Mary's hostility crumpled in a second. She began to cry, softly, clutching Katharine's arm tighter, and with her other hand scuffling in her pocket for a handkerchief.

"Oh, I'm sorry, Katharine," she gulped. "Of course I know it's not your fault. It's nothing to do with you—or Stephen either, of course. I know that really. But sometimes I feel I can't trust *anybody*. I feel hemmed in by people, all watching . . . guessing . . . talking about me . . . and I think and think, and picture it all, until the very sight of a man's raincoat sets me shivering. I know it's silly—I know really it was just a burglar, but somehow I can't believe it. I keep feeling that there's something else . . . something worse . . . closer to us—"

"But *Mary*—you *know* it wasn't—" Katharine burst out in astonishment. "You and I know it wasn't—" "A burglar" she was going to finish, but suddenly, urgently, Mary squeezed her arm. There seemed to be a message in that squeeze—some desperate, forbidden message to be smuggled in code across that invisible frontier which even the closest friendship cannot leave unmanned. For a second Katharine was utterly at a loss; and then, slowly, a possible meaning of the message began to dawn.

Perhaps Mary had been lying to her. Right from the very beginning. When she had confessed to Katharine that she had stabbed Alan herself, the confession might have been false. Alan's story about the dark man in the raincoat might have been quite simply true—which would explain why he had stuck to it so obstinately! How simple—and how obvious—an explanation!

But *why* should Mary have lied like this? To shield someone, perhaps? A lover, as suggested by Mrs. Forsyth? At the thought that Mrs. Forsyth's vulgar, uncalled-for aspersions might turn out to be perfectly correct, Katharine's whole soul squirmed in revulsion. As so many others have done, she fought briefly and vainly against the hard realisation that opinions are not necessarily false because they are held by people you don't like, any more than they are necessarily true because they are held by people you do.

And this was a terribly plausible opinion. For what other motive could be strong enough to induce a woman gratuitously to draw upon herself the blame for such a crime?

But it was still queer. For, given that Mary was telling these lies to shield her lover, why should she tell them only to Katharine? To everyone else—even to the police—she had backed up Alan's story—if not in actual words, then by silent acquiescence. What sort of shielding was this, which shielded the criminal from one person only, and that a person who had nothing whatever to do with any of it?

It almost began to make it look as if Katharine *had* got something to do with it—or as if Mary thought she had. Suddenly Katharine became aware that they had been walking along in silence for several minutes: and with this awareness came a strange feeling that Mary had been listening all the time—listening to Katharine's very thoughts as they paced along the rainy street towards their destination. For her head was turned half sideways, attentively, towards Katharine.

Or was Katharine mistaken in how long they had been walking in silence? For when Mary spoke, it was to answer Katharine's last remark, just as if there had been no intervening pause.

"Of course I know it wasn't," she echoed Katharine's unfinished protest. "Things can't really be—uncanny—can they? Of course I know that really. But all the same, I have this queer feeling that—"

"Mummy!"

Jane's small, ecstatic figure whirled like a missile through the glitter of rain, and into Katharine's arms. She was followed at a more leisurely, lordly pace by Flora.

"We thought we'd better start home," announced the latter, reprovingly, as she drew near. "You're terribly late, do you know, Mummy. Mrs. Moffat was getting awfully fed up with us—you know, in that extra welcoming sort of way that mothers have to get fed up with not their own children. We were nearly the last. Jane said we ought to wait for you, and that Mrs. Moffat didn't mind, but *I* could tell that she did. And anyway, I know the way home perfectly well."

"But where's Angela? Has she gone with someone else?"

It was Katharine, not Mary, who spoke; and Flora turned round and peered vaguely into the dazzle of darkness behind her.

"No. Yes. That is, she said her Auntie Pen was coming for her," she explained perfunctorily. "She wasn't ready to come with us, anyway: she'd lost her propelling pencil, or something, and Mr. Moffat was helping her look for it down all the sides of the armchairs. They found nearly two shillings all in pennies and threepennies, and he said she could have it. She took it, too. *I* wouldn't have if it had been me. It would have been politer to refuse, don't you think, Mummy?"

"Not necessarily," retorted Katharine, irritated by Flora's smug self-assurance. "In fact, to refuse might have been rather snubbing—it would depend on the circumstances. But anyway—"

"Oh, Mummy, there were such lovely prizes!" burst out Jane, clutching her mother's arm and dragging all her exultant weight on it. "I got a sweet little teeny red monkey in a matchbox—look! Isn't he a darling; he's going to live on my shelf. And, oh, Flora's so *lucky*! Do you know what she got? She got a mouth-organ!"

"You can have it if you like. *I* don't want it."

Flora thrust the instrument towards her sister with an off-hand, rejecting gesture which somehow (and was this deliberate?) took all the pleasure out of the transaction. Well, not all of it; and not for long. Jane was a resilient child, and a mouth-organ was, after all, a mouth-organ. Soon she was running joyfully ahead, clutching both her treasures, while Flora loitered behind with her elders, ears pricked for the snippets of unsuitable gossip that she had learned were never long in making themselves heard once her mother and Mrs. Prescott were together, and once she had succeeded in making them forget her existence.

"Oughtn't we to go back and make sure about Angela?" Katharine was saying, hesitating on the pavement. "Did you know that her Auntie Pen was fetching her?"

Mary shrugged; and there was unconcealed bitterness in her voice as she answered.

"Oh, don't worry! Nobody ever tells *me* anything! If she says Auntie Pen's fetching her, then Auntie Pen *is* fetching her. It's all been arranged over my head, naturally. I dare say she'll go home with Auntie Pen and spend the night there, and *I* shan't know anything about it unless I like to go down on my knees and ask!"

Katharine was aware of Flora's ears almost tingling aloud at her elbow, so she could not allow herself to encourage Mary in this sort of talk, consumed by curiosity though she herself was.

"Oh well. That's all right, then," she said brightly and unconvincingly, quickening her pace in the direction of home. "But it's a pity you've had to come for nothing. Such a wet, miserable night, too."

But Mary wasn't so easily put off. She stared belligerently at the aforesaid night, as if summoning its wetness and miserableness to her side in some incommunicable battle.

"Oh yes. It's all right," she commented sourly. "Perfectly all right. Why shouldn't it be? Did you know, Katharine, that Alan has asked Auntie Pen to have Angela to stay with her indefinitely? For the rest of this term, I mean; and to go back with her for the Christmas holidays?"

"No—I didn't know," said Katharine cautiously, and terribly aware of Flora breathless with interest at her side. "But mightn't it be quite a good idea, Mary? For the holidays, anyway. Didn't you tell me that Mrs. Quentin lives in the country for most of the year? I should think Christmas in the country would be lovely for Angela—a real change. And a rest for *you*, Mary. You told me you were dreading the Christmas preparations this year. A real rest is just what you need."

Slowly, Mary turned her face towards Katharine, her eyes so large and shining that one should have been struck by their beauty. But somehow their brilliance seemed to go beyond beauty tonight; and Katharine was somehow afraid.

"*Rest!*" repeated Mary in a harsh undertone. "A real rest! Do you know that that's exactly what Alan said—those very words?" Her voice dropped almost to a whisper: through the spitting and swishing of the cars on the wet road, Katharine could hardly hear the next words:

"Why has he done it, Katharine? Why is he so anxious to get Angela out of the house? Sometimes—I almost think—that he knows something. That he knows—he expects—that something is going to happen. . . ."

It was impossible that Flora shouldn't have heard something of this. No, not heard; Mary had admittedly kept her voice too low for that; but that sort of whisper doesn't need hearing, exactly, for its meaning to be conveyed. Mary should really have been more careful—should have remembered that Flora was with them.

Katharine could not stop to analyse the source of her dismay. Was it really anxiety lest Flora should be frightened or distressed—Flora, so tough, so self-confident, and so reassuringly self-centred into the bargain—surely she, more even than most children, was well insulated against other people's troubles? Or was she afraid for Mary's sake, lest Flora should spread even more silly, ill-informed gossip than had been going around already? Whatever it was, she knew with certainty that this conversation must cease forthwith. It could be continued some time when they were alone—any time.

"Look—the bus!" she exclaimed. "If we run we'll just catch it. Quick, Flora—you run on, and tell Jane to wait when she gets to the bus stop...."

And in the ensuing whirl of hurry, light and noise, Mary's ill-timed confidences were indeed obliterated. It did not occur to Katharine that by the time she should again find herself alone with Mary, the chance for renewing them might be over; that it might already be too late.

CHAPTER XX

STEPHEN WAS still out when Katharine got home, and at first she felt nothing but relief. It was so easy to give the children just crisps and bread and jam for supper; so easy, too, to deal single-handed with the argument about why Flora as well as Jane should go straight to bed afterwards. Not that she dealt with it very efficiently, and certainly not very quickly; but this way at least it was only *one* argument. It wasn't followed by another argument about why she allowed Flora to argue so much, and yet another about why they were always arguing about whether Flora should be allowed to argue so much.

By half-past nine it was all over, and Katharine was sitting quiet and relaxed by the fire, with Clare chewing her penholder gently in the armchair opposite. After dawdling vaguely through the day, doing a little knitting, a little reading, and making a batch of coconut macaroons, Clare had suddenly decided to settle down to her homework after supper. And, of course, she wanted to do it by the fire in the sitting-room.

But it was all right so far. She wasn't crying, even though it was Latin again. Strands of straight fair hair fell across her face, as they always did when she was working, but the effect tonight was somehow pleasantly casual rather then distraught. The gentle, expressive mouth looked grave, even determined, but no longer desperate.

As Katharine studied her daughter with cautious satisfaction, the girl looked up.

"It's a funny thing, Mummy," she observed, "but I seem able to understand the gerunds quite well so long as I don't think about them. Like the way you can see the Pleiades best if you don't look right at them—do you know how I mean? It's just the opposite from algebra—the more you think about that, the better you understand it. It's very interesting, isn't it, the different ways there are of understanding different things."

Katharine smiled, and with her thirteen-year-old daughter embarked boldly and cheerfully on the ancient puzzle of the Nature of Understanding. But it was Clare's nature, of course, that she had in mind as she talked. Perhaps, after all, it hadn't been a mistake to have sent her to the grammar school. Perhaps in her own plodding, worrying, difficult way she would get more out of it than any of them?

And now Clare was deep in her books again, and everything was very quiet. There had been a few unexplained thuds from upstairs a few minutes ago, and a sharp, perfunctory shriek of protest; but whatever it was must have beeen settled—probably in Flora's favour—quite quickly, for there had been no more sounds.

The fire was dying down now, ash already beginning to whiten near the bars, but it didn't seem worth making it up. Soon it would be bedtime. In fact it had been Clare's bedtime long ago, but it seemed a shame to interrupt her just when she was getting on so nicely with her work. But as she sat there, lapped in quietness and what should have been peace, Katharine was aware of a now familiar uneasiness nibbling away at her tranquillity.

How was Mary now? Should Katharine have stayed with her for a little after they got home? Had it been right to allow her, in her nervous state, to go alone into her empty, darkened house?

Hang it all, she wasn't Mary's keeper, was she? And hadn't she had enough on her hands, with her own clamorous, excited pair just back from their party; both claiming after their huge party tea, to be "starving", and both having to be absolutely driven to bed? And anyway, Mary wouldn't have been alone for long.

156

Auntie Pen and Angela would probably have turned up soon, and Alan too, presumably, some time or other. Mary would have been busy enough getting a meal ready for them all—or if she hadn't, then she ought to have been, Katharine reflected censoriously. Besides, Mary had seemed cheerful enough, almost back to normal, by the time they'd all got off the bus and hurried up the road—though Katharine was aware that she'd more or less forced normal behaviour on her companion by her own briskness, her bright, superficial chatter. And I was quite right, Katharine went on reassuring herself. It was just what Mary needed—someone to make her pull herself together and behave sensibly. Too much sympathy and attention would simply encourage her to brood, to get more wrapped up in herself than ever.

So Katharine's sensible, reassuring reflections ran their course, and in doing so made not the slightest dent in her growing uneasiness; her slow, unwilling consciousness that something was building up next door; was mounting, even now, to some climax; and that she, Katharine, was inextricably involved. The dying fire stirred, as yet another once glowing cinder dropped softly into darkness; Clare's pen scratched unevenly and then stopped, poised in doubt; and Katharine sat very still, her sewing untouched in her lap, her newspaper unread at her side.

The sudden, sharp ring at the front door was like a long-awaited summons, and Katharine leapt to her feet, her heart beating wildly. Clare glanced up, vaguely startled.

"Who is it, Mummy?" she asked—quite absurdly from one point of view, since Katharine could not know any more than she did; and yet from another point of view quite understandably, for Katharine's feeling of having expected just this must surely have got across to her.

"I don't know," said Katharine, almost feeling that she was lying; and hurried out into the hall.

The tall, elegant young woman in the doorway was a total stranger, and Katharine in her surprise stared almost rudely at the unfamiliar face under a cloud of high-piled hair. Delicately plucked brows arched beautifully over lustrous, greenish eyes with black, thickly mascaraed lashes. The scarlet mouth smiled confidently at Katharine as the young woman stepped, uninvited but with assurance, into the hall. There she hesitated, poised gracefully on her three-inch heels, her light blue swagger coat swaying round her.

"Where's Clare?" she asked. "I've forgotten the Latin homework again, and old Fossie'll be furious, so I . . ."

Katharine's mind lurched into focus . . . spinning as down a helter-skelter in the effort of adjustment. So this glittering vision was simply Brenda Forbes, whom Katharine had last seen (surely only a few weeks back?) as an inky schoolgirl, barely as tall as Clare, her satchel bumping against her stout bare legs as she ran for the school bus.

"Of course. Come along in, Brenda," gulped Katharine, still trying to readjust herself to the transformation, and led the visitor into the sitting-room.

Clare greeted her classmate without any great enthusiasm, but without surprise, and soon the two girls were crouched on the sofa, marking pages in Clare's Latin book, and arguing about whether Miss Foster had said they could or they couldn't leave out questions 8 and 9 because they weren't about the pluperfect subjunctive. One of Brenda's three-inch heels was tucked awkwardly under her as she sat, coat rumpled, just where she had flung herself, the other had fallen from her foot, inky under its 15-denier nylon, and lay on its side under the table. Feeling that perhaps the transformation in Brenda was less than she had at first supposed, Katharine left them to it, and went into the kitchen to tidy up and put things ready for the morning.

But it was hard to concentrate. All those useful, and indeed perfectly justifiable, thoughts about Mary's affairs being none of her business, and about the whole thing being a lot of hysterical nonsense anyway—all these thoughts seemed to whirr in her mind like so many road drills, both distracting and meaningless. By the time Brenda had been got out of the house, and Clare had been sent gradually to bed, Katharine's feeling of impending disaster had become unbearable. Softly she unbolted the scullery door and stepped out into the night.

From here, at the far end of the lawn, just before you stepped backwards into the brussels sprouts, you could see all the Prescott back windows—and the lights were on in every single one.

Was this a good sign, or a bad one? What, indeed, had Katharine expected to discover by staring up at the windows? She had started out into the garden simply on impulse—a sudden, unreasoning dread lest the windows should still be as dark, the house as silent, as when she had let Mary go into it on her own three or four hours ago. But even if they had been, what would it have signified? Probably simply that the whole family were already in bed and asleep—and why not, at half-past ten on a wet winter's night?

Katharine shivered a little in the heavy, autumn air. Not that it was cold, exactly: only wet, and dismal, and forbidding. And it certainly wasn't dark; all those lighted windows, even though most of them were curtained, threw a suffused, shapeless brightness over the gardens. Katharine, standing here, must be clearly visible to anyone who cared to look.

Even as the thought crossed her mind, Katharine was aware of a sudden movement behind the curtains at one of the Prescotts' windows—Mary's bedroom window, Katharine recognised in the instant. A darkness—a shadow, a something too vague to be called a silhouette—appeared at the join of the curtains. For a moment they swung apart, and a streak of brilliant light flashed across the garden. . . . Then they closed again.

Nothing in it, of course. Someone had simply pulled them apart for a second, readjusting them, and then dropped them back again. Nothing extraordinary: there could be a thousand reasons for such a gesture.

But of these thousand reasons, only one found a foothold in Katharine's tense, alerted mind tonight. Suddenly, involuntarily, and with distracting vividness, she recalled the evening last week when she had been sitting in with Angela: recalled the swift, silent way Mary had slipped between the long curtains of the sitting-room, and then had stood there, behind them, for long minutes, staring out into the gardens. And had never, in the end, explained to Katharine at *what* she was staring.

At this very moment Mary might once again be standing up there in the darkness, silently staring down at Katharine—who was silently staring up towards her. An eerie, almost superstitious terror kept Katharine for a moment standing absolutely still. . . . Though, of course, this was the worst thing she could possibly do if Mary *was* watching. She seemed to hear again Mary's absurd accusation earlier in the evening "Why are you following me, Katharine?" To stand staring like this, motionless and in silence, would surely give foundation to whatever idiotic suspicion Mary was harbouring.

Quickly, idiotically, Katharine began trying to behave naturally in her unsought limelight. She bent down, pretending to examine the brussels sprouts—as if anyone could in this darkness! Then she pretended she was pulling up a weed—as if anyone would at this time of night! And then, her meagre resources at an end, she simply fled: across the lawn, and into the blessed anonymous darkness of the side passage with the dustbins.

Well! Of all the silly, childish ways to behave! And probably Mary hadn't been watching anyway, Katharine scolded herself, as she felt her way along the passage, crashing first into Curfew's tin of sawdust and then into the broken mowing machine that the dustmen wouldn't take.

But still, just in case Mary *had* been watching, Katharine ought to go round and apologise. Well, not apologise, exactly, but explain . . . get out of it somehow before Mary got any more odd, suspicious ideas into her head. And if it turned out that Mary hadn't seen her—well, no harm would be done. Half-past ten wasn't so *very* late to be calling on a close friend, especially when they were all so obviously wide awake, with all those lights on everywhere.

CHAPTER XXI

IT WAS not Mary who answered the door, but Auntie Pen. She showed neither pleasure nor surprise at Katharine's visit, but led her matter-of-factly into the sitting-room, ordered rather than invited her to sit in one of the two armchairs by the bare hearth, and then seated herself, very straight, in the one opposite.

"Well?"

Mrs. Quentin's tone was not encouraging: but nor, on the other hand, did it demand any great politeness in Katharine's response. So she replied, almost equally brusquely: "I came to see Mary, really. Is she around?" Then, as Mrs. Quentin did not answer, but simply sat there watching as if waiting for Katharine to incriminate herself in some way, Katharine found herself, quite against her will, becoming apologetic.

"I'm sorry to butt in on you so late. It was just that—well—I wanted to see Mary. I wanted to see that she was all right."

"And why shouldn't she be?"

Mrs. Quentin was shooting out her questions like little sharp pebbles from a catapult. Her hostility was unmistakable. The black, snapping eyes rested on Katharine's face censoriously, just as they had done in the bus queue that first evening. But what was it all about? What had Katharine done? She tried to answer Mrs. Quentin's question reasonably.

"Just that she seemed a little—upset—this evening," she explained carefully. "She was all alone in the house . . . and wasn't sure when anyone would be back. . . ." Her voice slithered to a stop as the black eyes raked her face, fury mounting in their glittering depths.

"'Mary seemed a little upset.'" Mrs. Quentin quoted mockingly. "Only a little, eh? And after all the time and trouble you've spent—you and your chattering, gossiping, back-biting friends—hovering round my poor Mary with your crocodile sympathy . . . your curiosity . . . your vulgar, unfeeling, prying, vicious scandal-mongering. . . ."

Mrs. Quentin's voice choked on the flood of her own epithets, and Katharine stared at her aghast. The tiny thread of truth that her conscience could detect in the intemperate accusations only served to sharpen her astonishment. And in any case, of what significance was this tiny thread, embedded as it was in such a vast, warm, generous tangle of genuine concern for Mary; of real kindness, of desire to help?

"I—we—were only trying to help," Katharine began dazedly to stammer out her thoughts. "You know—we were sort of rallying round—"

"'Rallying round!' That's what you call it! And I suppose that's what your friend Stella calls it when she starts lecturing Mary about her 'unconscious aggression' when a pair of scissors happens to fall out of her handbag! And I suppose Mrs. Forsyth calls it 'rallying round' too, when she comes prying and needling and trying to trap Mary into saying that she hates Alan. Just because Mrs. Forsyth hates and despises *her* husband, she loves to feel that other women hate and despise theirs. It makes her feel better about it. It makes Stella feel better too, but in a different way. *She* loves to watch Mary messing up her life because it shows up how marvellously she, Stella, is managing hers. Everything lovely in *her* garden—that's Stella; and to keep it looking that way, of course, everything has to be pretty frightful in everyone else's garden."

"And me? What am I supposed to be getting out of it?" asked Katharine in a tone of icy sarcasm that helped to mask her uneasy knowledge of the answer. But the answer was more hurtful even than her conscience had warned her.

"Oh, *you*! *You're* just another Mrs. Forsyth, only feebler. You don't say the really nasty things—Oh no. You just enjoy letting Mrs. Forsyth do it for you. You get all the fun that way, *and* a reputation for being a little less spiteful than the others. But you're not: not by the least fraction. There's not a pin to choose between the lot of you, that's the truth. You're just a gang of trouble makers—all of you engaged on the same activity, stropping your egos on Mary's troubles like cows scratching themselves on a gate . . . until, finally, between them they break it down. Yes, they break it down. Do you realise that between you you're driving Mary insane?"

The anger was receding from the black eyes now; they looked sombre, desolate. Katharine felt her own anger seeping away, leaving a sharp pity for this uncompromising woman whose harsh and hard-won wisdom had shown her so much of the truth—and yet had blinded her to so much. Katharine answered gently, and with absolute honesty.

"You're quite right," she said slowly. "I admit it. Everything you say is true—but it's not all of the truth. We *do* have these awful spiteful, selfish motives, exactly as you say—but we also really do want to help. We really *do* care about Mary—at the same time as being spiteful. Can't you understand that? Perhaps it's because you're not a born gossip yourself," Katharine smiled a little ruefully, "you don't understand the—the sort of *warmth* there is about it. Take me, for instance—I'm a born gossip, so I can understand if from both sides. Of course I know that when I'm not there my friends gossip about me just as much as I do about them when they're not there. They say the most dreadful things about me—I'm certain they do. But I don't *mind*. Can't you understand that? Of course, now and again one feels the spitefulness like a sort of prick—but it seems a trifle compared with the all-over warm feeling of knowing that people are interested. Even if nobody stirs a finger actually to help you—and even you must admit that they *sometimes* do—but even if they don't, I still think that to have your troubles chewed over, picked to pieces, and put together again—it gives you a feeling of support. I don't quite know how to describe it, but it would take an *awful* lot of spite to cancel out that feeling. For me it would, anyway."

"For you, perhaps, but what about Mary?"

Mrs. Quentin spoke thoughtfully: the belligerent air was gone. "Mary *isn't* a born gossip, you see, any more than she's a born doormat, which is what she's tried to make of herself for years, for Alan's sake. Not that Alan would have liked it if she'd succeeded, any more than he likes what he's got now. He liked her as she was when he married her—light-hearted, simple, rather tomboyish. Everything that he *wasn't*, in fact. She had all the qualities that he lacked—all the qualities that he *needed*, to get him out of his narrow, prim ways. . . ."

"But if he liked her like that . . . ?" queried Katharine tentatively; and Mrs. Quentin banged her fist agonisedly on the table.

"*Liked* her like that—yes. But also he couldn't *stand* her like that—that was another matter altogether, as they both found all too soon. And yet, if she'd been left alone, Mary could have *taught* him to stand it—just simply taught him, and he would have been grateful to her for ever. If only the average wife would understand that! She always thinks that if her way of looking at life is different from her husband's, then she must either 'give in' and change to his ways, or else she must 'stand up for herself', 'preserve her integrity' and so forth through a lifetime of rows and scenes. But usually she doesn't need to do either. All she need to do is to teach him to *like* her way of seeing things. But actually to like it—to enjoy seeing the world in this new way. And usually he's ready enough to learn. He probably *wants* to learn—that's why he married her in the first place, because this was something he wanted.

"Mary could have done all that—easily—if only she'd been left alone."

"But how wasn't she left alone?" asked Katharine nervously, fearful of bringing down on her head another tirade; as indeed she did.

"How wasn't she left alone?" The black eyes were flashing again. "Living here among you lot, all paddling in and out of each other's matrimonial troubles like ducklings in a pool! All of you running in and out, sympathising with one another about your husbands' faults and failings—it may be warm and comforting, as you say, but I would say it's a warm, comforting morass in which a young wife may well drown. It's a sort of mutual running-home-to-mother which is naturally consoling, but doesn't help your marriages, any of you. Or only in the very rarest cases." Mrs. Quentin sighed, and as once before, Katharine had the feeling that she was speaking from deep and perhaps tragic experience. From her own mistakes, perhaps, or her imagined mistakes, with the still unmentioned Mr. Quentin.

"Anyway," she resumed wearily, "it's too late now." Did she mean for herself, or for Mary and Alan? Presumably the latter, for she continued: "I only hope that Angela may not suffer. Did Mary tell you, I'm taking Angela away with me tomorrow, to stay for a while. I—we"—Mrs. Quentin looked confused for a moment—"that is, my brother feels that she'd be better away, out of this atmosphere. I'd be only too glad to keep her for good, if that were possible. There's something about that child—a toughness, a resilience, a sort of nine-lives quality— which just answers to something in *my* nature. I understand her, somehow; though I'm too hard a person to understand the rest of you—as I dare say you've noticed." She smiled now, a little stiffly, and with a gesture silenced Katharine's protest: "I noticed you, you know, before we ever properly met. In a bus queue, one rainy night. I don't suppose you remember, but I was standing there in the rain, worrying about Mary— she had just rung me up, sounding distressed—and suddenly

I caught sight of you, and something made me think: That's just the kind of inquisitive, restless, foraging sort of woman who's causing half my brother's troubles. Always hovering round sympathising, advising, interfering—I know the type. Of course, I may have unconsciously recognised you as a neighbour of Mary's—I suppose I must have caught sight of you occasionally when I've been visiting here before. But it was only after quite a time that I realised that the woman in the queue was *you*. You look quite different without that headscarf on."

"Less inquisitive, restless and interfering?" asked Katharine, with a rueful smile; and Mrs. Quentin nodded.

"A bit less," she allowed grudgingly, looking Katharine up and down, and seeming to assess the precise extent of these qualities like an expert dressmaker assessing the waist and bust measurements of her client. "But I still don't really feel I can trust you." She sat silent for a moment, and then spoke again, abruptly:

"You know, don't you, that Mary stabbed Alan herself? I suppose she told you?"

"Well—yes—she did," answered Katharine quickly, almost eagerly in her relief at finding that there was after all one other person who shared Mary's secret, and who might, therefore, be able to elucidate Mary's queer behaviour this evening. "She did tell me, but now I'm beginning to wonder—"

"You see?" Mrs. Quentin was truculent. "It's just as I thought! Your inquisitiveness obliterates all other considerations. You betray Mary's confidence—and I'm sure Mary *did* tell you this in confidence—simply because I gave you a lead, and you are dying to talk it over with someone. Isn't that true?"

"It may be true, but it certainly isn't fair," retorted Katharine hotly. "If Mary tells both of us, separately, she surely shouldn't mind if—"

"Ah, but she *didn't* tell me," returned Mrs. Quentin softly. "I only guessed—from what I've heard, from what I've seen. From your behaviour, among other things. Mary told me nothing. *You're* the one who told me—just now. Mary was a fool to trust you."

Katharine stared into the heavy, lined face, fear and anger mingling as she threshed about for a suitable retort. Surely she hadn't really betrayed Mary? No one could say she had. And anyway, Auntie Pen was wholly on Mary's side, and wouldn't use the knowledge to harm her.

"And now you're frightened!" commented Auntie Pen scornfully. "It's all right—I won't tell Mary you've told me. Not that you've told me anything I didn't know, of course. It's all so absolutely in character for Mary, you see. The impulsive, hysterical striking out in the first place: the subsequent conscience-pricking so that she *had* to confess to someone—to you, as it happened, but don't flatter yourself that it was due to anything more than chance and propinquity. There was no *need* for her to confess, you understand—my brother would never have exposed her in a hundred years. She could have kept it all dark from everyone, for ever. If it had been me I would have; but, of course, Mary is a weak person. Weak, and kind, and guilt-ridden, and terribly aware of having failed Alan. And silly, too, and unpractical. Do you know, I found her jumper, covered with blood, just stuffed into the bottom of her wardrobe? *Anyone* could have found it. Angela, the charwoman—anyone. It was a marvel of Providence that it was only me. It was past washing, of course, so I wrapped it in newspaper and stuffed it deep into the next-door dustbin one night, after they were all asleep; and Mary's never even missed it. I'll swear to you that she never thought of it as a dangerous clue at all. She's so naïve—so hopeless at any kind of dissembling. So suggestible, too, and so trusting . . . chattering about it to *you* of all people. *You*, who can never keep quiet about anything; who'll keep on chewing it over with her, discussing it, probing her feelings, glorying in your position of confidence—of power. I'm sorry—'rallying round' is the technical term for all this, isn't it."

"You've no need to be so disagreeable," said Katharine sharply. "I don't talk to her about it at all, if you want to know. Never. We more or less agreed not to, as a matter of fact. We thought— in fact, I suggested to her—that she'd more quickly forget the whole thing if neither of us ever referred to it again, but spoke and acted as if the burglar story was true. And *I* think she ought to forget it. It's no use letting a single isolated action haunt your whole life."

"Indeed no. No use at all. But people rarely choose their ghosts on the grounds that they are any *use*," responded Mrs. Quentin sombrely. "And Mary agreed to this?" she went on. "I'm surprised. She's such a truthful girl—or used to be. It was one of her sterling qualities. A narrowing one, perhaps—a little childish— and not altogether loveable. But sterling—and very much a part of her nature. Yes, you surprise me. However," she continued, "I suppose I can't really criticise you on this score, because I have been doing exactly the same myself. I, too, have been plugging the burglar idea for all it was worth. Not entirely for Mary's sake, I must admit; I was thinking of my brother, too. I didn't want Mary to start confessing all round the place, causing endless trouble for him—for his job, for his reputation, everything. And it's just the kind of impulsive, childish, inconsiderate thing that she *would* do. Poor Mary—she's never really grown beyond the ethics of the Bravest Girl in the Fourth. You know—clear your own conscience regardless of the upset and inconvenience to everyone else. My poor Mary—this sort of thing takes her right outside her natural range. That's why I felt I had to guide events a little."

It occurred to Katharine that Mrs. Quentin—with the best of intentions, like the rest of them—had been interfering as much as anyone; but she felt it would be tactless—as well as futile, at this stage—to point this out.

"Where *is* Mary, by the way?" she asked suddenly, realising that she and Mrs. Quentin had been sitting there talking for over an hour, and all that time there had been no sound from the rest of the house. "Is she upstairs? I thought she couldn't have gone to bed, because there were all the lights on everywhere. Every single room."

Mrs. Quentin looked at Katharine pityingly from under her heavy, wrinkled lids. "All the lights on? Yes, I suppose they are. But I told you, didn't I? Between you, you have been driving Mary insane."

CHAPTER XXII

SWIFTLY UP the lighted stairs ran Katharine. Up, up into a white blaze of light from the unshaded hundred-watt bulb on the little landing; and all the bedroom doors wide open, too, pouring out their quota of shadowless brilliance. On went Katharine, unhesitating, through Mary's bedroom door, and only then, right inside the room, did she pause.

For the room was empty. Bright, and bare, and empty. No: no, it wasn't. On the big bed the coverlet was slightly humped by what must be a long, slender shape lying perfectly still. Wisps of Mary's dark hair were just visible on the far edge of the pillow, the coverlet pulled up smooth and nearly flat over her face. As if she had covered her head, like a child, to shut out the terrors of the night . . . or as if someone else had covered it for her, after she was asleep. . . .

Katharine's movements were still swift, but now, quite without her knowledge or volition, they had also become stealthy. With scarcely a sound, she was across the room and lifting the coverlet from Mary's silent head. Even as she did do, Mary's eyelids twitched, and she gave a little sigh. So swiftly had it all happened that Katharine experienced the great pulsating relief at these signs of life almost before she had registered the fear from which the slight movements had released her; and she stood, recovering herself, and staring down into Mary's sleeping face.

For Mary *was* sleeping, of that there was no doubt; and sleeping very deeply, too, for after that single flicker of awareness she had made no further movement. Her breath was soft and even, and her usually anxious, expressive face was blank and calm.

For some reason, Mary must have gone to bed very, very frightened. Why else would she try to sleep with the light blazing right into her eyes . . . and with the door wide open . . . and the window too, on this damp, dismal night, with fog already pricking at your throat? Yes, Katharine confirmed, moving the curtains slightly—wide open, and at the bottom, too, as if to make sure that her screams would be heard. . . .

What screams? Why? Why should Katharine leap to the conclusion that this was the purpose of the open window? For what sort of danger, real or imagined, could all this be a preparation?

In the bright silence of the room, Katharine tried to recall Mary's first words to her when they had met in the Building Site that evening. Katharine had been too much startled at the time to pay much attention, but she remembered them now: "Hush, Katharine, he'll hear us!" Who was "He"? At the time, Katharine had taken for granted that it referred to the man from under the lamp-post, and had been quick to point out the silliness of anticipating any danger from such a source. But suppose Mary had been referring not to this man at all, but to Alan? Alan, the reserved, the mysterious, the unforgiving? Alan, who had stored up that envelope of hair, dated and labelled? . . . Who had refused to accept his wife's confession to the stabbing, and had thereby, in one subtle stroke, made the crime for ever unforgivable?

But forgotten was just as good as forgiven. Better, Katharine assured herself. And as for the hair, perhaps a punctilious, hoarding kind of man like Alan could have done exactly that, with no more motive than to have everything about himself and his life recorded, classified, and dealt with? To him, the labelling, classifying and putting away of such a relic might be a way of getting the whole episode under control, and hence of being able to dismiss it. Just as in his business the only way to get a document off his mind would be to file it in its proper place. Merely thrown away it would be on his conscientious mind for ever.

But who could tell how Alan Prescott's mind worked? Grim, and tortuous, and resentful unto death, as you would think if you listened to Mary? Or was it a mind baffled, tied up in its own severities, and longing to be released, as his sister, rightly or wrongly, presented it? Certainly Mary was not the one to know the answer—at first too wayward and self-centred, and latterly too frightened, she had never come within a mile of understanding her husband.

Or had she? Once again Katharine found herself up against this blank, impenetrable possibility that perhaps Mary really had good reason for fearing Alan?

The first uneasy wisps of fog were fingering their way into the room now, creeping, clammy and soft, round the edges of the curtains. With a little shiver, Katharine moved back to the window and closed it. For all her care, the noise of it seemed tremendous in the silent house: and Katharine felt oddly shocked at what she had done.

But Mary did not stir; and Katharine stood for a while pondering.

For really, there seemed no point in staying here any longer. It was late; she was growing sleepy. This feeling that she ought to wait till Mary woke was absurd, because Mary wouldn't wake till morning—why should she? The obvious thing was to go downstairs, say good night to Auntie Pen, and go back home. That is, if Auntie Pen was still there. Was she supposed to be staying the night? Katharine couldn't remember anyone having mentioned it; perhaps she had gone home already.

Everything seemed very quiet. Quiet, that is, if people were awake. You wouldn't think anything of it if the house had been dark as well as quiet; it was all this light combined with all this silence that seemed so queer.

And then Katharine heard a sound; a sort of shuffling thud. Not from downstairs, though; from the bedroom right next to this one.

For one bizarre moment Katharine fancied that Mary, as she lay sleeping so quietly there, must be dreaming: dreaming that Katharine was standing by her bed listening to a noise in the next room. Don't let her be having a nightmare, Katharine almost prayed, for there is no limit to what may happen next in a nightmare. . . . But then the full absurdity of her fancy swept over her. Rousing herself, rubbing her eyes, she moved softly towards the door and peered out on to the landing.

The completeness of the anticlimax almost made her reel back against the bed. Whatever furtive figure she had expected to see tiptoeing from the adjoining room, it was not this one—tall, loose-limbed, and already falling over the flex of Angela's reading lamp that trailed across the doorway.

"Sorry to startle you," apologised Stella in a noisy whisper, "but Auntie Whatsit said I could just barge up and say goodbye to Angela. You know—give her a good luck message from Jack and Mavis. That sort of thing. I hear she's going away tomorrow."

"What do you mean, you barged up?" asked Katharine sourly, still not recovered from her shock. "I didn't hear a sound. You must have crept up on tiptoe. I don't call that 'barging'!"

Stella looked affronted.

"Well, all right, I *walked* up, then. Let's not argue about a word. You know, when people start quibbling about words, I always just simply agree with them, because I know they must be on edge about something. It's nothing to do with the word at all. *Whatever* word I'd used you'd have picked on it because you're in a nervy sort of state, I can see. Anyway, you were making a lot of noise yourself, opening or shutting windows or something. It's no wonder you didn't hear me."

Right on all counts as usual—or at least totally insulated against any possibility of being wrong, which was very nearly the same thing. And anyway, it was none of Katharine's business—it wasn't *her* house that Stella was prowling round at this time of night. But all the same, it seemed odd. Who would call to say goodbye to a child of ten at nearly midnight?

"But isn't Angela asleep?" Katharine voiced her doubts guardedly, curiosity and reproof mingling in her tones. "It's very late, surely?"

"Yes, she is, as a matter of fact," answered Stella lightly. "I only thought she might be awake because I happened to notice that her light was on. Anyway, I've left a note for the poor little thing. I thought that a little message from really *secure* children, like Jack and Mavis, would give *her* a feeling of security in the midst of all this upset."

You didn't, thought Katharine disagreeably. You thought that the contemplation of Angela undergoing all this upheaval would give you a lovely, superior feeling about how much better cared for Jack and Mavis are, and how much better a mother you are than Mary. *I* know. . . . You can't kid me. . . . You don't even think you can. . . . Set a thief to catch a thief. . . .

The two women eyed each other cautiously under the glaring light bulb—and Katharine suddenly realised that Stella had just as much reason to wonder about her, Katharine's, motive for being here as she had to wonder about Stella's. Curiosity, of course, they could both recognise in each other. But was Stella discounting Katharine's real concern for Mary—just as Katharine was discounting the possibility that there was an element of real kindness in the mixed motives which had prompted Stella to leave a friendly message for Angela to find, with surprise and pleasure, when she woke in the morning?

"Of course," Stella was saying, "Jack and Mavis don't actually know about any of it yet, but I know they would want me to write a note on their behalf. It's a funny thing, isn't it, how really happy, secure children can understand the feelings of an insecure one much better than another insecure child can? I suppose it's because they're better able to *face* things . . . to release their sympathies in valid directions. . . ."

Even while Katharine longed to hit Stella over the head with Mary's heavy silver hairbrush, she still found herself, maddeningly, having to remember that Jack and Mavis were in fact quite pleasant, well-disposed children, who probably *would* want the note written. One expects, as if of right, that all boasting should be empty—that the boaster should always be a hollow sham, covering up his inadequacies by his bragging. It comes as an unpleasant shock, every time, when the boaster turns out to be quite a competent person with quite a lot to boast about. And you couldn't get away from it, Jack and Mavis *were* nice children in spite of their mother's praises of them; and she *was* giving them quite a good life, in spite of her ceaseless advertising of the fact. After all, there must be something to be said for having a mother who unfailingly assumes that you are the best children, your home the best home, your father the best father, your school the best school, and even your coffee-grinder the best coffee-grinder, in the whole world. Less to be said for having a neighbour like that, of course: I don't actually have to *like* it, reflected Katharine with relief, as Stella's barbed panegyric hissed to a stop and she set off down the stairs, the steps and bannisters creaking in agonised chorus at her painstaking efforts to be quiet.

Katharine had been going to follow her, but now she stood still, listening all over again, for she fancied she had heard a sound from Mary's room. But she did not move immediately; whatever was going on, she did not want Stella to come back and get involved in it: Stella would be back up those stairs like a ball on a piece of elastic if she once got any inkling that anything more was going to happen tonight. So Katharine waited until she heard the front door close, and then hurried softly back into Mary's room.

Once again the room was full of damp night air and wisps of fog: once again the window was open at the bottom: and Mary herself, intent and furtive, was clambering softly back into bed. She glanced up at Katharine without surprise.

"You shouldn't have shut the window," was all she said. "People keep *on* shutting it—it's so tiresome. I *like* it open."

She sat, hands clasped round her knees under the bedclothes, and stared accusingly at Katharine. Her shoulders were bare above her flimsy nightdress, and Katharine could see that already she was shivering.

"But it's so cold, Mary," she objected, moving in the direction of the window. "And foggy, too. You'll be frozen." She reached up towards the sash once more, but with a sharp cry Mary halted her.

"No! *Please* not, Katharine! *Please* leave it alone. It's safer, you see. I feel safer with it open."

"Safer? Safer from what?" Katharine felt all her former uneasiness returning. Something was going on . . . something was mounting to a climax; and in spite of all Mary's confidences, all her heart-to-heart talks, there was still some vital, central fact which she was keeping to herself.

"What are you afraid of, Mary?" she asked bluntly. "Are you afraid of Alan?"

A curious look came on to Mary's face—half shocked, half sly.

"Afraid *of* Alan?" she asked uneasily . . . cautiously. . . . "Why should I be afraid *of* Alan? I'm afraid *for* him, naturally. The dark man—the burglar—he's coming again tonight: I know he is. This is the night when he plans to strike again."

"But, *Mary*—!" Once and for all, Katharine meant to get this puzzle cleared up. "What do you mean, the dark man? Were you lying to me when you said there wasn't any such man? That Alan was making it all up—that you'd stabbed him yourself?"

Mary stared at her in the strangest way—frightened, defensive—yet somehow triumphant. Then, without warning, her eyes filled with tears.

"It's not fair, Katharine, to accuse me of such awful things. You promised—that day in the cafeteria—that you'd never say such a thing again. You *promised*. And we had a long talk, and decided it *must* have been the man in the raincoat. Why, it was you who were so positive about it—don't you remember? You absolutely *insisted* that it must have been him. You seemed to think it was quite absurd of me to doubt it. . . ."

Katharine stared down at the anxious, petulant face, and understanding slowly overwhelmed her. She remembered the tepid cups of coffee, the desolate cafeteria, and she remembered her own words: "You'll find that you'll forget all about it yourself—really you will."

And it had come to pass exactly as she had prophesied. Mary had forgotten.

CHAPTER XXIII

FOR A long time that night Katharine lay awake, wondering. Wondering if she had been right to come back home like this, leaving Mary alone. Well, not alone really, because Auntie Pen was still there—and Alan was expected home, too, though not until very late. He still hadn't come when Katharine left, but he *would* come, of course he would. And Mary had declared that it wasn't him she was afraid of—not now.

Now Mary was afraid of a ghost—a non-existent man. But how could one convince her of his non-existence? Katharine felt bewildered by the irony of the situation. She recalled again her own ill-judged insistence that Mary should try to put the truth, the real facts, out of her mind; should talk, and think, and behave, as if they did not exist. This way, Katharine had airily predicted, Mary would soon forget them herself, and all would be well.

But I didn't mean *actually* forgetting! Again Katharine experienced the blank sense of shock she had felt as the import of Mary's peevish words had taken possession of her understanding; a sense of confronting the utterly unknown.

But was Mary's state of mind so utterly unknown? Wasn't it after all within the bounds of an ordinary person's comprehension? A highly suggestible young woman, by nature utterly frank and truthful—indeed, almost childishly devoid of guile—how would such a young woman feel when confronted by a situation in which she was prevented, in a most absolute sense, from confessing to a crime about which she felt deeply and justifiably guilty? And on to this unsteadily toppling base had been piled pressure upon pressure. First Katharine herself, urging Mary with all the weight of her friendship (and with complete disregard, she now realised, of the basic differences between Mary's nature and her own) to forget; to disregard the truth, and to pretend to herself, day in and day out, that the false story was the true one. And then the surging, inquisitive, well-meaning hordes of Mary's other neighbours, and her family: all of them extracting from her the false story, believing it, repeating it to each other, and then bringing it back to her, ever more vivid, ever more colourful, ever more solidly fixed in its framework of social acceptance. "Dark man in a raincoat. . . ." "Dark man in a raincoat. . . ." How relentlessly they had all of them, in their various ways, kept this image before Mary's unhappy mind . . . pressing it deeper and deeper into her guilty conscience, into her very soul, until in agony she had cried out to Katharine: "I begin to feel I am haunted by dark men in raincoats. . . ."

Did that despairing cry mark the moment when the real forgetting had begun—when she could stand the pressures of suggestion no longer? Katharine remembered the evening when Mary had roamed the house like a lost, uneasy spirit, staring out into the dark gardens . . . locking and relocking her doors—against a non-existent man already growing real? Or was there not a precise moment of forgetting at all? Did it begin, instead, with a sort of prolonged, uneasy holding of memory in abeyance—a shrinking in horror from any threat of having recollection stirred? Again Katharine seemed to hear Mary's urgent cry of "Hush!" on the stairs that night, when Katharine had seemed about to finish her sentence with the words, "He doesn't exist."

Wildly, crazily suggestible? Who could say, who hadn't actually been through it as Mary had been through it? Why, even Katharine herself, scarcely involved at all, had nevertheless experienced that momentary shock of seeing a dark man in a raincoat sitting behind them on a bus—had had to recall, with a conscious effort, that the dark man in a raincoat that they had been talking about so intently was wholly imaginary, and that therefore this real man on the bus couldn't possibly be he. And if you could experience this moment of illusion after only half an hour's concentration on the nonexistence, then what would it be like after hours ... and days ... and weeks of it? Suggestion piled on suggestion.... Wouldn't the false picture, always before you, gradually grow more and more vivid, until at last it filled your mind, and you would think it was the truth?

And what then? Would the false picture remain static, or would it then begin to grow? To grow, to change ... to add a false detail here ... a bit of false dialogue there? Would it throw out strange, twisted side branches, thrown up of necessity from its basic, inner falsity ... where ... how would it all end?

As she lay there, staring up into the swirling patterned darkness under her closed lids, Katharine began to realise that the situation had gone beyond her. It was out of control, and she did not know what to do. For a moment she had a rash impulse to rouse Stephen, to talk it over with him then and there, to ask his advice.

But would this not be a betrayal of Mary's confidence? *Was* it still a betrayal, in any ordinary sense, if Mary had herself forgotten all about it? And anyway, wasn't the whole situation becoming too dangerous, too explosive, for promises to be still binding? When she had promised to keep Mary's secret, it surely wasn't a burden on this scale that she had undertaken to bear?

So much for the ethics of it. But what about Stephen? How would he—or indeed any man—react to being woken at three in the morning to discuss such a problem? It wasn't even as if he was already in touch with it, she'd have to explain the whole thing from the very beginning. "For pity's sake, can't it wait till the morning?" he'd say—and he would be right. Of course it could wait till the morning. First thing in the morning . . . before breakfast . . . before the children came down . . . she'd tell him all about it.

But it didn't work out like that. When she woke, Stephen was already up; and when she went into the kitchen to make tea there he already was; and it was he, not she, who broke the silence with the words, "There's something I want to say to you."

He looked moody and tired, and Katharine felt her whole body stiffening resignedly. So there was going to be a row: Mary's affairs would have to wait. Even though she did not know yet what the row was to be about, she could feel all her faculties already taking up their familiar positions of defence—moving up into line like a platoon of seasoned soldiers, trained and drilled over the years into absolute precision. Against a defence like this he will have to attack very, very hard, it suddenly occurred to her. Was that why he always *did* attack hard, even—or was it particularly?—about trifles?

"I hear that Angela Prescott stayed the night here last Wednesday," he began, his hand resting on the handle of the kettle, and his weight slumped warily against the sink. "Why didn't you tell me?"

Katharine stared, then laughed, with dreadful artificial lightness.

"But Stephen, she didn't," she exclaimed. "Who told you she did? I suppose it was Stella?"

It must have been Stella, of course. Katharine remembered Stella's casual reference to Mary's having told her that Angela was spending the night with Katharine's children; and how she, Katharine, had not denied it; refraining from doing so out of a bewildered sense of loyalty to Mary, who presumably must have had *some* motive for the lie. "I don't know how Stella got the idea," she continued, confusedly, when Stephen still did not speak. "I suppose she must have misunderstood something Mary said. But anyway, Angela *didn't* stay the night. I went over there to look after her instead."

Stephen didn't even look suspicious. He just simply didn't believe her at all.

"I suppose you are trying to hide it from me because I'd said I thought Jane's friendship with Angela ought to be discouraged," he surmised wearily. "I wish you wouldn't do this sort of thing, Katharine. I've given up feeling hurt at the way you tell lies to me all the time, but I still find it a nuisance."

"But I *don't* tell lies," began Katharine in fury—and did not know how to go on. Because, of course, she did tell lies—little, tiny, trivial ones, like that one about the washing-up mop. Such tiny ones, though. It wasn't fair to call them *lies*.

"I'd never tell lies about—well—something that mattered, like whether Angela'd stayed the night or not. *Really* I wouldn't."

She felt baffled, affronted. Like all small-scale liars, she felt that there should be some special, super-convincing form of language that could be used when one really *was* speaking the truth: something that would automatically carry total conviction. It seemed more like a flaw in the language than a flaw in herself that this should not be so.

"I *wouldn't* tell a lie about a thing like that," she could only repeat, helplessly.

"Well, how am I to know what sort of categories are to be included in 'like that'?" demanded Stephen. "What about that mop business the other day? You knew damn well that Jane had taken it for her bloody rabbit, and you pretended you'd thrown it away. What category does *that* come in, in your complicated system?"

"I—I didn't know you'd noticed," said Katharine feebly, as if that was some kind of defence, "I mean, I don't count it exactly a lie if it's only to keep the peace."

"Well, and wouldn't it 'keep the peace' as you call it to deceive me about Angela staying the night? It would stop me making a scene about it, wouldn't it? Just like the mop. What you call 'Keeping the peace' simply means 'Keeping Stephen out of it'. I think that's what I hate most about your lying, Katharine. I'm not bothering about whether it's wicked or not any more than you are. But every single lie you ever tell has the sole and express purpose of keeping me out of something. Out of the family's life. Jane's rabbit. Clare's homework. Everything. Do you think I don't notice?"

Katharine had thought that he didn't notice. There was something both terrifying and immensely stimulating in finding that he did. But for the moment she could put none of this into words.

"Well, you always make such a fuss," she retorted. "And you seem to hate it so, too—I mean all the children's games—and their tiresomeness—the way I let them be a nuisance. I *can't* bring them up strictly—I expect I'm too weak, or something, but anyway, I can't. Everybody can only bring children up in the way they *can* bring them up," she concluded, her eyes filling with tears. "The books all make it sound as if you have some sort of choice, but you haven't. You have to bring them up according to the sort of person you *are,* and that's all there is to it."

Stephen's face had softened strangely. Wildly and forlornly the kettle boiled unnoticed, and he absently moved his hand out of range of the scalding steam.

"I know, Katharine, I know," he said gently. "But the same goes for me—has that never occurred to you? I can only handle them in the way I can, too: and it's not the same way as yours, I know. But surely this must be very common? And it can't be the answer for one parent simply to shut the other one out, just to save the trouble of sorting out conflicting methods. To the one who's doing the shutting out I daresay it looks like 'keeping the peace'. But to the other one—the shut out one—it looks quite different, I assure you."

The neglected kettle was spitting, jerking, clattering, the lid pounding up and down under the savage swell of steam. Mechanically, Katharine moved across the room and turned down the gas; and for a second, as she stood there, she thought that Stephen's arm was about to come across her shoulder in the old caressing gesture. . . .

"Mummy. Do you know it's a quarter to eight? When are you going to wake us?"

The idiocy of Flora's question would have made Katharine laugh if she had not been so near to tears—and so outraged by the interruption. Something like this *always* happened just when she and Stephen were coming to some flicker of understanding.

Well, it was all spoilt now. Briskly, angrily, she set about preparing breakfast—hurrying the children to get dressed. The atmosphere became again busy, distant, hostile, as it so often was in the mornings. And to crown all, Jane had to jump hastily up from the table the moment she had finished her breakfast and announce that she had to clean Curfew's hutch before she went to school.

"And could you come, Mummy, and hold him for me for a minute? You see, I've got to—"

Stephen looked up irritably, maddened as always by clatter and upheaval about Curfew. As always, too, Katharine grew tense and nervous, racking her brains for some way of shelving the situation—distracting attention—blurring the issues. Like murmuring something about fetching the washing in, so that Stephen wouldn't fully realise that she was going out to help Jane with the rabbit. They were both of them reacting in exactly the way they had always done. Nothing was changed. And then Katharine realised that in this moment, by simply behaving in her usual way, and allowing Stephen to behave in *his* usual way, she could allow that moment of understanding before breakfast to close over for ever.

Quietly she stood up, followed Jane into the garden, and obediently took Curfew into her arms. But then, instead of standing there waiting till Jane was ready to have him back, she turned, and walked purposefully back into the kitchen, while Jane followed, wide-eyed and puzzled.

"But Mummy—why?" she kept protesting; but Katharine still kept on, across the kitchen, right up to her husband's chair.

"Here, Stephen," she said, clearly and confidently, "You hold Curfew for a few minutes, will you, while Jane cleans his hutch," and, bending down, she plumped the warm, tremulous creature right into his lap.

For a second there was absolute silence. Every single person in the kitchen knew that something new, something momentous, was occurring. The three girls stared, bewildered, tense, uncomprehending, while their father slowly recovered from his astonishment. They waited for his anger to break loose; and saw instead a slow, wondering look spread over his face. Cautiously, inexpertly, with the tip of one finger, he tickled the rabbit between its ears.

"Curfew—curse you!" he commented slowly: and surely no comedian, ever, anywhere, has had so feeble a pun greeted with such riotous applause. Relief, surprise, excitement, a new sense of rare, unaccustomed unity were all released in the shrieks and screams of laughter which now filled the kitchen. Tears of laughter ran down the girls' faces: Clare's elbow went into her tea-cup unnoticed, and Stephen looked round in understandable bewilderment at the success of his inane remark. Bewilderment, but evidently not displeasure; for as soon as the noise abated enough for him to be heard, he said it again.

CHAPTER XXIV

KATHARINE KNEW that she was happy because she was polishing the little oak table in the sitting-room for the first time in weeks. The outcome of the Curfew affair this morning had been so great a surprise—even a shock—that at first neither triumph nor happiness had registered on her mind at all: only total astonishment. Astonishment less, she now realised, at Stephen's favourable response to the unprecedented situation, than at her own dare-devil courage in initiating it. I didn't know I had it in me! she thought with awe, and with trepidation. And—yes—with happiness.

Because you didn't polish little oak tables first thing in the morning unless you were happy. Nor did you go out into the damp, wintry garden straight after breakfast to pick the last ragged chrysanthemums, your heart beating in anticipation of seeing their dim colours reflected on the newly shining wood. No. When you were anything less than happy, you did the absolutely essential tasks first: the washing-up, the bed-making, the emptying of rubbish. "I'll do the polishing and fill the vases when I've finished everything else," you said: and of course you never had finished everything else. Nobody had, ever. The beautiful, the inessential, must be given priority if it was to exist at all.

Katharine gave a final stiff rubbing to the little table, set the vase in the centre of it, and stepped back. She gazed with pride, with wonder, and with a sort of trepidation at the massed, heavy-headed flowers, their muted colours touched into radiance by the still, wintry sunshine. The mauves, the pinks, the fading purples were caught by the newly polished wood and reflected back like jewels; and Katharine was suddenly reminded of Esmé's loving, laughed-at canvas of purple pansies.

But already the shifting winter sunshine was moving on; soon it would leave the flowers in shadow. Katharine was aware of a vast, precarious poignancy in which she seemed to be sharing for the very first time—right now, as she stood here with the polishing rag still in her hand, and the open, half-used tin of polish balanced injudiciously on the arm of the sofa behind her.

And now, before she could pin down or analyse the fleeting mood, the telephone began to ring. She left the shining, newly cherished corner of the sitting-room, and went out into the still unswept hall.

"Katharine," came Mary's voice, small and tinkling, as if she was speaking from very far away. "Could you—do you think you could—well—come in for a minute? As quickly as you can?"

"Well, all right," said Katharine, recognising instantly, and with compunction, the grudging quality of her response. She was aware that it mirrored a shockingly self-centred and unreasonable annoyance that Mary should still be unhappy early in the morning, just when Katharine was busy. One's friends should only be in trouble in the evenings, or sometimes at week-ends.

"What is it, Mary?" she amended, trying to sound kinder, more interested: trying to force herself back, by an effort of will, into the state of total involvement in Mary's troubles, of real, desperate anxiety on Mary's behalf, in which she had been immersed last night. Katharine could recall clearly how frightened she had felt then; yet now, in the busy morning light, the whole thing seemed trivial as a dream. She glanced at the clock as if for support: and the clock, ticking vigorously onwards towards five-past nine, seemed to be entirely on her side. How could anyone be frightened of anything at five minutes past nine in the morning? Beds still unmade, the washing-up still to do, the gas man expected any minute to see to the Ascot—surely these things should be insulating Mary, too, from fear?

"What is it, Mary?" she repeated patiently. "What's the matter? What's happened?"

Mary's voice had grown even fainter now, so thin and shrill it sounded down the wire, like a bird chirruping.

"He's coming!" came the weak, whistling words out of the earpiece. "The dark man in the raincoat. He's just phoned to say he's coming! Oh, Katharine, come quickly! Quickly, before he gets here!"

It is true that Katharine delayed long enough to turn out the saucepan of boiling stock, and to pin a note on the door for the gas man: but wouldn't any other housewife have done the same? And the delay couldn't have been more than a minute, she was to assure herself afterwards. Less than a minute in fact. Why, it was practically no time at all before she was running down the Prescotts' side passage, and pushing at their back door that always jammed.

But this time it was more than jammed. Katharine felt the resistance of the bolts at top and bottom, and now, for the first time since she woke up this morning, she began once more to feel the reality of last night's alarm. Trivial as a dream, she had thought it, not more than five minutes ago. But a dream is only trivial after one has woken up; and as she struggled with the resistant door, Katharine felt stealing upon her the conviction that in this locked, silent house there had been no awakening. Here the dream was still going on . . . perhaps even now sliding into nightmare. . . . Wildly, as though trying to rouse the house itself from coma, Katharine beat upon the door with her fists, her feet, and finally with a milk bottle snatched from the sill beside her.

At that there was a slight stir within—a swift, pattering run— the grinding bolts scraped back, and Mary, wide-eyed and trembling, stood before her.

"*Katharine!*" she hissed in fury, clutching her friend by the arm. "How *could* you make such a noise? He'll hear you—he

may be here already! Don't you understand? He may be *here!*"
She dragged Katharine into the little, stone-floored scullery, and
swiftly closed and rebolted the door behind her.

"You're so *stupid,* Katharine!" she chided; but there was a note
of relief now in her harsh whisper as she pushed the last bolt
home. "Don't you realise he might have been just near you, hiding, ready to rush in when I opened the door? He's prowling
about somewhere . . . somewhere near. I know he is."

"Then why don't you ring the police?" asked Katharine, a little
hesitantly: because surely the whole thing must really be Mary's
imagination. "I mean, if you really think—"

But Mary interrupted, clutching her arm.

"Listen, Katharine," she said—no longer in a whisper, but low
and firm, and her face suddenly looked strangely composed, "I
know you're going to think it's all nonsense—and there's not
time to try and convince you—but will you, all the same, do
something to help me? Will you, Katharine? Just one thing? It
won't take more than a few minutes."

"Well, of course I will," said Katharine heartily—and in her
relief at Mary's new decisiveness of manner she gave no thought
to what sort of thing it might be that she was promising to
undertake.

And in fact it turned out to be the simplest thing in the world.

"Just stand here," Mary instructed her, leading Katharine into
the narrow hall. "Stand here for a few minutes, where you can
see all the doors, and make sure that no one—absolutely *no
one*—goes in or out of Alan's study in the next five minutes. Will
you do that? Just while I go out and look round the garden, and
in the shed, just to make sure? . . ."

"Well, all right," agreed Katharine. "But you don't really expect,
do you, that . . . ?" But Mary had already dragged a coat at random
from the pegs—Stephen's old coat, Katharine noticed—flung it
round her shoulders, and was off into the scullery once more,
where Katharine could hear her drawing back the bolts. For a
moment a draught of wild damp air swirled round Katharine's

feet: then the outer door must have been closed again, for the draught ceased, and Katharine was alone.

It was rather dark in the hall, lit only by a square of frosted glass above the front door, and by the dregs of light from an upstairs window beyond the turn of the stairs. It was quiet, too, with a strange enveloping quietness of extraordinary power; so powerful indeed, that it seemed able to keep at bay the bustle of the morning; to drown by its own strength the tapping of busy footsteps on the pavement outside, the grinding diminuendo of the cars as they slowed at the corner.

Five minutes, Mary had said, and five minutes is a very long time to stand still, doing absolutely nothing. Absorbed now into the waiting silence of the house, Katharine did not care to walk about, or yawn, or lean with a rustle and scrape of her nylon overall against the bannisters. So she stood, silent and self-conscious, in a state of nebulous expectancy which grew and grew until she found herself alert, and trembling, and watching each closed door with straining eyes.

And within the five minutes Mary returned. So white and shaken did she look that for a moment Katharine stared in total credulity. The intruder must be here at last.

"No—no. I haven't found him," Mary whispered in answer to Katharine's urgent query. "And I've locked the door again. But—Katharine—I think it's too late. I think he's somewhere in the house already!"

"But he can't be. I've been standing here watching the whole time," objected Katharine; but Mary gestured her to silence.

"No—I mean *before*," she whispered. "Before you ever got here. Oh, Katharine, why didn't you come immediately when I phoned? Then he could never have got in. But come with me now, anyway. Let's look in every room. . . ."

How it took Katharine back to that other time when she had crept round this house, looking into every room. It had been evening then, and dark, whereas now it was morning, with the white winter light falling clear and still across a rumpled blanket here, a stretch of dusty linoleum there. Then, she had had Stella for company—tactless, and full of ghoulish but somehow reassuring curiosity. Now it was Mary who moved at her side, ghostlike—so white, so silent, and—somehow—so devoid of curiosity. Almost as if she already knew.

Knew what? Katharine could not begin to guess: and yet, when they came to Alan's study, it was exactly as it had been three weeks before, when she and Stella had come to the end of their search in this same room. Once again Katharine had the calm, unsurprised feeling that these smears of blood were just what she had been expecting. And this time, there, in the midst of them, lay Alan, face downward on the floor. She stood there, perfectly unmoved, unable to think or feel anything at all.

But not so Mary. With a wild, despairing shriek, she flung herself across the room towards her husband's motionless body.

"He's killed him!" she screamed. "I knew it! I knew it! We're too late! Oh, Katharine, why were you so slow? I begged you—I besought you—to come at once, and you didn't! It was too late!" She fell to frantic sobbing, which forced Katharine to rouse herself from her stunned emptiness of spirit.

"I'll ring a doctor—" she began helplessly, and Mary, in the midst of her sobbing, turned to her thankfully.

"Yes, yes, Katharine," she cried. "Do that. And the police. Ring them too, won't you, Katharine? *Quickly!*" and Katharine rushed out into the hall to obey.

"They'll be here in ten minutes," she turned to call to Mary as she laid the receiver down; but Mary was no longer in the study, but right beside her.

"Quick, Katharine," she whispered hoarsely. "Up to my room—we can lock ourselves in there. He's heard you phoning and he's coming!"

She turned and raced headlong up the stairs, Katharine following in a daze of confusion and fear. They darted into Mary's bedroom, and Mary swiftly turned the key in the lock, pocketed it, and turned round panting.

"There! We're all right now," she gasped; and then leaned towards the door, head on one side, listening.

"He's coming!" she whispered very softly. "Can't you hear him, Katharine? Can't you . . . ?" her voice quivered to a stop; the listening look became more intent.

"But he can't get in; we're all right," pointed out Katharine, reiterating Mary's own words. "Besides, the police will be here in a very few minutes now. . . ."

"So they will," rejoined Mary stiffly, her lips scarcely moving, "It'll be all right, won't it, Katharine? They'll be here before he can get in, won't they? . . . Won't they Katharine? Oh! Listen! Katharine listen! Can't you hear his footsteps . . . ?"

Katharine bent to the door crack, but could hear no sound but Mary's quick breath and the thudding of her heart.

"He's after you, Katharine," Mary whispered again, straightening up. "He's after you because he heard you phoning. He's trying to get you before the police arrive . . . but he won't! He won't! Look, I've foiled him!"

With a gay laugh of triumph, Mary whipped from the pocket of the raincoat, which she was still wearing, a long, sharp-bladed carving knife, and brandished it in triumph.

"Look I've taken it! He won't be able to find it now, he'll waste all his time looking for it, and by that time the police will be here. Won't they, Katharine? Won't they?"

The last words were spoken in desperate urgency: and as Katharine stood there, watching Mary with the raincoat clutched about her, and with the terror growing in her big, bright eyes, she knew suddenly that everything she had guessed last night was true. She, Katharine, with the help of Mrs. Forsyth, of Stella, even of Auntie Pen herself—yes, all of them together had caused the Dark Man in the Raincoat to come alive: and now, today, he had come into his twisted inheritance.

Behind the great, frightened eyes staring into hers, Katharine saw a strange purpose growing: and it was as if a light had been switched on, blazing into Mary's soul, into the shadows where all this time the Dark Man had been maturing—with Katharine's eager co-operation, and with that of all the neighbours. It was Katharine who had forced Mary at first to accept this alien growth, and then all of them together had helped her to rear it. Yes, like a dedicated team of midwives, welfare workers, teachers, they had helped Mary to raise this monstrous thing, to bring it to maturity. Katharine could see now, in this moment, that as the Dark Man grew in strength, so did Mary's fear of her husband. Her initial fear of what Alan might do to her had merged imperceptibly into a fear of what she might do to him; this it was that had made her afraid to embark with him on that lonely walk from the station when she knew she had a pair of sharp scissors in her bag; this that made her rush round to Stella's in the small hours rather than spend a night alone in the house with him. And now, this morning, she had not dared to stay alone with him at all, after Auntie Pen and Angela had gone. "The dark man in the raincoat has phoned," she had said; and even as she spoke it had become true: he had.

"But he can't hurt you. The door's locked, and I've got the knife," cried Mary again, desperately: and even as she spoke Katharine noticed that the hand holding the knife stopped trembling. It was strange to watch the Dark Man's eyes beginning to look out from between Mary's tear-swollen lids.

"Oh, Katharine!" her voice rose in a last despairing appeal. "Make the police come! Open the window! Tell them to hurry . . . hurry . . . because he's coming. . . ." Her voice dropped nearly to a whisper. "He's coming . . . nearer . . . nearer. . . . Scream, Katharine! Scream out of the window! It's your only chance! . . ."

And leaning out of the window, Katharine screamed and screamed.

A CATALOG OF SELECTED
DOVER BOOKS
IN ALL FIELDS OF INTEREST

A CATALOG OF SELECTED DOVER
BOOKS IN ALL FIELDS OF INTEREST

100 BEST-LOVED POEMS, Edited by Philip Smith. "The Passionate Shepherd to His Love," "Shall I compare thee to a summer's day?" "Death, be not proud," "The Raven," "The Road Not Taken," plus works by Blake, Wordsworth, Byron, Shelley, Keats, many others. Includes 13 selections from the Common Core State Standards Initiative. 112pp. 0-486-28553-7

ABC BOOK OF EARLY AMERICANA, Eric Sloane. Artist and historian Eric Sloane presents a wondrous A-to-Z collection of American innovations, including hex signs, ear trumpets, popcorn, and rocking chairs. Illustrated, hand-lettered pages feature brief captions explaining objects' origins and uses. 64pp. 0-486-49808-5

ADVENTURES OF HUCKLEBERRY FINN, Mark Twain. Join Huck and Jim as their boyhood adventures along the Mississippi River lead them into a world of excitement, danger, and self-discovery. Humorous narrative, lyrical descriptions of the Mississippi valley, and memorable characters. 224pp. 0-486-28061-6

ALICE STARMORE'S BOOK OF FAIR ISLE KNITTING, Alice Starmore. A noted designer from the region of Scotland's Fair Isle explores the history and techniques of this distinctive, stranded-color knitting style and provides copious illustrated instructions for 14 original knitwear designs. 208pp. 0-486-47218-3

ALICE'S ADVENTURES IN WONDERLAND, Lewis Carroll. Beloved classic about a little girl lost in a topsy-turvy land and her encounters with the White Rabbit, March Hare, Mad Hatter, Cheshire Cat, and other delightfully improbable characters. 42 illustrations by Sir John Tenniel. A selection of the Common Core State Standards Initiative. 96pp. 0-486-27543-4

THE ARTHUR RACKHAM TREASURY: 86 Full-Color Illustrations, Arthur Rackham. Selected and Edited by Jeff A. Menges. A stunning treasury of 86 full-page plates span the famed English artist's career, from *Rip Van Winkle* (1905) to masterworks such as *Undine, A Midsummer Night's Dream,* and *Wind in the Willows* (1939). 96pp. 0-486-44685-9

THE AWAKENING, Kate Chopin. First published in 1899, this controversial novel of a New Orleans wife's search for love outside a stifling marriage shocked readers. Today, it remains a first-rate narrative with superb characterization. New introductory note. 128pp. 0-486-27786-0

BASEBALL IS . . .: Defining the National Pastime, Edited by Paul Dickson. Wisecracking, philosophical, nostalgic, and entertaining, these hundreds of quips and observations by players, their wives, managers, authors, and others cover every aspect of our national pastime. It's a great any-occasion gift for fans! 256pp. 0-486-48209-X

THE CALL OF THE WILD, Jack London. A classic novel of adventure, drawn from London's own experiences as a Klondike adventurer, relating the story of a heroic dog caught in the brutal life of the Alaska Gold Rush. Note. 64pp. 0-486-26472-6

CANDIDE, Voltaire. Edited by Francois-Marie Arouet. One of the world's great satires since its first publication in 1759. Witty, caustic skewering of romance, science, philosophy, religion, government — nearly all human ideals and institutions. A selection of the Common Core State Standards Initiative. 112pp. 0-486-26689-3

THE CARTOON HISTORY OF TIME, Kate Charlesworth and John Gribbin. Cartoon characters explain cosmology, quantum physics, and other concepts covered by Stephen Hawking's *A Brief History of Time.* Humorous graphic novel–style treatment, perfect for young readers and curious folk of all ages. 64pp. 0-486-49097-1

Browse over 10,000 books at www.doverpublications.com

THE CHERRY ORCHARD, Anton Chekhov. Classic of world drama concerns passing of semifeudal order in turn-of-the-century Russia, symbolized in the sale of the cherry orchard owned by Madame Ranevskaya. Showcases Chekhov's rich sensitivities as an observer of human nature. 64pp. 0-486-26682-6

A CHRISTMAS CAROL, Charles Dickens. This engrossing tale relates Ebenezer Scrooge's ghostly journeys through Christmases past, present, and future and his ultimate transformation from a harsh and grasping old miser to a charitable and compassionate human being. 80pp. 0-486-26865-9

CRIME AND PUNISHMENT, Fyodor Dostoyevsky. Translated by Constance Garnett. Supreme masterpiece tells the story of Raskolnikov, a student tormented by his own thoughts after he murders an old woman. Overwhelmed by guilt and terror, he confesses and goes to prison. A selection of the Common Core State Standards Initiative. 448pp. 0-486-41587-2

CYRANO DE BERGERAC, Edmond Rostand. A quarrelsome, hot-tempered, and unattractive swordsman falls hopelessly in love with a beautiful woman and woos her for a handsome but slow-witted suitor. A witty and eloquent drama. 144pp. 0-486-41119-2

A DOLL'S HOUSE, Henrik Ibsen. Ibsen's best-known play displays his genius for realistic prose drama. An expression of women's rights, the play climaxes when the central character, Nora, rejects a smothering marriage and life in "a doll's house." A selection of the Common Core State Standards Initiative. 80pp. 0-486-27062-9

DOOMED SHIPS: Great Ocean Liner Disasters, William H. Miller, Jr. Nearly 200 photographs, many from private collections, highlight tales of some of the vessels whose pleasure cruises ended in catastrophe: the *Morro Castle, Normandie, Andrea Doria, Europa,* and many others. 128pp. 0-486-45366-9

DUBLINERS, James Joyce. A fine and accessible introduction to the work of one of the 20th century's most influential writers, this collection features 15 tales, including a masterpiece of the short-story genre, "The Dead." 160pp. 0-486-26870-5

THE EARLY SCIENCE FICTION OF PHILIP K. DICK, Philip K. Dick. This anthology presents short stories and novellas that originally appeared in pulp magazines of the early 1950s, including "The Variable Man," "Second Variety," "Beyond the Door," "The Defenders," and more. 272pp. 0-486-49733-X

THE EARLY SHORT STORIES OF F. SCOTT FITZGERALD, F. Scott Fitzgerald. These tales offer insights into many themes, characters, and techniques that emerged in Fitzgerald's later works. Selections include "The Curious Case of Benjamin Button," "Babes in the Woods," and a dozen others. 256pp. 0-486-79465-2

ETHAN FROME, Edith Wharton. Classic story of wasted lives, set against a bleak New England background. Superbly delineated characters in a hauntingly grim tale of thwarted love. Considered by many to be Wharton's masterpiece. 96pp. 0-486-26690-7

FLATLAND: A Romance of Many Dimensions, Edwin A. Abbott. Classic of science (and mathematical) fiction — charmingly illustrated by the author — describes the adventures of A. Square, a resident of Flatland, in Spaceland (three dimensions), Lineland (one dimension), and Pointland (no dimensions). 96pp. 0-486-27263-X

FRANKENSTEIN, Mary Shelley. The story of Victor Frankenstein's monstrous creation and the havoc it caused has enthralled generations of readers and inspired countless writers of horror and suspense. With the author's own 1831 introduction. 176pp. 0-486-28211-2

THE GARGOYLE BOOK: 572 Examples from Gothic Architecture, Lester Burbank Bridaham. Dispelling the conventional wisdom that French Gothic architectural flourishes were born of despair or gloom, Bridaham reveals the whimsical nature of these creations and the ingenious artisans who made them. 572 illustrations. 224pp. 0-486-44754-5

THE GIFT OF THE MAGI AND OTHER SHORT STORIES, O. Henry. Sixteen captivating stories by one of America's most popular storytellers. Included are such classics as "The Gift of the Magi," "The Last Leaf," and "The Ransom of Red Chief." Publisher's Note. A selection of the Common Core State Standards Initiative. 96pp. 0-486-27061-0

THE GOETHE TREASURY: Selected Prose and Poetry, Johann Wolfgang von Goethe. Edited, Selected, and with an Introduction by Thomas Mann. In addition to his lyric poetry, Goethe wrote travel sketches, autobiographical studies, essays, letters, and proverbs in rhyme and prose. This collection presents outstanding examples from each genre. 368pp. 0-486-44780-4

GREAT ILLUSTRATIONS BY N. C. WYETH, N. C. Wyeth. Edited and with an Introduction by Jeff A. Menges. This full-color collection focuses on the artist's early and most popular illustrations, featuring more than 100 images from *The Mysterious Stranger, Robin Hood, Robinson Crusoe, The Boy's King Arthur,* and other classics. 128pp. 0-486-47295-7

HAMLET, William Shakespeare. The quintessential Shakespearean tragedy, whose highly charged confrontations and anguished soliloquies probe depths of human feeling rarely sounded in any art. Reprinted from an authoritative British edition complete with illuminating footnotes. A selection of the Common Core State Standards Initiative. 128pp. 0-486-27278-8

THE HAUNTED HOUSE, Charles Dickens. A Yuletide gathering in an eerie country retreat provides the backdrop for Dickens and his friends — including Elizabeth Gaskell and Wilkie Collins — who take turns spinning supernatural yarns. 144pp. 0-486-46309-5

HEART OF DARKNESS, Joseph Conrad. Dark allegory of a journey up the Congo River and the narrator's encounter with the mysterious Mr. Kurtz. Masterly blend of adventure, character study, psychological penetration. For many, Conrad's finest, most enigmatic story. 80pp. 0-486-26464-5

THE HOUND OF THE BASKERVILLES, Sir Arthur Conan Doyle. A deadly curse in the form of a legendary ferocious beast continues to claim its victims from the Baskerville family until Holmes and Watson intervene. Often called the best detective story ever written. 128pp. 0-486-28214-7

THE HOUSE BEHIND THE CEDARS, Charles W. Chesnutt. Originally published in 1900, this groundbreaking novel by a distinguished African-American author recounts the drama of a brother and sister who "pass for white" during the dangerous days of Reconstruction. 208pp. 0-486-46144-0

HOW TO DRAW NEARLY EVERYTHING, Victor Perard. Beginners of all ages can learn to draw figures, faces, landscapes, trees, flowers, and animals of all kinds. Well-illustrated guide offers suggestions for pencil, pen, and brush techniques plus composition, shading, and perspective. 160pp. 0-486-49848-4

HOW TO MAKE SUPER POP-UPS, Joan Irvine. Illustrated by Linda Hendry. Super pop-ups extend the element of surprise with three-dimensional designs that slide, turn, spring, and snap. More than 30 patterns and 475 illustrations include cards, stage props, and school projects. 96pp. 0-486-46589-6

THE IMITATION OF CHRIST, Thomas à Kempis. Translated by Aloysius Croft and Harold Bolton. This religious classic has brought understanding and comfort to millions for centuries. Written in a candid and conversational style, the topics include liberation from worldly inclinations, preparation and consolations of prayer, and eucharistic communion. 160pp. 0-486-43185-1

THE IMPORTANCE OF BEING EARNEST, Oscar Wilde. Wilde's witty and buoyant comedy of manners, filled with some of literature's most famous epigrams, reprinted from an authoritative British edition. Considered Wilde's most perfect work. A selection of the Common Core State Standards Initiative. 64pp. 0-486-26478-5

JANE EYRE, Charlotte Brontë. Written in 1847, *Jane Eyre* tells the tale of an orphan girl's progress from the custody of cruel relatives to an oppressive boarding school and its culmination in a troubled career as a governess. A selection of the Common Core State Standards Initiative. 448pp. 0-486-42449-9

JUST WHAT THE DOCTOR DISORDERED: Early Writings and Cartoons of Dr. Seuss, Dr. Seuss. Edited and with an Introduction by Rick Marschall. The Doctor's visual hilarity, nonsense language, and offbeat sense of humor illuminate this compilation of items from his early career, created for periodicals such as *Judge, Life, College Humor,* and *Liberty.* 144pp. 0-486-49846-8

KING LEAR, William Shakespeare. Powerful tragedy of an aging king, betrayed by his daughters, robbed of his kingdom, descending into madness. Perhaps the bleakest of Shakespeare's tragic dramas, complete with explanatory footnotes. 144pp. 0-486-28058-6

THE LADY OR THE TIGER?: and Other Logic Puzzles, Raymond M. Smullyan. Created by a renowned puzzle master, these whimsically themed challenges involve paradoxes about probability, time, and change; metapuzzles; and self-referentiality. Nineteen chapters advance in difficulty from relatively simple to highly complex. 1982 edition. 240pp. 0-486-47027-X

LEAVES OF GRASS: The Original 1855 Edition, Walt Whitman. Whitman's immortal collection includes some of the greatest poems of modern times, including his masterpiece, "Song of Myself." Shattering standard conventions, it stands as an unabashed celebration of body and nature. 128pp. 0-486-45676-5

LES MISÉRABLES, Victor Hugo. Translated by Charles E. Wilbour. Abridged by James K. Robinson. A convict's heroic struggle for justice and redemption plays out against a fiery backdrop of the Napoleonic wars. This edition features the excellent original translation and a sensitive abridgment. 304pp. 0-486-45789-3

LIGHT FOR THE ARTIST, Ted Seth Jacobs. Intermediate and advanced art students receive a broad vocabulary of effects with this in-depth study of light. Diagrams and paintings illustrate applications of principles to figure, still life, and landscape paintings. 144pp. 0-486-49304-0

LILITH: A Romance, George MacDonald. In this novel by the father of fantasy literature, a man travels through time to meet Adam and Eve and to explore humanity's fall from grace and ultimate redemption. 240pp. 0-486-46818-6

LINE: An Art Study, Edmund J. Sullivan. Written by a noted artist and teacher, this well-illustrated guide introduces the basics of line drawing. Topics include third and fourth dimensions, formal perspective, shade and shadow, figure drawing, and other essentials. 208pp. 0-486-79484-9

THE LODGER, Marie Belloc Lowndes. Acclaimed by *The New York Times* as "one of the best suspense novels ever written," this novel recounts an English couple's doubts about their boarder, whom they suspect of being a serial killer. 240pp. 0-486-78809-1

MACBETH, William Shakespeare. A Scottish nobleman murders the king in order to succeed to the throne. Tortured by his conscience and fearful of discovery, he becomes tangled in a web of treachery and deceit that ultimately spells his doom. A selection of the Common Core State Standards Initiative. 96pp. 0-486-27802-6

MANHATTAN IN MAPS 1527–2014, Paul E. Cohen and Robert T. Augustyn. This handsome volume features 65 full-color maps charting Manhattan's development from the first Dutch settlement to the present. Each map is placed in context by an accompanying essay. 176pp. 0-486-77991-2

MEDEA, Euripides. One of the most powerful and enduring of Greek tragedies, masterfully portraying the fierce motives driving Medea's pursuit of vengeance for her husband's insult and betrayal. Authoritative Rex Warner translation. 64pp. 0-486-27548-5

THE METAMORPHOSIS AND OTHER STORIES, Franz Kafka. Excellent new English translations of title story (considered by many critics Kafka's most perfect work), plus "The Judgment," "In the Penal Colony," "A Country Doctor," and "A Report to an Academy." A selection of the Common Core State Standards Initiative. 96pp. 0-486-29030-1

METROPOLIS, Thea von Harbou. This Weimar-era novel of a futuristic society, written by the screenwriter for the iconic 1927 film, was hailed by noted science-fiction authority Forrest J. Ackerman as "a work of genius." 224pp. 0-486-79567-5

THE MYSTERIOUS MICKEY FINN, Elliot Paul. A multimillionaire's disappearance incites a maelstrom of kidnapping, murder, and a plot to restore the French monarchy. "One of the funniest books we've read in a long time." — *The New York Times.* 256pp. 0-486-24751-1

NARRATIVE OF THE LIFE OF FREDERICK DOUGLASS, Frederick Douglass. The impassioned abolitionist and eloquent orator provides graphic descriptions of his childhood and horrifying experiences as a slave as well as a harrowing record of his dramatic escape to the North and eventual freedom. A selection of the Common Core State Standards Initiative. 96pp. 0-486-28499-9

OBELISTS FLY HIGH, C. Daly King. Masterpiece of detective fiction portrays murder aboard a 1935 transcontinental flight. Combining an intricate plot and "locked room" scenario, the mystery was praised by *The New York Times* as "a very thrilling story." 288pp. 0-486-25036-9

THE ODYSSEY, Homer. Excellent prose translation of ancient epic recounts adventures of the homeward-bound Odysseus. Fantastic cast of gods, giants, cannibals, sirens, other supernatural creatures — true classic of Western literature. A selection of the Common Core State Standards Initiative. 256pp. 0-486-40654-7

OEDIPUS REX, Sophocles. Landmark of Western drama concerns the catastrophe that ensues when King Oedipus discovers he has inadvertently killed his father and married his mother. Masterly construction, dramatic irony. A selection of the Common Core State Standards Initiative. 64pp. 0-486-26877-2

OTHELLO, William Shakespeare. Towering tragedy tells the story of a Moorish general who earns the enmity of his ensign Iago when he passes him over for a promotion. Masterly portrait of an archvillain. Explanatory footnotes. 112pp. 0-486-29097-2

THE PICTURE OF DORIAN GRAY, Oscar Wilde. Celebrated novel involves a handsome young Londoner who sinks into a life of depravity. His body retains perfect youth and vigor while his recent portrait reflects the ravages of his crime and sensuality. 176pp. 0-486-27807-7

A PLACE CALLED PECULIAR: Stories About Unusual American Place-Names, Frank K. Gallant. From Smut Eye, Alabama, to Tie Siding, Wyoming, this pop-culture history offers a well-written and highly entertaining survey of America's most unusual place-names and their often-humorous origins. 256pp. 0-486-48360-6

PRIDE AND PREJUDICE, Jane Austen. One of the most universally loved and admired English novels, an effervescent tale of rural romance transformed by Jane Austen's art into a witty, shrewdly observed satire of English country life. A selection of the Common Core State Standards Initiative. 272pp. 0-486-28473-5

Browse over 10,000 books at www.doverpublications.com